The Fahrenheit Twins

Michel Faber

THE FAHRENHEIT TWINS

CANONGATE

Edinburgh · New York · Melbourne

First published in Great Britain in 2005 by
Canongate Books Ltd, 14 High Street,
Edinburgh EH1 1TE

1

Earlier versions of some of these stories appeared in the following
publications: 'All Black' in *Edinburgh Review*, 'Andy Comes Back' in
Prospect, 'Beyond Pain' in *New Writing 11*, 'The Eyes of the Soul' in
Macallan Shorts, 'Finesse' in *Prospect*, 'Flesh Remains Flesh' in *V&A
Magazine*, 'A Hole With Two Ends' in *Damage Land*, 'Less Than
Perfect' in *Crimewave*, 'Serious Swimmers' in *West Coast*, 'The
Smallness of the Action' in *The Printers Devil*, 'Tabitha Warren' in
Scottish Book Collector, and 'Vanilla-Bright Like Eminem' in *Matter*.
A short excerpt from the title story first appeared in *Black Book*
magazine. The technical information in 'Explaining Coconuts' is
drawn from *Coconut Research Institute, Manado*, by Professor Doctor
T. A. Davis, Mr H. Sudasrip and Dr S. N. Darwis.

British Library Cataloguing-in-Publication Data
A catalogue record for this book is available on
request from the British Library

ISBN 1 84195 673 2 (hardback)
ISBN 1 84195 674 0 (paperback)

Text design by Pentagram
Typeset in Bembo by Palimpsest Book Production Ltd,
Polmont, Stirlingshire
Printed and bound in Great Britain by CPD Wales, Ebbw Vale

www.canongate.net

As always, I thank my dear Eva for her criticism and wise advice during the revision of these stories.

CONTENTS

THE SAFEHOUSE

I

I wake up, blinking hard against the sky, and the first thing I remember is that my wife cannot forgive me. Never, ever.

Then I remind myself I don't have a wife anymore.

Instead, I'm lying at the bottom of a stairwell, thirty concrete steps below street level in a city far from my home. My home is in the past, and I must live in the present.

I'm lying on a soft pile of rubbish bags, and I seem to have got myself covered in muck. It's all over my shabby green raincoat and the frayed sleeves of my jumper, and there's a bit on my trousers as well. I sniff it, trying to decide what it is, but I can't be sure.

How strange I didn't notice it when I was checking this place out last night. OK, it was already dark by then and I was

desperate to find somewhere to doss down after being moved on twice already. But I remember crawling into the rubbish really carefully, prodding the bin bags with my hands and thinking this was the softest and driest bed I was likely to find. Maybe the muck seeped out later on, under pressure from my sleeping body.

I look around for something to wipe my clothes with. There's nothing, really. If I were a cat, I'd lick the crap off with my tongue, and still be a proud, even fussy creature. But I'm not a cat. I'm a human being.

So, I pull a crumpled-up advertising brochure out of the trash, wet it with dregs from a beer bottle, and start to scrub my jacket vigorously with the damp wad of paper.

Maybe it's the exercise, or maybe the rising sun, but pretty soon I feel I can probably get by without these dirty clothes – at least until tonight. And tonight is too far away to think about.

I stand up, leaving my raincoat and jumper lying in the garbage, where they look as if they belong anyway. I'm left with a big white T-shirt on, my wrinkled neck and skinny arms bare, which feels just right for the temperature. The T-shirt's got writing on the front, but I've forgotten what the writing says. In fact, I can't remember where I got this T-shirt, whether someone gave it to me or I stole it or even bought it, long long ago.

I climb the stone steps back up to the street, and start walking along the footpath in no particular direction, just trying to become part of the picture generally. The big picture. Sometimes in magazines you see a photograph of a street full of people, an aerial view. Everyone looks as though they belong, even the blurry ones.

I figure it must be quite early, because although there's lots of traffic on the road, there's hardly any pedestrians. Some

of the shops haven't opened yet, unless it's a Sunday and they aren't supposed to. So there's my first task: working out what day it is. It's good to have something to get on with.

Pretty soon, though, I lose my concentration on this little mission. There's something wrong with the world today, something that puts me on edge.

It's to do with the pedestrians. As they pass by me on the footpath, they look at me with extreme suspicion – as if they're thinking of reporting me to the police, even though I've taken my dirty clothes off to avoid offending them. Maybe my being in short sleeves is the problem. Everyone except me seems to be wrapped up in lots of clothes, as though it's much colder than I think it is. I guess I've become a hard man.

I smile, trying to reassure everybody, everybody in the world.

Outside the railway station, I score half a sandwich from a litter bin. I can't taste much, but from the texture I can tell it's OK – not slimy or off. Rubbish removal is more regular outside the station than in some other places.

A policeman starts walking towards me, and I run away. In my haste I almost bump into a woman with a pram, and she hunches over her baby as if she's scared I'm going to fall on it and crush it to death. I get my balance back and apologise; she says 'No harm done,' but then she looks me over and doesn't seem so sure.

By ten o'clock, I've been stopped in the street three times already, by people who say they want to help me.

One is a middle-aged lady with a black woollen coat and a red scarf, another is an Asian man who comes running out of a newsagent's, and one is just a kid. But they aren't offering me food or a place to sleep. They want to hand me over to

the police. Each of them seems to know me, even though I've never met them before. They call me by name, and say my wife must be worried about me.

I could try to tell them I don't have a wife anymore, but it's easier just to run away. The middle-aged lady is on high heels, and the Asian man can't leave his shop. The kid sprints after me for a few seconds, but he gives up when I leap across the road.

I can't figure out why all these people are taking such an interest in me. Until today, everyone would just look right through me as if I didn't exist. All this time I've been the Invisible Man, now suddenly I'm everybody's long-lost uncle.

I decide it has to be the T-shirt.

I stop in front of a shop window and try to read what the T-shirt says by squinting at my reflection in the glass. I'm not so good at reading backwards, plus there's a surprising amount of text, about fifteen sentences. But I can read enough to tell that my name is spelled out clearly, as well as the place I used to live, and even a telephone number to call. I look up at my face, my mouth is hanging open. I can't believe that when I left home I was stupid enough to wear a T-shirt with my ID printed on it in big black letters.

But then I must admit I wasn't in such a good state of mind when I left home – suicidal, in fact.

I'm much better now.

Now, I don't care if I live or die.

Things seem to have taken a dangerous turn today, though. All morning, I have to avoid people who act like they're about to grab me and take me to the police. They read my T-shirt, and then they get that look in their eye.

Pretty soon, the old feelings of being hunted from all

sides start to come back. I'm walking with my arms wrapped around my chest, hunched over like a drug addict. The sun has gone away but I'm sweating. People are zipping up their parkas, glancing up at the sky mistrustfully, hurrying to shelter. But even under the threat of rain, some of them still slow down when they see me, and squint at the letters on my chest, trying to read them through the barrier of my arms.

By midday, I'm right back to the state I was in when I first went missing. I have pains in my guts, I feel dizzy, I can't catch my breath, there are shapes coming at me from everywhere. The sky loses its hold on the rain, starts tossing it down in panic. I'm soaked in seconds, and even though getting soaked means nothing to me, I know I'll get sick and helpless if I don't get out of the weather soon.

Another total stranger calls my name through the deluge, and I have to run again. It's obvious that my life on the streets is over.

So, giving up, I head for the Safehouse.

II

I've never been to the Safehouse before – well, never inside it anyway. I've walked past many times, and I know exactly where to find it. It's on the side of town where all the broken businesses and closed railway stations are, the rusty barbed-wire side of town, where everything waits forever to be turned into something new. The Safehouse is the only building there whose windows have light behind them.

Of course I've wondered what goes on inside, I won't deny that. But I've always passed it on the other side of the

street, hurried myself on before I could dawdle, pulling myself away as if my own body were a dog on a lead.

Today, I don't resist. Wet and emaciated and with my name writ large on my chest, I cross the road to the big grey building.

The Safehouse looks like a cross between a warehouse and school, built in the old-fashioned style with acres of stone façade and scores of identical windows, all glowing orange and black. In the geometric centre of the building is a fancy entrance with a motto on its portal. GIB MIR DEINE ARME, it says, in a dull rainbow of wrought iron.

Before I make the final decision, I hang around in front of the building for a while, in case the rain eases off. I walk the entire breadth of the façade, hoping to catch a glimpse of what lies behind, but the gaps between the Safehouse and the adjacent buildings are too narrow. I stretch my neck, trying to see inside one of the windows – well, it *feels* as if I'm stretching my neck, anyway. I know necks don't really stretch and we're the same height no matter what we do. But that doesn't stop me contorting my chin like an idiot.

Eventually I work up the courage to knock at the door. There's no doorbell or doorknocker, and in competition with the rain my knuckles sound feeble against the dense wood. From the inside, the *pok pok pok* of my flesh and bone will probably be mistaken for water down the drain. However, I can't bring myself to knock again until I'm sure no one has heard me.

I shift my weight from foot to foot while I'm waiting, feeling warm sweat and rainwater suck at the toes inside my shoes. My T-shirt is so drenched that it's hanging down almost to my knees, and I can read a telephone number that people are supposed to ring if they've seen me. I close my eyes and count to ten. Above my head, I hear the squeak of metal against wood.

I look up at the darkening façade, and there, eerily framed in the window nearest to the top of the portal, is a very old woman in a nurse's uniform. She flinches at the rain and, mindful of her perfectly groomed hair and pastel cottons, stops short of leaning her head out. Instead she looks down at me from where she stands, half-hidden in shadow.

'What can we do for you?' she says, guardedly, raising her voice only slightly above the weather.

I realise I have no answer for her, no words. Instead, I unwrap my arms from my torso, awkwardly revealing the text on my T-shirt. The sodden smock of white fabric clings to my skin as I lean back, blinking against the rain. The old woman reads carefully, her eyes rolling to and fro in their sockets. When she's finished she reaches out a pale, bone-wristed hand and takes hold of the window latch; without speaking she shuts the dark glass firmly between us and disappears.

Moments later, the massive door creaks open, and I'm in.

Even before the door has shut behind me, the sound of the rain is swallowed up in the gloomy interior hush of old architecture. I step uncertainly across the threshold into silence.

The nurse leads me through a red velvety vestibule lit by a long row of ceiling lamps which seem to be giving out about fifteen watts apiece. There is threadbare carpet underfoot, and complicated wallpaper, cracked and curling at the skirtingboards and cornices. As I follow the faintly luminous nurse's uniform through the amber passageway, I glance sideways at the gilt-framed paintings on the walls: stern old men in grey attire, mummified behind a patina of discoloured varnish like university dons or Victorian industrialists.

On our way to wherever, we pass what appears to be an office; through its window I glimpse filing cabinets and an obese figure hunched over a paper-strewn desk. But the old

woman does not pause; if my admission to the Safehouse involves any paperwork it seems I'm not required to fill in the forms myself.

Another door opens and I am ushered into a very different space: a large, high-ceilinged dining room so brightly lit by fluorescent tubes that I blink and almost miss my footing. Spacious as a gymnasium and cosy as an underground car park, the Safehouse mess hall welcomes me, whoever I may be. Its faded pink walls, synthetic furniture and scuffed wooden floor glow with reflected light. And, despite its dimensions, it is as warm as anyone could want, with gas heaters galore.

At one end, close to where I have entered, two fat old women in nurse's uniforms stand behind a canteen counter wreathed in a fog of brothy vapour. They ladle soup into ceramic bowls, scoop flaccid white bread out of damp plastic bags, fetch perfect toast out of antique black machines. One of them looks up at me and smiles for half a second before getting back to her work.

The rest of the hall is littered with a hundred mismatching chairs (junk-shop boxwood and stainless steel) and an assortment of tables, mostly Formica. It is also littered with human beings, a placid, murmuring population of men, women and teenage children – a hundred of them, maybe more. Even at the first glimpse, before I take in anything else, they radiate a powerful aura – an aura of consensual hopelessness. Other than this, they are as mismatched as the furniture, all sizes and shapes, from roly-poly to anorexic thin, from English rose to Jamaica black. Most are already seated, a few are wandering through the room clutching a steaming bowl, searching for somewhere good to sit. Each and every one of them is dressed in a white T-shirt just like mine.

Behind me, a door shuts; the old nurse has left me to fend for myself, as if it should be transparently obvious how

things work here. And, in a way, it is. The fists I have clenched in anticipation of danger grow slack as I accept that my arrival has made no impression on the assembled multitude. I am one of them already.

Hesitantly, I step up to the canteen counter. A bearded man with wayward eyebrows and bright blue eyes is already standing there waiting, his elbow leaning on the edge. Though his body is more or less facing me, his gaze is fixed on the old women and the toast they're buttering for him. So, I take the opportunity to read what the text on his T-shirt says.

It says:

JEFFREY ANNESLEY
AGE 47
Jeffrey disappeared on April 7, 1994
from his work in Leeds. He was driving
his blue Mondeo, registration L562 WFU.
Jeffrey had been unwell for some time and it was
decided he would go to hospital to receive treatment.
He may be seeking work as a gas-fitter.
Jeffrey's family are extremely worried about him.
His wife says he is a gentle man who loves
his two daughters very much.
'We just want to know how you are,'
she says. 'Everything is sorted out now.'
Have you have seen Jeffrey?
If you have any information, please
contact the Missing Persons Helpline.

Jeffrey Annesley reaches out his big gnarly hands and takes hold of a plate of food. No soup, just a small mound of toast. He mumbles a thanks I cannot decipher, and walks away, back to a table he has already claimed.

'What would you like, pet?' says one of the old women behind the canteen counter. She sounds Glaswegian and has a face like an elderly transvestite.

'What is there?' I ask.

'Soup and toast,' she says.

'What sort of soup?'

'Pea and ham.' She glances at my chest, as if to check whether I'm vegetarian. 'But I can try to scoop it so as there's no ham in yours.'

'No, it's all right, thank you,' I assure her. 'Can I have it in a cup?'

She turns to the giant metal pot on the stove, her fat shoulders gyrating as she decants my soup. I notice that the seams of her uniform have been mended several times, with thread that is not quite matching.

'Here you are, pet.'

She hands me an orange-brown stoneware mug, filled with earthy-looking soup I cannot smell.

'Thank you,' I say.

I weave my way through the litter of chairs and tables. Here and there someone glances at me as I pass, but mostly I'm ignored. I take my seat near a young woman who is slumped with her feet up on a table, apparently asleep. On the lap of her mud-stained purple trousers, a plate of toast rises and falls almost imperceptibly. The forward tilt of her head gives her a double chin, even though she is scrawny and small.

I read her T-shirt. It says:

CATHY STOCKTON
AGE 17
Cathy left her home in Bristol in July 2002
to stay in London. She has run away before
but never for this long. At Christmas 2003, a girl

claiming to be a friend of Cathy's rang Cathy's auntie
in Dessborough, Northants, asking if Cathy could
come to visit. This visit never happened.
Cathy's mother wants her to know that Cathy's
stepfather is gone now and that her room is
back the way it was. 'I have never stopped
loving you,' she says. 'Snoopy and Paddington are
next to your pillow, waiting for you to come home.'
Cathy suffers from epilepsy and may need medicine.
If you have seen her, please call the
Missing Persons Helpline.

Cathy snoozes on, a stray lock of her blond hair fluttering in the updraft from her breath.

I lean back in my chair and sip at my mug of soup. I taste
nothing much, but the porridgy liquid is satisfying in my
stomach, filling a vacuum there. I wonder what I will have to
do in order to be allowed to stay in the Safehouse, and who I
can ask about this. As a conversationalist I have to admit I'm
pretty rusty. Apart from asking passers-by for spare change,
I haven't struck up a conversation with anyone for a very
long time. How does it work? Do you make some comment about the weather? I glance up at the windows, which
are opaque and high above the ground. There is a faint
pearlescent glow coming through them, but I can't tell if it's
still raining out there or shining fit to burst.

The old woman who escorted me here hasn't returned
to tell me what I'm supposed to do next. Maybe she'll escort
somebody else into the hall at some stage, and I can ask her
then. But the canteen ladies are cleaning up, putting the food
away. They seem to have reason to believe I'm the last new
arrival for the afternoon.

I cradle my soup mug in both my hands, hiding my

mouth behind it while I survey the dining hall some more. There is a susurrus of talk but remarkably little for such a large gathering of people. Most just sit, staring blindly ahead of them, mute and listless inside their black-and-white texts. I try to eavesdrop on the ones who are talking, but I barely catch a word: I'm too far away, they have no teeth or are from Newcastle, Cathy Stockton has started snoring.

After about twenty minutes, a grizzled bald man walks over to me and parks himself on the chair nearest mine. He extends a hand across the *faux*-marble patio table for me to shake. There is no need for introductions. He is Eric James Sween, a former builder whose business had been in financial difficulties before he disappeared from his home in Broxburn, West Lothian, in January 1994.

I wonder, as I shake his surprisingly weak hand, how long ago his wife said she would give anything just to know he was safe. Would she give as much today? The baby daughter she desperately wanted to show him may be experimenting with cigarettes by now.

'Don't worry,' he says, 'It's a doddle.'

'What is?' I ask him.

'What you have to do here.'

'What do you have to do?'

'A bit of manual labour. Not today: it's raining too hard. But most days. A cinch.'

The old women seem to have melted away from the canteen, leaving me alone in the dining hall with all these strangers.

'Who runs this place?' I ask Eric James Sween.

'Some sort of society,' he replies, as if sharing information unearthed after years of painstaking research.

'Religious?'

'Could be, could be.' He grins. One of his long teeth is

brown as a pecan nut. I suspect that if I could read the lower lines of his T-shirt, obscured by the table, there would be a hint of bigger problems than the failure of a business.

Which reminds me:

'No one must know what's become of me.'

Eric James Sween squints, still smiling, vaguely puzzled. I struggle to make myself absolutely clear.

'The people who run this place . . . If they're going to try to . . . make contact, you know . . . with . . .' I leave it there, hoping he'll understand without me having to name names – although of course one of the names is printed on my breast in big black letters.

Eric James Sween chuckles emphysemally.

'Nobody's ever gonna see you again,' he assures me. 'That's why you're here. That's why they let you in. They can tell you're ready.'

He is staring at me, his eyes twinkling, his face immobile. I realise that our conversation is over and I wonder if there is something I can do to bring it to a formal conclusion.

'Thank you,' I say.

I sit in my dining room chair for the rest of the afternoon, getting up occasionally to stretch my legs, then returning again to the same chair. No one bothers me. It is bliss not to be moved on, bliss to be left unchallenged. This is all I have wanted every day of my life for as long as I care to remember.

Everyone else in the hall stays more or less where they are, too. They relax, as far as the hard furniture allows, digest-ing their lunch, biding their time until dinner. Some sleep, their arms hanging down, their fingers trailing the floor. Some use their arms to make little pillows for themselves against the headrest of their chairs, nestling their cheek in the crook of an elbow. Others have their knees drawn up tight

against their chin, perched like outsized owls on a padded square of vinyl. A few carry on talking, but by now I have reason to wonder if they are really talking to the people they sit amongst. Their eyes stare into the middle distance, they chew their fingernails, they speak in low desultory voices. Rather than answering their neighbours or being answered, they speak simultaneously, or lapse simultaneously into silence.

Eric James Sween, perhaps the most restless soul of them all, ends up seated in the most crowded part of the room, drumming on his thighs and knees with his fingertips, humming the music that plays inside his head. He hums softly, as if fearful of disturbing anyone, and his fingers patter against his trouser legs without audible effect. A little earlier, he found a handkerchief on the floor and wandered around the room with it, asking various people if it was theirs. Everyone shook their heads or ignored him. For a while I was vaguely curious what he would do with the handkerchief if no one accepted it, but then I lost focus and forgot to watch him. My concentration isn't so good these days. The next time I noticed him, he was hunched on a chair, empty-handed, drumming away.

Occasionally someone gets up to go to the toilet. I know that's where they're going because at one point a hulking arthritic woman announces to herself that she had better have a pee, and I follow her. She walks laboriously, obliging me to take childish mincing steps so as not to overtake her. I notice that on the back of her T-shirt she has a lot of text too, much more than on the front. In fact, there is so much text, in such tiny writing, that her back is almost black with it. I try to read some as I walk behind her, but I can't manage it. The letters are too small, and the woman is contorting her muscles constantly in an effort to keep her ruined body from pitching over.

She leads me to two adjacent toilet doors on the opposite

end of the dining hall from the canteen. Fastened to one door is a picture of a gentleman in a frock coat and top hat; the other has a lady in a long crinoline dress, with a bonnet and parasol. I enter the gentleman toilet. It is bigger than I thought it would be and luridly white, more like a room in an art gallery. Above the washbasins is a faded illustration painted directly onto the wall; it depicts a pair of hands washing each other against a green medicinal cross. REINLICHKEIT, it says underneath.

I select one of a long row of teardrop urinals to stand at. They look ancient and organic, as if they have been fashioned from a huge quantity of melted-down teeth. There are caramel stains on the enamel like streaks of tobacco. Yet the drain-holes are bubbly with disinfectant, showing that they are clean.

I stand for a while at the urinal, giving myself permission to let go of my little reservoir of waste, but nothing happens, so I leave. At least I know how to find it now.

Finally it is time for the evening meal. The two old nurses arrive and start cooking, in the kitchen behind the canteen. A watery miasma emanates from their labours, floating out into the hall, ascending to the ceiling. There is a general murmur of anticipation. I go to the toilet, successfully clear my bowels, and find myself disturbed almost to tears by the soft-ness of the toilet paper. I wash my hands under the sign of the green cross. A dark coffee of grime swirls in the sink, dilutes and gurgles away.

When I return to the dining hall, a queue is forming at the canteen counter. I wonder whether the Safehouse is the sort of set-up where all the really decent food is snatched by the early birds and there's only scraps and clammy leftovers for the latecomers. I take my place in the queue, even though I'm not particularly hungry. It's an opportunity to stand close

behind someone, trying to read what's written on their back.

I'm standing behind a young man with bad acne on his neck and head. He has very short hair, like felt, lovingly clipped to avoid any trauma to all the bulbous little eruptions dotting the flesh of his skull. I wonder if a hairdresser charges a great deal more for that: to exercise such care, such restraint, such understanding. What has brought this young man here, if he so recently had a hairdresser who was prepared to handle his head so gently?

On the back of the young man's T-shirt is an unbelievable amount of text, a dense mass of small print which I can't imagine to be anything more than a random weave of symbols, a stylish alphabet texture. Starting near the top of his left shoulder, I read as much as I can before my attention wanes:

n:12/5/82, M:pnd(s), F:ai, pM1:30/5/82}gs(!vlegLnd),
hf8B, M2:31/5/82}gs(!vlegLsd), @n7, gH, ^MGM:ingm, ¬b,
c(T)@m, pMGM3:4/6/82(v[#]penisd++), >@m, ¬X+,
Hn>j, pF4:8/12/82,

and so on and on, thousands of letters and numbers right down to his waist. I peek over the young man's shoulder, at the back of the woman standing in front of him, and then, leaning sharply out from the queue, I glimpse the backs of half a dozen people further on. They're all the same in principle, but some of them have text that only goes as far down as the middle of their backs, while others have so much that their T-shirts have to be longer, more like smocks or dresses.

My own T-shirt is pretty roomy, come to think of it. Definitely XL. I wonder what's on it.

There is a man standing behind me, a tall man with thick glasses and hair like grey gorse. I smile at him, in case he's been reading the back of my T-shirt and knows more than me.

'Lamb tonight,' he says, his magnified bloodshot eyes begging me to leave him be.

I turn and face front again. When my turn comes to be served, I am given a plate of piping-hot lamb stew. The fat nurse has dished it up in such a way that there is a big donut-shaped ring of mashed potato all around the edge of the plate, with a puddle of stew enclosed inside it. As she hands it over she smiles wanly, as if admitting she just can't help being a bit creative with the presentation, but maybe I'm reading too much into it. Maybe she's learned that this is the best way to prevent people spilling stew off their plates on their way back to the tables.

I sit down somewhere and eat the stew and the potato. There's quite a lot of lamb in the gravy and there's a few carrots and beans floating about as well. I haven't had anything this wholesome since my . . . well, for a long time anyway.

When it's all over, I stare into space. I'd meant to keep an eye on the others, to ascertain how much food the last ones in the queue got. But I forgot. My memory is not what it was; thoughts and resolutions crumble away like biscuits in a back pocket. The important thing is that no one is moving me on. I could weep with gratitude. Except of course I don't weep anymore.

After another little while, I become aware that the windows of the Safehouse have turned black. Night has fallen on the outside world. I feel a cold thrill of anxiety, the instinctive dread that comes over you when you realise you've foolishly put off the essential business of finding a soft enclave of rubbish or an obscure stairwell until it's too late. I imagine the bony old nurse coming up to me and saying it's time for me to go home now, and that the Safehouse opens again at ten o'clock tomorrow. But deep down I know this isn't going to happen. I'm here to stay.

I sit for another couple of hours, staring at the people but not really seeing them. I also stare at my shoes, mesmerised by the metal eyelets of the laces, the scuffs and grazes on the uppers. I stare at the black windows, the reflection of the fluorescent light on the table nearest me, the damp canteen counter, empty now. I wonder if I should be shamed or even alarmed by my lack of boredom. I hadn't realised before today how completely I have made my peace with uselessness. Out in the world, I was hunted from sitting-place to sitting-place, never still for more than an hour, often rooted out after a few minutes. In warm shopping malls detectives would lose patience if I loitered too long without buying; on stone steps outside shops people would swing the door against my back and say 'Excuse me'. Even at nights, watchmen would shine torches into my face, and unexpected vehicles would cruise close to my huddled body.

With so much outside provocation to keep me moving, I never noticed that inside myself I have, in fact, lost any need for action or purpose. I am content.

I wish my wife could know this.

Eventually a bell rings and people start filing out of the dining hall. I look around for Eric James Sween in case he might be making his way over to me to explain what happens now, but he's already gone. So, I fall into step with the others and allow myself to be herded into a new corridor.

It's a shabby passage, not very long. On one wall hang naïve paintings of meadows and farm animals, slightly skew-whiff and with incongruous gilt frames. The opposite wall is blank except for a very large laminated board, screwed securely into the plaster well above eye level. It looks like those lists you see in war memorials of soldiers who died between certain dates, or the lists of old boys in ancient universities. At the top, it says:

KEY TO ABBREVIATIONS

There are columns and columns underneath, five square feet of them, starting with:

n: = born
M = mother
F = father
PGM = paternal grandmother
MGM = maternal grandmother

and so on. I dawdle to a standstill under the board, allowing the other people to pass me. I read further down the columns, straining to understand and to remember. The further I read, the more complicated it gets. **p** means punished, for example, but it only really makes sense when learned in combination with other symbols, like **!**, meaning an act of physical violence.

I glance ahead. The last few columns are full of fearsome strings of algebra which, if I could decode them, would apparently explain highly complicated things involving social workers and police. Even the most compact-looking formula, $\{$**F∉>M/-](δn*)** , unfurls to mean 'birthday present sent by father, withheld by mother and never mentioned'.

I pull my T-shirt over my head, exposing my naked torso to the draughty corridor. The soft white fabric flows like milk over my fists as I try to get it sorted out. It's not the front I want to see: I know my name and I don't want to be reminded who might be worried about me. I hold the back of the T-shirt aloft and check its left shoulder. **n:13/4/60**, it says. That's my date of birth, right enough.

After that, it's hard going. My text makes no sense because I don't know what I'm looking at, and the key is no

help because I can't see what I'm looking for. I try to tackle it one symbol at a time, hoping that a moment will come when it suddenly all starts falling into place. At least I have the advantage of having had quite a simple childhood.

Unfortunately, just as I'm a couple of lines into my text and am searching for an explanation for **pM9**, the ninth time my mother punished me, I feel a tap on my naked shoulder and almost jump out of my skin.

I spin around, my T-shirt clutched to my breast like a bath towel. Confronting me in the hollow corridor is the old nurse who admitted me to the Safehouse. My heart beats against my ribs as she glowers straight into me, face into face. Her withered hand remains raised, as if she is about to administer a Catholic blessing, but she merely scratches the air between us with a hovering fingernail.

'You mustn't take your garment off here,' she warns me, *sotto voce.*

'I was just trying to see what it says on my back,' I explain.

'Yes, but you mustn't.' Her eyes, fringed all round with dull silver lashes, glow like sad heirloom brooches. I cannot disobey her.

As I pull my T-shirt over my head, she retreats one small step to avoid my flailing arms. Then, when I'm decent again, she touches me lightly on the elbow, and escorts me along the corridor, away from the KEY TO ABBREVIATIONS board.

'It's bedtime now,' she says.

I am led into the Safehouse's sleeping barracks. It's an even larger space than the dining hall – more like some massive, echoing warehouse whose ceilings must accommodate the comings and goings of forklifts and cranes. It is harshly lit and draughty and smells like a vast kennel, with a faint whiff of

chlorinated urine. The ceiling is so high that rafts of fluorescent lights are dangled on long chains, down to where the highest ladder might be able to service them. Each raft contains four strips nestled side by side. Suspended so far above my head, luminous, airborne and still, they remind me of childhood visits to the Natural History Museum – fibreglass dolphins and sharks, dusty with time and grimy at the seams.

I tilt my head back, trying to see beyond these glowing mobiles to the ceiling above. I glimpse the silhouettes of wooden beams and steel pipes, a shadowy Cartesian plane supporting a transparent, or at least translucent, roof.

I feel a prod at my elbow.

'Time for that later,' the old nurse chides me gently, and I walk on.

The floor we tread is an old pool of concrete worn smooth as bone, silent under my feet. The rubber crêpe soles of the old nurse go *vrunnik, vrunnik, vrunnik* as she walks beside me, leading me deeper in.

I keep my eyes downcast, reluctant to see what this great warehouse is, after all, for. I feel a glimmering constellation of eyes on me, I fancy I can hear the massed sighing of breath.

'This is your bed, up here,' I hear the nurse say, and I have to look where she is pointing.

All along the walls, stacked like pallets of produce, are metal bunk-beds, a surreal Meccano bolted straight into the brickwork. The beds go twelve-high, each compartment a little nest of white sheets and oatmeal-coloured blankets. A few of these beds are empty, but very few. Almost every rectangular nook contains a horizontal human being – man, woman or child, installed like *poste restante*. Some lie with their backs already turned, their rumpled heads half-buried under bedclothes. But most stare straight at me, blinking and passionless, from all heights and corners of the room.

The old nurse is pointing at a vacant bed, eleven beds off the ground, which I can only get to by climbing an iron ladder up the side of the bunk tower. I look round at her awkwardly, wondering if I can bring myself to tell her that I have a fear of high places.

She purses her thin dry lips in what could almost be a smile as she waves her fingers brusquely upwards.

'No one falls here,' she lets me know. 'This is the Safehouse.'

And she turns and walks away, *vrunnik vrunnik, vrunnik*.

I climb the ladder to my bed. On the way up, I am conscious of my progress being watched by a great many people, and not just from a distance, but at close and intimate range by the inhabitants of each of the ten beds I climb past. Half in shadow, half illuminated by shafts of harsh light, they haul themselves onto their elbows, or merely turn their heads around on the pillow, staring hollow-eyed into my face as I ascend. They stare without self-consciousness, without mercy, reading what they can of the text on my T-shirt, or appraising my body as I haul it upwards only inches from their noses. Yet they stare, too, without any spark of real interest. I am an event, a physical phenomenon, occurring on the rungs of the ladder that is bolted to their own bunk. To ignore me would require a greater fascination with something else, and there is nothing. So, they stare, mute and apathetic, their gaze eyeball-deep.

Man or woman, they have all kept their T-shirts on, like white cotton nightgowns. I glimpse names and ages, and a word or two of history, incomprehensible without the remainder. Their other clothes are bundled up under their pillow – trousers, skirts, socks, even shoes, all to raise the level of the thin cushion in its envelope of stiff white cotton.

I reach the eleventh bunk and crawl in. Under cover of the sheet and blanket, I take off all my clothes except the T-shirt, and arrange them under my pillow like the other people here. I notice that my feet are quite black with dirt, that the flesh of the insides of my knees is scarred with a rash from sleeping too many nights in damp jeans, that my genitals are as small as a child's.

The sheet is so old and often-mended that I'm afraid of tearing it as I try to make myself comfortable, but the blanket is thick and soft. I wrap it around me, tucked snug around my neck, and am just about to make a decision about whether I'll pull it right over my head when the barracks falls into darkness.

Relieved to be invisible at last, I venture my head a little way out of my bunk, looking up at the ceiling. It is glass, as I'd thought: huge tessellated panes of tinted glass through which moonlight smoulders, indistinct and poorly defined. The dangling rafts of extinguished fluorescent tubes loom at black intervals in the air, suspended between me and the people on the other side. I stare into the gloom, waiting for my vision to adjust. But as soon as it does, and I begin to see pale shoulders and the feeble candlepower of wakeful eyes, I turn away. I don't know what I expected to see or what I expected to feel, but these shadowy towers of scaffolding, these tiers of hidden bodies and glow-worm faces, fail to strike awe or pity into my heart. This indifference shames me, or I imagine it ought to, and I make a conscientious attempt to feel *something*. After some effort, I decide that I feel gratitude, or at least absence of anxiety, owing to us all being here for the night, assigned to our places. Often since going missing I've daydreamed of going to prison, but of course the gift of brute shelter is not easy to earn. Whatever crime you may commit, the world still wants you to keep playing the game. Even murderers are visited by their wives and children.

I lay my head back on the pillow, quite carefully, for fear of dislodging my shoes and sending them plummeting to the floor below. The nurse was right, though: I feel no fear of falling myself. The rectangle of steel and wire on which I lie feels as secure as the ground. I relax.

Above me, there sags another mattress held in a metal web, bulging down under the weight of a heavy body. I reach up and touch the mattress and the metal that holds it, very gently, just for something to do. I wouldn't, for the world, wish to attract the attention of the sleeper above.

I close my eyes, and as my brain begins to shut down I realise that for the first time in months I don't have to worry about being found.

In the morning, after a blissfully dreamless sleep, I wake to the sound of coughing. From various recesses in the honeycomb of bunks, gruesomely distinctive snorts, hacks and wheezes are flying out. In time, I will come to recognise each cough and associate it with a name and a history. On that first morning, I know nothing.

I lean over the side of my bed and look down. On the floor far below, lit up brilliantly by the sunlight shining down through the transparent ceiling, is a silvery pool of urine. The metal towers of sleeping berths are mirrored in it; I scan our reflections trying to find myself, but can't tell the difference between all the tiny dishevelled faces. I raise one hand, to wave into the glowing pool, to clinch which one is me. Several hands – no, half a dozen – wave back at me.

I am no longer missing.

ANDY COMES BACK

His eyes fluttered open, and he was surprised to find himself alive.

If he'd thought about himself at all in the last five years, he'd considered himself dead. Occasionally he'd peek out at the world, and for his peekhole he would use the gibbering, shrieking idiot the nursing staff called Andy.

But today he'd dropped in to the idiot's head to have a look, and there he was: alive as anything. It was a hell of a shock.

He sat up, immediately aware of the institutional pyjamas he was in.

'Morning, Andy!' said the old man in the next bed.

'Morning,' he responded vaguely, looking at his bedside cabinet, which had nothing on it but flowers and orange juice.

'Ha! Good for *you*, Andy boy!' said his neighbour, as if impressed.

Andy checked inside the cabinet. It was empty. He twisted around to look at the wall behind his bed. A flimsy plastic bas-relief of Father Christmas had pride of place there, connected by a barbed wire of tinsel to other identical Father Christmases behind other beds. Blu-tacked under Andy's Santa were photographs of a woman and three children, in various combinations. A child's painting, rather tattered and signed *Robert*, was almost hidden behind the bedhead.

A nurse strolled into the ward and said hello to everyone. She was wearing disposable gloves.

'Andy said good morning just now,' the old man informed her at once.

'That's nice,' she said, obviously not believing it. She strode over to Andy's bed and without warning pulled back the covers. Briskly uninhibited, she inspected his crotch, then slipped a hand under his bottom to check the white undersheet.

'You been a *good* boy tonight, Andy?' she cooed approvingly, addressing his lower half.

'What?'

She carried on instinctively, before she'd had a chance to decode the sound he'd made.

'Not poo'd the bed?'

'I should hope not,' he said. 'What do you think I am?'

She stared at him openmouthed, stuck for an answer. Then she ran away.

It turned out he'd been a drooling imbecile for five years. He'd contracted a rare disease, survived it, but lost his mind. When first admitted to an acute ward, he'd presented an exciting challenge to medical science. All sorts of experts had tried to pursue his consciousness wherever it had gone, and bring it back. Then the weeks had passed, and life went on,

and the hospital needed his bed. He'd been shifted to a nursing home, and that's where he'd lived ever since.

He gathered he'd been very difficult to care for, twitching convulsively and flinging his limbs about whenever the nurses tried to shave or wash him, sending cereal bowls and cutlery flying across the room with one slam of his fist, waking the other patients up at night with dog-like howls. His howls, in fact, could be heard even beyond the nursing home environs. Despite stiff competition from all the other mournful cries these walls had ever contained, his howls had achieved legendary status.

Calm and soft-spoken now, he asked for a mirror and a razor.

A nurse fetched him the electric shaver that had been shoved across his squirming face every day for five years. He asked for a blade and some soapy water. Their eyes met. Only a couple of days ago, she and a burly porter had had to restrain him when a Christmas singalong provoked him to a frenzy. The memory of his feral strength was fresh in her mind.

'Thank you,' he said, when she brought him the razor.

He was disturbed by what had happened to his face. It was very much older in one way, with hard, rubbery folds and wrinkles, and whitish-grey hairs amongst his usual black stubble. But it was obscenely young as well, like the face of a chimpanzee infant. Shaving the stubble off it didn't seem to make much difference.

The nurse watched him as he struggled to carve out something familiar.

'Your wife . . .' she began.

'What?'

'Your wife is coming today. It's her visiting day.'

He thought this over for a second; suddenly remembered his wife very well.

'I suppose you've rung and told her the news?' he said.

'I'm afraid not,' replied the nurse. 'We tried to, but there was no answer. She's got a surprise coming, hasn't she?' She snorted, then blushed and left abruptly.

Andy's wife arrived after lunch, when the nursing home was at its busiest. She was at his bedside before any of the staff noticed her.

'Hello Andy-boy,' she said as she sat down on the end of his bed. Yanking her shoulderbag onto her lap, she rummaged in it. 'Brought you some donuts. And a can of soft drink.' She reached past him and put the treats on the bedside cabinet. She ruffled his hair, squinting and pouting.

'How've you been behaving, eh Andy? Not causing the nurses too much bother? Not being a naughty boy at breakfast? Mustn't be a naughty boy at breakfast, Andy.'

She seemed quite content, steaming ahead without really noticing him, like a primary school inspector breezing through a class of cheerfully preoccupied children. It seemed a shame to tell her the truth, but as a nurse was running towards them he thought he'd better get in first.

'I'm all right now, Brom,' he said quietly.

'Uh ... yes,' panted the nurse, squeaking to a stop on the polished linoleum.

Andy's wife didn't speak, only looked from the nurse to Andy and back to the nurse.

'I mean,' said the nurse, 'we've called in the specialist, and the test results aren't in yet, but ...' She flashed a goofy grin and gestured towards Andy, as if to say *see for yourself*.

Andy's wife smiled too, a grin of infinite foolishness and shock, as if she were the victim of a surprise birthday party on the wrong day.

'Really?' she said.

It was her husband, rather than the nurse, who answered now.

'Really,' he said.

'How wonderful, darling,' said Andy's wife. She reached across the bed and embraced him awkwardly, like a member of the Royal Family embracing a deformed child.

There followed an excruciating silence.

'Well,' said the nurse, feeling herself being sucked into its vortex, 'I expect this will take a bit of getting used to. On both sides.' Counselling over, she walked off to do a bit of nursing, which was what she was paid for, after all.

The embrace broke. Andy and his wife settled back into their previous positions like pool players after a shot. Bromwyn stared straight ahead of her, at the narrow corridor at the far end of the ward.

'I'm sorry if I don't seem delighted, Andy,' she began.

'Have you been calling me Andy these past few years, Brom?' asked Andrew, who didn't like to be called Andy.

'Sorry. Yes. Sorry,' said Bromwyn, who didn't mind being called Brom.

He stayed in the nursing home for another two days, reading *Reader's Digest*s, chatting to astounded medical experts. Every capability he'd ever had seemed to have come back to him. When the time came for him to go home, however, he was advised, for no explicit reason, not to do the driving.

After some embarrassing farewells and best wishes for the new year from the nursing staff, Bromwyn took Andy home. A staunch non-driver all the years that he'd encouraged her to learn, she'd bitten the bullet and got her licence barely six months after his mind had gone. He would never know if mastering the controls had come easily to her. She drove mechanically and without undue concern for the other

traffic, like all experienced drivers. He found this oddly unbecoming.

The old neighbourhood had scarcely changed. This seemed to him an indictment of the sort of neighbourhood it was. He had moved here, reluctantly, for the sake of his job, which of course no longer existed.

His wife had found work, though. It was all she talked about on the way home, understandably.

At the front door of their house she could not, for a moment, find her key. This flustered her immoderately. Key found, she insisted on going in ahead of him when she'd opened the door. The house, from what he could glimpse as he followed her through, was cluttered and untidy: young boys' mess.

'I'm sorry the place is in such a state,' said Bromwyn, although she sounded irritated, not sorry. He knew damn well he was unwelcome, that he had come back to life at much too short a notice for her. He didn't care.

The house was a single mother's place now. Everything of his had been removed. He found this interesting, but didn't mind much. Nothing he had ever possessed had been quite what he wanted anyway. He guessed correctly that his den had been given to the eldest of his sons, and he approved of that: Robert would be nine now, an age at which a boy deserved a room of his own.

Andy wasn't looking forward to meeting his children, though.

His wife seemed hell-bent on taking him through a guided confessional tour of what had changed, and why. Extra space had been required for X, which meant that Y had to be shifted to Z, where it got in the way of . . . He told her he could wait until later for all that, and suggested she make them both a cup of tea.

The kitchen bench was littered with the mess made by children who'd been too young to serve themselves last time he'd seen them. He cleared a spot to lean his elbow on as his wife stiltedly made the tea.

'Now,' she said, her back to him, 'Is it two sugars or one?'

'Two,' he said absently. They seemed mutually agreed to let this exchange pass as if unnoticed. Instead, they sat at the breakfast bench and drank their tea in silence. This, as far as he could remember, was not unusual for them, although of course it felt that way in the circumstances.

'I have to clean up,' said Bromwyn at last.

'I'm not stopping you,' he said.

She stared pointedly at his elbow leaning in the midst of the plates. He understood he was in the way, got up and walked into the living room.

He sat down in the old armchair and picked up a news-paper to see what sorts of things the world was up to these days.

Meeting his sons was not as much of an ordeal as he'd thought it would be. The eldest was in fact ten (a miscalcula-tion on his part) and seemed uninterested in him or, for that matter, in Bromwyn.

'See you later, Dad,' he said, and went up to his room.

The younger boys were curious, shy, and friendly, as if he were an interesting visitor. They asked him how he got well.

'I don't *know*,' he said. '*Nobody* knows. It's a mystery of science.'

They seemed to like that.

They asked him, too, what it was like to be mad. The seven-year-old asked,

'Can you still make that noise you made when you were mad? You know, like *woo-woo-woooo*?'

'Sure,' he said, oblivious of his wife going rigid with

mortification behind him. Craning his head back and opening his mouth as wide as possible, he did an impression of his old howl.

'What do you think?' he asked his son.

'Mm,' said the seven-year-old dubiously. 'It was better before.'

'Sorry,' he said, amused.

'That's quite enough,' said his wife, sounding very careworn, which he supposed she was.

He could no longer see in her the young woman he'd married, the young woman with the black hair and the big dreamy eyes and the inviting satiny neck. If he had lived with her these past five years he'd probably still be able to see her the way she used to be, but he couldn't. She was from an older generation.

That evening, the family watched television, the way they'd always done, even when the boys were babies. Later in the night, when the children had gone to bed, Andrew and Bromwyn watched television as a couple. They changed channels a couple of times, caught the second half of a murder mystery. Having both missed the start, they were on equal footing and were able to talk a little, conjecturing who the murderer might be. He felt marginally closer to her, but knew it wouldn't last.

In bed she lay beside him like a folded-up deck chair. He stared at the wrinkles on her neck.

'Do you want to make love to me?' she asked. He could tell that if he touched her she would recoil.

'Not tonight,' he said. It was true. His erection, hidden away in his oversized pyjamas, was not for her. It was for women in general.

Eventually his wife turned over.

'I'm falling asleep,' she announced thickly. 'Good night, Andy.'

'Good night.'

At about 2:45 by the strange new alarm clock on his side of the bed, Andrew got out and put on his dressing-gown and slippers. Carefully making his way through the black corridor in case he tripped on foreign junk, he finished up in the living room, trying to look out through the gauzy curtains. It grew in him how good it would feel to be outside.

He stepped out onto the veranda, leaving the door unlocked. There was nothing in the house he would mind a burglar stealing.

The night was indigo and sultry, with a full moon. Static trickled up and down his neck. The world was as still as a forest that had been cut down. He felt like a small bird, hopping uncomprehendingly from stump to stump in the darkness.

Pushing off from his letterbox as if for good luck, Andrew set off down the street. In the dark the neighbourhood was not as familiar as he'd first thought. He didn't know if he'd be able to find his way back.

THE EYES OF THE SOUL

The view from Jeanette's front window was, frankly, shite.

Outside lay Rusborough South. There was no Rusborough North, West or East, as far as Jeanette knew. Maybe they'd existed once, but if so, they must have been demolished long ago, wiped off the map, and replaced with something better.

Jeanette's house was right opposite the local shop, which had its good and bad side. Not the shop itself: that had four bad sides, all of them grey concrete with graffiti on. But having your house right near the shop: there was a good side to that. Jeanette could send Tim out for a carton of milk or a sack of frozen chips and watch him through the window in case he got attacked. The bad side was that the shop was a magnet for the estate's worst violence.

'Look, Mum: police!' Tim would say almost every evening, pointing through the window at the flashing blue lights and the angry commotion just across the road.

'Finish your supper,' she would tell him, but he would keep on watching through the big dirty rectangle of glass. He couldn't really do anything else. The blinds were never drawn on the front window, because as soon as you blocked off the view, ugly though it was, you immediately noticed what a poky little shoebox the sitting room was. Better to see out, Jeanette had decided, even if what you were seeing was Rusborough South's substance abusers arguing with the law.

'What are police for, Mum?' Tim had asked her once.

'They keep us nice and safe, pet,' she'd replied automatically. But deep down, she had no faith in the boys in blue, or in the zealous busybodies who tried to get her interested in Neighbourhood Watch schemes. It was all just an excuse for coffee mornings where other powerless people just like herself complained about their awful neighbours and then got shirty about who was paying for the biscuits.

Positive action, they called it. Jeanette much preferred to buy lottery scratchcards, which might at least get her out of Rusborough South if she was lucky.

The one thing that pissed her off more than anything else was window companies. They would ring her up about once a week, telling her they were doing a special promotion on windows just now, and could they maybe send someone round for a free quote. 'I don't know,' she said the first time. 'Can you just tell me how much you'd charge to replace my front window when kids throw a rock through it?' But the window companies didn't do that sort of thing. They wanted to do the whole house up with security windows, double glazing: serious money. Jeanette didn't have serious money. The window companies kept phoning regardless.

'Look, I've told you before,' she would snap at them. 'I'm not interested.'

'Not a problem, not a problem,' they'd assure her. 'We

shan't trouble you again.' But a week later, someone else would call, asking her if she'd given any thought to her windows.

Then one day somebody called in person. A woman with an expensive haircut, dressed like a politician or a weather girl on the telly. She stood in Jeanette's doorway, clutching a leatherbound folder and what looked like a video remote control. Parked against the kerb behind her was a bright green van with a burly, shaven-headed man at the wheel. The side of the van was decorated with the words OUTLOOK INNOVATIONS and a stylised picture of a window looking out onto a landscape of trees and mountains.

'You're not a window company, are you?' said Jeanette.

The woman hesitated a moment, seemed a bit nervous. 'No, not really,' she said. 'We offer people an alternative to windows.'

'You're a window company,' affirmed Jeanette irritably, and shut the door in the woman's face. She hated to do this to another human being, but when she'd first moved to Rusborough, a bunch of red-faced, panting little kids had come to the door asking if they could please have a drink of water. She'd considered shutting the door in their faces, but let them into the kitchen to have a drink instead. Next day, her house was burgled.

Shutting the door in people's faces had got a little easier after that.

But the lady with the leatherbound folder popped up at the window and looked awfully embarrassed.

'I'm honestly not selling windows,' she pleaded, her voice muffled by the grubby pane of glass between her and Jeanette. 'Not what you'd think of as a window, anyway. Couldn't I please have five minutes of your time? I can actually show you what we're offering right here and now.'

Jeanette wavered on the spot, trapped. She should have drawn the blinds, but it was too late for that. Her eyes and the eyes of the other woman were locked, and all sorts of hum-drum intimacies seemed to be flowing between them, like *I'm a woman, you're a woman*, and *I'm a mother, are you a mother too?*

Her shoulders slumping in defeat, Jeanette walked back to the door and opened it.

Once allowed into the living room, the saleswoman didn't waste any time.

'What do you think of the view through your window?' she said.

'It's shite,' said Jeanette.

The saleswoman smiled again, and tipped her head slightly to the side, as if to say, *I'd have to agree with you there, but I'm too polite to say so.*

'Well,' she purred, 'If you had a choice, what would you be seeing out there?'

'Anything but Rusborough South,' replied Jeanette without hesitation.

'Mountains? Valleys? The sea?' persisted the saleswoman.

'Listen, when I win the lottery I'll let you know where I move to, how's that?'

The saleswoman seemed to sense she was annoying Jeanette. Cradling her folder against her immaculate breast, she pointed her remote control thingy towards the window, straight at the man in the van. There was a soft *neep*. The man got the message, and the van door swung open.

'At Outlook Innovations we like to say, windows are the eyes of the soul,' said the saleswoman, reverently, almost dreamily.

Jeanette considered, for the first time, the possibility that she had let some sort of religious loony into her home.

'That's very deep,' she said. 'Look, my son's going to be home from school soon . . .'

'This won't take a minute,' the saleswoman assured her.

The man had flipped open the hatches of the van, and was leaning inside. His overalls were bright green, to match the vehicle, and had OI emblazoned on them. Jeanette thought of skinheads.

Out of the back of the vehicle and into the arms of the man slid a large dull-grey screen. It looked like an oversized central heating radiator, but was apparently not as heavy, as the man lifted it by himself without much effort. He carried it across Jeanette's horrible little 'lawn' and lifted it up to the window of her horrible little house. He manoeuvred it onto the windowsill, grunting with the effort of not getting his fingers squashed. Then he shoved the screen right up tight against the window, with a scrape of metal on prefab something-or-other. It blocked the entire view snugly, with no more than a millimetre to spare on all sides.

Jeanette laughed uneasily. 'You've had me measured, have you?' she said.

'We would never take such a liberty,' demurred the saleswoman. 'I think you'll find that almost every front window on the estate is absolutely identical.'

'I'd wondered about that, actually,' said Jeanette.

Slid so securely into place, the screen sealed the room with claustrophobic efficiency, making the electric light seem harsher and yet at the same time more feeble, like the mournful glow inside a chicken coop.

Jeanette tried to be well-behaved about the way it made her feel, not wanting to make a scene in front of a stranger. But to her surprise the saleswoman said,

'Awful, isn't it?'

'Pardon?'

'Feels like a prison, yes?'

'Yeah,' said Jeanette. There were scrabblings going on outside the house, which must be the technician making adjustments. He wasn't screwing the bloody thing in, was he?

'If this particular Outlook were installed permanently, the seal would be soundproof, too.'

'Yeah?' said Jeanette. Being boxed in was already driving her mental, so the thought of being shut off from all sound as well wasn't exactly the thing to cheer her up. That cowboy out there had better take his damn panel off her window and put it back in his van ASAP. Jeanette wondered if it was going to be difficult to get these people to leave.

'Now,' said the saleswoman. 'I'll hand you the control, and you can switch it on.'

'Switch it on?' echoed Jeanette.

'Yes,' said the saleswoman, nodding encouragingly as if to a small child. 'Do go ahead. Feel free.'

Jeanette squinted at the remote, and pressed her thumb on the button marked ON/OFF.

Suddenly the screen seemed to vanish from her window, as if it had been whipped away by a gust of wind. Light beamed in again through the glass, making Jeanette blink.

But it was not the light of Rusborough South. Where the hell was Rusborough South? The shop across the road was gone. The dismal streets the colour of used kitty litter were gone. The bus shelter with the poster about saying no to domestic violence was gone.

Instead, the world outside had changed to a scene of startling beauty. The house had seemingly relocated itself right in the middle of a spacious country garden, the sort you might see in a TV documentary about Beatrix Potter or somebody like that. There were trellises with tomatoes growing on

them, and rusty watering cans, and little stone paths leading into rosebushes, and rickety sheds half-lost in thicket. Much love had obviously been poured into the design and the tending of this place, but nature was getting the best of it now, gently but insistently spilling over the borders with lush weeds and wildflowers. At its wildest peripheries the garden merged (just about at the point where the Rusborough shop ought to be) into a vast sloping meadow that stretched endlessly into the distance. The tall grass of that meadow rippled like great feathery waves in the breeze. In the sky above, an undulating V-formation of white geese was floating along, golden in the sunlight.

Entranced, Jeanette moved closer to the window, right up to the windowsill. The smudges on the glass were just as they had been for weeks, years maybe. Beyond them, the world really was what it appeared to be, radiant and tranquil. The perspective changed subtly just the way it should, when she turned her head or looked down. Just underneath the window, a discarded slipper had moss growing on it, and flower petals were being scattered across the ground by a tiny sparrow. Jeanette pressed her nose against the glass and tried to peek sideways, to see the joins. All she could see was some kind of ivy she didn't have a name for, nuzzling at the edges of the window, dark green with a spot of russet red at the heart of each leaf. Her ear, so close now to the glass, heard the little beak of that sparrow quite clearly, the infinitely subtle rustle of the leaves, the distant honking of the geese.

'It's a video, right?' she said shakily. To keep her awe at bay, she closed her eyes and tried to see the view through her window objectively. She imagined it as a sort of endless re-run of the same film of a country garden, with the same birds flying the same circuit at intervals like in those shop window displays at Christmas, those mechanical tableaux in which

Santa Claus lowered a sack of presents into a chimney end-lessly without ever letting it go.

'No, it's not a video,' murmured the saleswoman.

'Well, some sort of film anyway,' said Jeanette, opening her eyes again. The geese were out of sight now, but the golden light was deepening. 'How long does it go for?'

The saleswoman chuckled indulgently, as though a small child had just asked her when the sun would fall back to the ground.

'It goes *forever*,' she said. 'It's not any kind of film. It's a real place, and this is what it's like there, right now, at this very moment.'

Jeanette struggled with the idea. The sparrow had jumped onto the windowsill. It was utterly, vividly real. It opened its minuscule mouth and chirped, then shivered its wings, shedding a couple of fluffs.

'You mean . . . I'm looking into somebody else's back garden?' asked Jeanette.

'In a way,' said the saleswoman, opening her leather-bound folder and leafing through its waterproofed pages. 'This is a satellite broadcast of . . . let me see . . . the grounds of the Old Priory, in Northward Hill, Rochester. This is what is happening there right now.'

Jeanette became suddenly aware that she was gaping like an idiot. She closed her mouth and frowned, trying to look cynical and unimpressed.

'Well,' she said, staring out across the meadows. 'There's not a great deal happening there, is there?'

'That's a matter of opinion, of course,' conceded the saleswoman. 'We do have Outlooks which view onto more . . . *eventful* landscapes. There is the Blue Surge Outlook, which broadcasts the view through the lighthouse at Curlew Point, Cruidlossie, the third-stormiest beach in the British Isles. For

those who like trains, we have the Great Valley Crossing Outlook, which has three major railways running services past it. For animal lovers, we have the Room To Roam Outlook, viewing onto an organic sheep farm in Wales . . .'

Jeanette was watching her little sparrow hop away across the garden, and the saleswoman's voice was a twitter in the background.

'Mm?' she said. 'Oh well actually, this is . . . fine.'

'It's particularly lovely at night,' added the saleswoman in a soft, beguiling tone. 'Owls come out. They catch mice in the garden.'

'Owls?' echoed Jeanette. She had never seen an owl. She had seen a lot of things. She'd seen kids sniffing glue, she'd once stumbled onto an attempted rape, she'd had to pick bits of hypodermic syringe out of the rubber soles of her son's trainers. About a fortnight ago, sitting at this same windowsill late at night, she'd watched a drunken, bloodied boy larking about on the roof of the shop, pissing over the edge, while his mates whooped and ran around below, dodging the stream. *Now I've seen everything*, she'd murmured to herself. But she'd never seen an owl.

'How . . . how much does this cost?' she breathed.

There was a pause while the wind blew a few leaves trembling against the window.

'You can buy,' said the saleswoman. 'Or you can rent.' Her eyes twinkled kindly, offering her customer the choice that was no choice at all.

'How . . . how much per . . . um . . .'

'It works out to a smidgen over fourteen pounds a week,' said the saleswoman. Observing Jeanette swallowing hard, she went on: 'Some people would spend that much on scratch cards, or cigarettes.'

Jeanette cleared her throat.

'Yeah,' she said.

Then, desperate for a reason to resist the pull of the beautiful world out there, Jeanette narrowed her eyes and demanded,

'What if some kid throws a brick through it?'

Again the saleswoman opened her leatherbound folder, and held a particular page out for Jeanette's perusal.

'All our Outlooks,' she declared, 'are designed and guaranteed to withstand the impact of any residential missile.'

'Full beer cans?' challenged Jeanette.

'Beer cans. Footballs. Rocks. Gunfire at point-blank range, if necessary.'

Jeanette looked at the saleswoman in alarm, wondering if she knew something about the Rusborough gangs that Jeanette didn't.

'We do a lot of business in America,' the saleswoman explained hastily.

Jeanette imagined movie stars and celebrities like Oprah gazing through these wonderful windows. The saleswoman let her imagine, keeping to herself her own more accurate vision of the urban slums of Baltimore and Michigan, where rows and rows of windows – twenty, thirty, fifty a day – were being plugged up with the grey screens of Outlook Innovations.

'Of course, they're the ideal security, too,' she pointed out. 'Nothing in the world can get through.'

Jeanette knew deep down she was already sold, but she made one last attempt to appear hard-headed.

'People could still get in through the other windows,' she remarked.

The saleswoman accepted this gracefully with another little tilt of the head.

'Well . . .' she said, hugging her folder-full of Outlooks to her breast with unostentatious pride. 'One thing at a time.'

Jeanette looked back at the garden, the fields. They were still there. The sky, the horizon, the overgrown paths, the tomato-vines: none of it had gone away. She felt like crying.

Minutes later, while the man outside laboured to fix the screen permanently into place, Jeanette signed a contract, pledging £60 per month to Outlook Innovations Incorporated. She knew she was making the right decision, too, because while the screen was being bolted onto her house, it had to be switched off briefly, and Jeanette missed her garden with a craving so intense it was almost unendurable. There was no doubt in her mind that this was an addiction she would gladly give up smoking for.

An hour later, long after the saleswoman and the green van had driven away, Jeanette was still kneeling at the windowsill, gazing out at Northward Hill. Some of the geese were returning, flying closer to her house this time. They beat their wings lazily, trumpeting their alien contentment.

Suddenly Tim burst into the house, safe and sound after another long day at his sink school. He came to a halt on the living room carpet, goggling in amazement at the view through the window. He pointed, unable to speak. Finally, all he could manage was:

'Mum, what are those birds doing there?'

Jeanette laughed, wiping her eyes with her nicotine-stained fingers. 'I don't know,' she said. 'They're just . . . they just live here.'

SERIOUS SWIMMERS

There were a couple of hiccups between Gail and Ant before they even got to the swimming pool.

For a start, 'My name's not Ant,' the child said. 'It's Anthony.' Now why did he have to say that, with the social worker right there in the car with them, listening to everything? For a few moments (none of Gail's emotions lasted very long) she hated her little boy so much she couldn't breathe, and she hated the social worker even more, for being there to hear Ant's complaint. She wished the social worker could die somehow and take the knowledge of Gail's humiliation with him; he deserved to die anyway, the parasite. But the social worker remained alive and at the wheel, noting Gail's come-uppance in his little black book of a brain, and then – Jesus Christ! – Ant went and did it again when they were almost there, by asking Gail, 'What was that little drink you had back there?'

'What little drink?'

'The little drink you had at the chemist. In the little plastic cup.'

'Medicine, cutie.'

'My name's not cutie,' stated the child. 'It's Anthony.'

Then, as the car was drawing to a halt in front of the Melbourne public baths, this kid, this Anthony who had grown out of being the Ant she'd lost to the State five years ago, said to her,

'Are you still sick?'

'I used to be really sick,' was Gail's answer. 'Now I'm a lot better.'

The boy looked unimpressed.

'Moira says people shouldn't take medicine if they're not sick.'

Moira was Anthony's foster-carer. He didn't call her Mum. But then he didn't call Gail Mum either. He was careful not to call her anything.

'Your mum is only a little bit sick now,' the social worker chipped in, his head twisted away as he parked the car. 'The last bit.'

Gail hadn't expected this from him. She was glad the social worker was alive now, grateful. She was willing to do anything for him, anything he wanted, like for free. Although she'd better be careful who she slept with these days, if she wanted to get Ant back.

'Two,' she told the swimming pool cashier. 'One child and one . . . ah . . . grown-up.' She flinched at the stumble: years of addiction had half-dissolved lots of words she'd once had no problem coming out with. They were like things you leave in a box in the garage and then when you look for them years later you find the water's got to them.

* * *

This visit to the swimming pool was Ant's idea, as far as Gail knew. She didn't know very far, though. The social worker would suggest an outing with Anthony, like going to the movies, and Gail would go to the movies with Anthony. Everything was arranged: which movie, which cinema, which session time. Who decided? Gail wasn't sure, except that it wasn't her. Maybe Anthony had told Moira he really liked swimming and Moira had told the social worker, and the social worker had taken it from there. Maybe it was the other way around.

Gail had never been to this swimming pool before, had never been to any swimming pool since she'd been a schoolgirl, slouching in the audience at the water sports finals, distracted by nicotine craving. Those trials had been held in the open air, in a giant complex of pools. This place she and Ant were entering now was different altogether, an indoor place, like a railway-station-sized bathroom built around a railway-platform-sized bath. A combination of electric light and sunshine from the many windows and skylights made it a kind of in-between world, neither inside nor out.

The water was warm, something Gail didn't really believe until she dangled her naked foot off the edge. She'd imagined that 'heated' meant the water sort of had the chill taken off it, but it was as warm as a bath: body temperature maybe. She couldn't be sure. Her own body thermostat had been well and truly fucked for years.

Gail and Ant didn't need to go to the changing rooms; they both had their swimgear on underneath their street clothes – another detail overseen by the social worker, this man who brought them together and, just by existing, kept them officially apart.

There were only about ten or eleven people in the pool, half of them adults swimming or hanging off the sides near

the deep end. One length of the pool had been roped off by a floating divider of coloured plastic, to give serious swimmers one narrow lane to do their laps in. A well-muscled Japanese man prepared to enter this strip; a well-fleshed Australian woman was doing the backstroke. Everyone else was in the unrestricted part of the pool. Teenagers, children and their parents played at the shallow end, taking no notice of Gail and Anthony climbing in. Anthony was six and the water was up to his chest; Gail was twenty-three and the water was up to her navel. She squatted to come down to his level, and because it was warmer underwater.

'Can you swim?' she asked, noticing how awkwardly Ant was looking down at the water around his chest and his faraway feet on the bottom of the pool.

'Yeah, I swim all the time,' he said. 'I swim real good,' and immediately he gave a succession of startling demonstrations which consisted of throwing himself forward in the water, sinking, thrashing his arms and legs as rapidly as he could, and surfacing in a blind sputter. He couldn't even tell which direction he was facing when he surfaced, and he would swivel his head, blinking and burping, trying to orient himself to where he had started.

'I can swim too,' said Gail. 'But not very well.'

She'd learned to swim in a backyard swimming pool, one of those round, blue, free-standing things from the Clark Rubber store in Ferntree Gully, and she had been Anthony's age. The boy whose family owned the pool had shown her how to float and how to move forward. He also tried to show her how to synchronise the arm and leg movements and turn her head from side to side to get the breaths in, but she hadn't mastered that part. Then he had shown her his penis, and she had shown him her chubby little vulva: the pre-agreed reason for the game.

She wasn't chubby now. She was thin and grown-up. It had cost her $2.80 to get into the pool, twice as much as Ant. That was where growing up got you: ADULTS, $2.80.

A grotesquely overweight man climbed in at the children's end and waded out towards the deep, rolls of fat on his back humping in and out of the water as he began to swim.

'How come that man's swimming when he's so fat?' Anthony whispered to her, his awe overwhelming his reserve. Anxious to have the answer, Gail had to think hard. Other people's motivations, or even her own, were not her strong point.

'His doctor probably told him to,' she said at last.

She didn't perceive the man as being particularly grotesque. He was a member of the straight world, and members of the straight world were normal, they had their place. The fat man belonged here with the mothers and their paddling children, the idle athletes and goggled teenagers; he could claim the right to displace as much water as he wished, whereas Gail, pale from night-living and wasted by narcotics, was an alien object which might at any moment be fished out of the pool by an angry official. She looked down at herself in the water, at the spindly white legs coming out of the oversized red shorts, and then looked at Ant. His shorts were oversized too, yet they were very cute on him: he looked as if he was about to grow into them, whereas she seemed to be shrinking out of hers.

Anthony continued to demonstrate his mastery of swimming for her, throwing himself, thrashing furiously underwater, and surfacing: Gail tried to look as if she were looking on approvingly, but really she was staring at the well-fleshed woman swimming backstroke in the roped-off lane. This woman was so powerful and steady, completing length after length, from the deep end to the shallow and

back to the deep, a serious swimmer, her breasts sticking up out of the water. She was another species, as different from Gail as a seal or a porpoise. Gail laid one hand across her own breast. Her tube top had almost nothing inside it; her wrist rested against bone. Heroin had wasted her. The first time the social workers had taken Ant away from her, they had given her a milk expresser, but there had been nothing to express.

On impulse she started swimming, in her own way. All she could do was lie face-down in the water until her body started to float up to the top, and then with slow, sweeping strokes she moved forward. Once again, for the first time since learning to swim in that backyard pool, she tried the breathing part, but as soon as she lifted her head out of the water the rest of her started to sink. She was disappointed; she had hoped that somehow during the long and horrible lifetime she'd lived since first trying, she might have gained the knack sort of automatically.

She lay face down in the water again, waiting to be buoyed up, and then she swam and swam, back and forth across the shallow end of the pool. At first she swam with her eyes closed, anticipating the touch of her fingers against the pool's side or the floating rope, but after she'd hit her head on the tiles twice, and been kicked by one of the serious swimmers, she swam with her eyes open, surprised to find it didn't hurt. She couldn't see much except luminous chlorine blue, disturbed every now and then by a psychedelic glimpse of an approaching body. Sometimes it was Anthony's body trying to swim beside her, a blur of flailing little arms and legs distorted by motion and diffusion.

Eventually she worked up the courage to touch him, to signal him up.

'It's better if you float first,' she said. 'Watch me.'

She demonstrated, and he watched, and then, when she'd surfaced and was waiting for him to imitate her, he said,

'I've been watching you. I've been doing the same as you for ages.'

'You don't wait long enough. You start trying to move around before you're floating.'

His answer to that was to throw himself forward in the water next to her, to demonstrate that no matter how many long, long microseconds he could bear to wait, his body wasn't borne up the way hers was. Gail thought of telling him to keep still longer, but suddenly she was sickened by an image, rammed into her mind like a slide into a slide-viewer, of Ant floating on top of the water, dead.

'How about you hold on to me while I swim?' she suggested, so shaken by the dead son still floating in her head that she forgot to be afraid of rejection.

Anthony looked away from her, ignoring her suggestion it seemed, towards a part of the pool where a burly Italian man was playing a game with his daughter. Over and over the man would lift the child out of the water, arrange her weight carefully in his arms, and toss her as far and as high as he could. The girl shrieked with delight every time she made her splash.

'Can you do that to me?' Anthony asked.

No, Gail thought automatically, the way she'd always done when asked to attempt anything not related to heroin. Everything else was too hard.

'I'm only little,' she tried to explain.

Anthony looked at her as if she was crazy: couldn't she see the difference between them? To make him happy was so easy: a simple physical act. He was a child, she was a grown-up, therefore she could do it: the pleasure was hers to give or withhold.

Gail looked down at him, trying to assess how big or small he really was. Excitement shone on his face, like a sheen

of chemical which could contort his features into joy or distress depending on what happened next.

What happened next was that she picked him up and threw him as far as she could. He shrieked with delight, just like the Italian man's little girl. It was as simple as that.

'Again! Again!' he squealed, wading back to her, and they did it again. He had forgotten to be wary of her, and Gail felt secure enough to cope with the possibility of his remembering. It wouldn't last, but she was happy, incredibly happy, treating herself to dose after dose of infectious excitement.

Eventually when she was too exhausted to toss him anymore she did some more swimming, and this time he held on to her, pulled through the water at first by his hands on her ankle, then by his arms around her neck. His weight was the most satisfying physical sensation she could ever remember having.

She couldn't get over how easy physical intimacy was in the water. They were more buoyant; if they moved towards each other they were together so suddenly that there was nothing to do about it but accept. Also the water was a reassuring medium between them – she could even embrace him, his legs wrapped around her waist, and the water would keep their bodies discrete and a little unreal, just enough to make it possible. An embrace in the empty air out there in the real world would be so much more difficult. How could you start it out there, with nothing helping you towards the other person, and how could you end it, with no medium to ease you apart, only the awkward unclenching of decision? She remembered their previous outings together, which had been visits to the movies mostly. Gail had sat there in the dark next to Anthony, wondering if she could get away with laying her arm along the top of his seat so that when he sat back he might feel it there around his shoulders. She remembered the

mingled taste of Methadone and choc-top ice cream, and the gigantic images of robots, monsters and explosions whose reflected light flickered on the face of her son.

Never again, she thought. *It's the pool from now on.*

But already there was a problem.

The familiar pain in her guts had come.

'We have to get out soon,' she said to Anthony, but he played on as if he had water in his ears.

'We have to get out now,' she said a few moments later, as the pain screwed deeper.

'Oh please, not yet Mum!'

Hearing it, she realised she would do anything, anything for that last word.

'OK, you stay for a while,' she said. 'But I have to get out now. I'll come back and watch you from the edge.'

He seemed happy with that, so she climbed up the little steel ladder out of the pool. The unheated air felt freezing. Her shorts stuck heavily to her goose-pimpled flesh, and underneath her sodden tank top her nipples tightened painfully. She hobbled to where she had left her clothes, scooped them up and rushed to the changing room.

Her body temperature seemed to be dropping at the rate of one degree per second, and she undressed in a clumsy frenzy. The vision of Anthony floating face down in the water slotted into her mind again; he looked dead, as only a dead child can look.

The well-fleshed woman, the serious swimmer, was in the changing room too, observing Gail's anxiousness with mild curiosity as she stepped backwards into a steaming shower. Her pubic hair was thick and black; she was probably wondering why Gail had none. *Really*, thought Gail, *now that I'm off the game I should stop shaving it, let it grow . . .*

Every twenty seconds or so Gail hurried to the door of

the changing room, towel wrapped around her, to make sure her boy was still alive. Then she would hurry back inside and dry herself some more. Her skinny limbs seemed to slip through the fabric of the towel untouched, remaining cold and wet no matter how much she rubbed. There was water in the hollows of her collarbones, water running down the hardened lines of her arms and legs. The pain in her guts grew and grew as she dressed, and finally she couldn't contain it any longer. After checking on Anthony one more time, she shut herself into the toilet and stayed there, doubled up, for many minutes.

The diarrhoea took its sweet time as usual, and all the while her son was in the pool gasping blue water into his lungs, thrashing around under the surface in such a way that the others would think he was just playing, no different from when his mother had been in there with him. She was dizzy with pain and panic, considered staggering out there with her jeans around her ankles. Then suddenly the pain subsided. Something had rearranged itself inside her.

Back at the poolside moments later, she determined at a glance that none of the heads above water was Anthony's, and she peered anxiously at the indistinct bodies underneath. In the outside world the sun was setting, so that the indoor light was all electric now, cold and brutal. Running sideways along the edge of the pool, Gail became aware of the social worker standing on the other side, looking in also, but she didn't really care. She understood that if he was blaming her for Anthony's death, this was less important than Anthony's death itself.

'Anthony!' she called.

A hand on her arm sent a shock through her, like a stray electric spark. Anthony had emerged from the other changing room, dressed and dry, his hair neatly combed. Of course

she'd imagined that when the time came for him to come out of the pool she would have to take him into the changing room with her, the way she'd always taken him into toilets when he was a baby, but she could see now that that was half a lifetime ago.

With an inarticulate noise of relief and effort, she swept him up into her arms, swaying a little, surprised at his weight out of the water.

Simultaneously she wished never to let him go, and yet longed to put him down; his intrusion into her was so shocking, deeper and more merciless than anything she had ever suffered from men or needles. How could they compare, those thousand shallow, anaesthetic penetrations, when here she was fully clothed at a suburban swimming pool, blasted open and infused by this little alien she herself had made?

She'd had enough for one day, she was ready to call it quits, to sleep alone in her empty flat for fourteen hours and hand this heavy, heavy child of hers over to the social worker, and on to Moira Whatsername, until she'd recovered and was ready to cope with this feeling again.

But as the social worker walked towards them, Anthony leaned close to her face and whispered in her ear,

'That was fun, Mum. What next?'

EXPLAINING COCONUTS

The blood-red double doors swing open, sending a false breeze through the recycled tropical air, and yet another sweaty foreigner walks in. The desk clerks and cleaners and bellboys look up for an instant, then revert to their standby mode. *Just another coconut man,* they think.

Dozens of foreigners have been arriving from all over the world all day, many hours before the advertised starting time of the event. They are wealthy men, important men, not the sort of men who would usually sit around waiting for anything, especially not on ugly stainless-steel chairs upholstered in lime-green velour. They glance at wristwatches that resemble the counterfeits on sale throughout Indonesia, but are worth a hundred times more. They fiddle with gold and silver cuff-links that were gifts from business associates or absent spouses. Nothing will make the time go faster. They are determined – even the ones who are alcoholics – to stay sober.

The conference room is in a hotel in Jakarta that describes itself as world class. Of course the men know that any hotel which feels the need to describe itself as world class is not. Subtle *faux pas* in the brochure bear this out: misspellings, unnecessary capitalisations, references to 'authentic atmosphere' and the 'lucious green paddy fields that surround the Hotel's classic temple style architeture'. None of this matters to the men, not even to the ones who are architects and hotel owners by trade.

Nor do these men care that the Magdalaya Hotel's echoing gymnasium lacks the facilities to which they're accustomed, that the water of the swimming pool lies chlorinous and still, and that, outside in the shimmering heat, the nets of the tennis courts are crawling with bees. They have not come here for these things. They have come here for pleasures that are available nowhere else on earth.

The unique ritual spectacles of Indonesia? No, no, no. They have not come to see the re-enacted ancient battles, the whip duels, the spirit drummers, the funeral feasts. They've perused photographs of these phenomena in the inflight magazine on the journey here, and what small appetite they might have had for them is satisfied.

They have not come to dive in Padangbai, snorkel in Komodo or surf in Grajagan. They are unhealthy men, most of them: overweight, fiftyish, wearing expensive, roomy suits and white shirts already ringed with crystallising antiperspirant stains. Many of them have wives who would have adored visiting the temples and soaking up the sun, but they've left their wives at home – at home in London, New York, Montreal, Munich, Vienna, Tokyo, Melbourne, and many other places.

Some of the men have brought cameras, simply because they're in the habit of taking a camera on overseas trips, or

because their wives urged them not to leave home without one. These cameras will remain unused, for none of the men would dare take a photograph during Miss Soedhono's presentation, nor would there be much point in doing so. After all, one's own rapture cannot be captured on film.

Mounted high on one of the walls of the conference room is a slender grey surveillance camera, pointed not at the empty expanse of purple carpet where Miss Soedhono will soon stand, but at the audience. It moves from left to right in an oiled, leisurely arc, like a snake half-dozing over an uneventful hole in the earth. Its dark glassy eye glints each time its slow-motion swivel catches the light from the spherical lamps hanging from the ceilings. These lamps, switched on despite the noonday sunshine penetrating the thin fabric of the curtains, cast an ambiguous luminosity over the men, yellowing them in much the same way that a grimy refrigerator bulb discolours leftover hunks of beef and neglected jars of mayonnaise.

The conference room is filled to capacity, or it will be when the men who are smoking outside have finished sucking nicotine into their bloodstreams. Once Miss Soedhono's presentation is underway, no one will think of their more mundane addictions, but in the meantime these still exert their pitiful tyranny. Tobacco, chewing-gum, an early-morning sniff of cocaine in the sauna-like lavatories. Some of the men have vomited or had diarrhoea: the indigestible overload of waiting.

Finally all the cigarette butts are extinguished, all the bowels purged, all the mouths rinsed and sprayed, all the foreheads mopped one last time before such things cease to matter. The last stragglers — although that word is unjust, because no one dares to be even a second late, and the 'stragglers' are merely those who take their seats five minutes rather

than an hour early – walk self-consciously into the room, nodding blindly at the fellowship of strangers among whom they must find their place. No one speaks, apart from grunts of permission as knees are swung aside to allow ungainly male bodies to squeeze past, and grunts of relief as buttocks settle on the velvety green seats and trousers are adjusted.

The oversized clock on the back wall, slightly fogged with condensation, ticks towards the agreed geometry of the long and short hands. The men make no attempt to converse or even acknowledge each other's existence, preferring to stare at the long hand of the clock as it approaches the appointed hour. Very likely the Magdalaya's clocks are wrong, compared to the wristwatches of the men, which are precision instruments guaranteed not to lose a second in ten million years. However, that's irrelevant here. Here, nothing can be hurried, and none of the men – even those who might ordinarily need to humiliate several inferiors per hour – has uttered a word of complaint all day.

At last, when the Magdalaya's foggy clock says the time has come, Miss Soedhono appears from a curtained anteroom like a carved effigy on a revolving clocktower display. The wait is over.

Miss Soedhono is tall for an Indonesian woman, but no taller than an average Western adolescent. Her outfit is demure by the standards of an English or American boardroom: her legs are shrouded in a long, sarong-like skirt, and her high-collared jacket is buttoned up to the throat. The colours – emerald green, with bright gold brocade – are more sensuous than the greys and blacks these men are accustomed to seeing on their female colleagues back home, but on the other hand, there's something affectedly formal, even antiseptic, about Miss Soedhono's clothing, redolent of the livery of flight attendants. Her hair is pinned back severely, and her lips

are painted pale orange, with a gloss as thick as wax. Her teeth are white, faintly delineated with pale brown, as though she was once a smoker and has spent many years trying to polish the damage away. Yet if she is a person of any vulnerability, this is not betrayed by her expression. She's as calm as a bronze sculpture, her eyes so dark that pupil and iris are indistinguishable, even up close. No one gets close.

Miss Soedhono lifts her hands into the air, allowing them to hover near her brocaded bosom, displaying the flawless shape and yet mature flesh of her fingers, the whitish pink of her palms contrasted with the dark honey of her knuckles, the orange fingernails in all their pellucid lustre. Her hands cradle air as though it were a dossier of papers, a dossier she holds for the sake of protocol but which she has no need to consult. Already the men are attentive: affecting to shuffle in their seats in casual preparation, they are staring at Miss Soedhono's hands, at those sculpted orange nails hovering in front of them, almost eerie in the jaundiced light.

Miss Soedhono opens her mouth to speak. A hundred male mouths open too, their lips parting in anticipation.

'You will forgive me,' she says, 'if some of what I say is already well known to you.' Her accent is thick, though the words are all her own, not recited from a script or reconstituted from a phrasebook. She's fluent in five Asian languages, but English is the *lingua franca* to which she condescends as a special favour to this crowd of perspiring, pink-faced non-Indonesians.

'There is always a possibility,' she continues, 'that there will be someone here for whom the subject is ... virgin territory.'

A subtle thrill goes through the audience, as though the air temperature had momentarily dropped ten degrees. The combination of the word 'virgin' and the way Miss Soedhono

pouted her glossy orange lips to speak the word is what caused that thrill to pass among the men. The presentation has begun; nothing can stop it now.

'We are here,' says Miss Soedhono, 'to examine the physiology of the coconut, particularly in areas of exudation – that is, bleeding – of spadix sap, analysis of the sieve tube sap in all its components, translocation of ferro-cyanide in the sieve tube, and the factors which influence the nut's copra content.'

'Oh God,' whispers one of the men, scarcely able to believe that only yesterday morning he was exchanging meaningless pleasantries with his wife at the breakfast table, and now here he is, in the same room as Miss Soedhono, breathing the same air she exhales from her glossy mouth, from her honeyed throat.

'We have been busy here,' says Miss Soedhono, 'since you attended my last presentation.' She gestures in the air, a soundless snap of the fingers, and a large video screen, nestled in an enclave in the wall behind her, switches itself on. A brilliant image of green coconuts clustered against a ribbed tree-bough appears, haloed by the miraculous Kodachrome blue of Sulawesi sky. The men's eyes appraise it for an instant, then revert to the woman.

'We have developed – created, if you will – a new variety of coconut,' she says. 'It produces fifty-five fruits per bunch, aggregating to six hundred and sixty nuts per palm per year. You will note that the size is small. Do not be deceived. The usable contents, once the epicarp, mesocarp and endocarp have been discarded, account for a greater proportion of the whole than in large-sized fruits. In particular, there is a great deal more . . .' (she gestures again, and the picture dissolves into an extreme close-up of a whitish substance) 'endosperm.'

The men squirm collectively; there is an audible creaking of metal chairs.

'This endosperm yields as much as fifty-one per cent copra, with hardly any husk,' continues Miss Soedhono, her voice, on that last word, growing almost husky. 'We have given the germ-plasm priority in our breeding programme, and are confident that we will soon evolve D x T hybrids, using a dwarf known as Kelapa Raja as the seed parent.'

An image of the mighty Kelapa Raja, embraced by an adolescent Indonesian boy wrapped around the vertiginous upper reaches of its bough, comes on the screen.

'But let us now examine, briefly, what happens to the root system in swampy soil.' Miss Soedhono gestures again, and the screen is filled with pink rhizomes, a jostling crowd of them like starveling baby carrots. 'When the tips of main roots come into contact with the permanent water table, they immediately begin to rot. Death, gentlemen, certain death. To compensate for this extinction, branch roots develop directly from the tip, below the rotting portion. New roots also spring out from the bole and the stem. These abundant rootlets ramify into a densely-woven mat within one metre from the bole. Also, closer to the bole, we see' (another gesture, another dissolve) 'super-abundant pneumatophores or respiratory organs.'

A helplessly synchronised intake of breath passes through the audience. Miss Soedhono's eyes narrow in contempt, and she glances over the ranks of blushing faces, as if searching for the worm who dared to gasp out of turn.

'Also of prime importance,' she hisses, 'is the life span of the leaves. From the day a coconut leaf primordium distinguishes itself from the apical meristem, springing up from the throat of its immediate older leaf, a long period elapses before it is finally shed, exhausted and senile, from the crown. Illustrations of each phase of this metamorphosis from emergence to death are shown here. Please take a moment to study them.'

The men take a moment only. The supreme object of their focus is Miss Soedhono, whose jaw, turned towards glowing images of leaves and wooden rulers, is perfection itself, and whose neck, were it not for the intervention of her jacket collar, would continue straight down to her breast, that exotic bosom whose precise nature the men can only guess at.

'In each fertile palm, super-abundant female flowers bloom,' she continues, her cheek catching reflected light from the screen's latest offering. 'A particularly prolific palm is capable of producing over a thousand female flowers, in each of several spadices.'

The sharp odour of sweat is beginning to permeate the atmosphere; deodorants and perfumes with pointedly masculine names are no match for tropical heat, decrepit air conditioning and the combined temperature of sixty-six overdressed bodies arrayed shoulder-to-shoulder and thigh-to-thigh.

'If you care to look,' declares Miss Soedhono, 'you will find trichomes on the abaxial lamina, mostly along the inter-costal regions, on the petiole and the rachis as well as on the leaf sheath, the spathe, the peduncle, the spikes. You will even see them, if you peer closely, on this young ovary, partially exposed in this picture. You will see them everywhere, in fact. They vary in shape, size and in the intensity of their occurrence in different organs. They are imbued with certain substances that are poisonous to insects.'

As she says this, some of the men fancy they detect a sardonic twitch at the edges of her lips, a venomous aftertaste in the honey of her voice. She clicks her fingers, and the screen offers another close-up.

'These leaves, as you can see, arrange themselves so that the periphery of the spear is composed of the margins of leaflets with their special protective thickening. The hairy outgrowths' (she sweeps her orange fingernails towards the

image) 'also provide physical impediments to any young larvae that may be trying to affix themselves to the leaf.'

From somewhere in the audience comes a single, bronchial cough. Miss Soedhono turns her head to find the man responsible. Sixty-six pairs of eyes blink innocently, for although each man longs for Miss Soedhono to look at *him* and him only, he fears it too, especially if it should be for the wrong reason. Most terrifying of all would be if she observed him lurching fumblingly out of his seat, a victim of indigestion or a shameful lapse of continence. So, they all sit tight, affecting impassivity, oozing sweat, their eyes wide and bloodshot, while Miss Soedhono continues her lecture, moving on to the subject of parasites.

'There may be those among you,' she says, folding her exquisite hands together in an interleaving of bright nails and dark flesh, 'who believe in the myth, the *lie*, perpetuated by naturalists, that the coconut crab is capable of nipping a fruit, peeling off its husk, fibre by fibre, and breaking open the shell through the soft eye, in order to make a meal of the endosperm.'

Again she gestures, a mere nod this time, and images of crustaceans materialise on the screen, extraterrestrial-looking creatures with orange highlights on their turd-brown armour, as though Miss Soedhono herself had lovingly decorated them with her nail-polish.

'Examine, if you will, these infra-red exposures of the coconut crab, *Birgus latro*, pictured with coconuts in various states of development, including young fruits with soft exteriors, and even one ripe nut from which the husk had been temptingly stripped. No penetrations were made.'

Miss Soedhono raises her chin, somewhat defiantly, and rests her hands on her waist, her fingers hooked over the sharp curves of her hips, which protrude through her tunic.

Her arms are thin. She breathes in, and her bosom swells slightly, the gold of the brocade glittering as the silken fabric adjusts its purchase on the flesh beneath.

Does she notice what effect her stance is having on her audience? Her unblinking eyes survey the men as if they were no more than wooden puppets, carved ceremonial effigies arranged in rows. Indeed they have done their best to maintain such composure, but the provocation is too great. Flesh must move.

Miss Soedhono raises one hand off her hip. This time the click of her fingers is audible. The image on the video screen dissolves and is replaced by a startling picture of curdled fluid, ever-so-slightly out of focus.

'When a tapped inflorescence is cut off close to the stem,' she says, serene in her self-possession, 'the flow continues for some time, reducing only gradually. Bleeding is strictly polar. At the cut-off lower surface of the inflorescence, not even a drop of the fluid appears, no matter how the inflorescence is positioned.'

To illustrate her argument, Miss Soedhono walks up to the video screen and touches the glass with her taloned forefinger, indicating first this example, then that. Her long skirt which, during the three or four steps she took to reach the video screen, delineated the curves of her backside in an evanescent shimmer of silk and shadow, hangs inscrutable. 'In coconut,' says Miss Soedhono, turning to face her audience once more, 'the bleeding tissue is found at the extremities of the lateral branches of the inflorescence, close to the cut from which the juice flows. No doubt you are curious about anatomical differences between bleeding and normal branches. Yes, I can see you are curious. The differences can be seen here, side by side. Bleeding spikes experience a high incidence of clogged vessels. Look at the bleeding spikes, gentlemen. Nearly all the vessels are closed.'

By now, throughout the audience, more and more men are giving in to the irresistible. The temperature in the room has risen to an unbearable level, and the ancient air conditioners begin to complain, bemoaning their futile labour with an irritating 'ar-ar-ar' sound. The oxygen has long since disappeared into the lungs of those assembled, and is being devoured in their blood; what remains of the atmosphere is dense with percolating aluminium chlorohydrate, alcohol, hydroxypropylcellulose, and the other ingredients of chemically deodorised armpit, as well as an excess of carbon dioxide and a miasma of pheromone.

Miss Soedhono appears wholly unaffected; the satiny skin of her throat is free of any perspirous sheen, her forehead is smooth and unreflective, her soft black hair not in the least tacky. Since beginning her presentation she has shown no interest in the glass of water that stands on the table to her right, nor has she even licked her lips – those lips whose gloss is undiminished. She speaks for minute upon minute, never faltering, never hesitating for the correct word, never running out of breath even during sentences whose polysyllable count is in the dozens. Now she moves onto the topic of pollination, keeping her gaze level, making contact only with the imploring eyes of her audience, ignoring the agitation lower down.

'The possible disadvantages of employing pollinating bags are these,' she announces. 'Use of damaged bags, or bags with large mesh that allow pollen, or mites carrying pollen, to pass through; not securely tying the mouth of the bag with the peduncle, thus keeping the bags open for longer durations during active female phase; and failure to emasculate properly. In dwarf coconuts, a small number of flowers are found to be bisexual, possessing both pistils and stamens. We conducted a random survey of two hundred Nias yellow

dwarfs, and fifty-four of the palms were discovered to have at least one hermaphrodite flower, which means, as a rule of thumb, that twenty-seven per cent of Nias dwarf palms are polygamo-monoecious. You will appreciate the threat this poses to our breeding programme.'

One of the men has begun to make a soft, rhythmic sound, but he is elbowed in the ribs by his neighbours on either side. If their passions can no longer be secret, let them at least be silent.

'The problem,' Miss Soedhono explains, 'is that at the time of emasculation, most of the hermaphrodites escape detection and pass for female flowers. We breeders must be vigilant, and act before fertilisation occurs.'

A birdlike flunkey dressed in a white Nehru jacket walks into the room, and carefully deposits two additional items on the table next to Miss Soedhono's untouched glass of water. A murmur passes through the men, as they watch first the gleaming machete, then the massive, furry coconut, being laid side by side.

'Each male,' Miss Soedhono continues, as her assistant pads away, 'each female, and each hermaphrodite flower, bears six perianth units or lobes. Everything you need to know, gentlemen, is governed by threes. The outer three whorls make up the calyx and the inner three the corolla. We also meet three kinds of aestivation within the coconut, where the members of unopened flowers just touch each other without overlapping: Firstly, valvate. Secondly, imbricate. Thirdly, contortion.'

Miss Soedhono's voice, though still calm and coolly modulated, has been raised somewhat, to compensate for the worsening 'ar-ar-ar' of the air conditioners, the rhythmic creaking of metal seats, occasional groans and grunts from the men.

'Individually,' she concedes, her eyes half-closing, her

head tilting slightly to one side, 'the male flowers may be sessile and small, but their aggregation on the spikes in large numbers with expanding petals and light-coloured stamens add to the allure of the spadix. The female flowers, when they are in this state of receptivity, offer excellent landing sites. The exposed portion of the ovary near the stigmatic end is covered with bright trichome units which can be irresistibly attractive for insects of all kinds.'

'Oh God,' cries a hoarse voice from the audience.

'Shut up,' hisses another. The noise of foot-shuffling, chair-creaking and heavy breathing has become obtrusive, and the air conditioner rattles louder, then abruptly dies away, like a lawn-mower whose blades have struck a boulder, fatally injurious to the mechanism. At once the room, which had seemed already as stifling as it could possibly be, is inundated with an invisible wave of additional warmth.

Miss Soedhono glances sidelong at the machete and the coconut, and someone in the audience cries 'Yes!' But she makes no move, content merely to verify that the sacraments are in place. Impatience can have no influence on her presentation; enthusiasm, even desperate enthusiasm, cannot alter the inexorable sequence of logic, the orderly progression of argument, the decorous enigma of learning. She parts her lips, licks her upper teeth, leaving the lustrous patina of her lipstick undisturbed, and continues: 'When a young coconut spadix, still snugly wrapped in the spathe, is trained at the correct stage of its maturity, it can be made to bleed a sweet sap known as toddy or neera. This sap is procured by tapping the palm's organs. What organ we tap depends on the species. For example, in *Cocos nucifera* and *Caryota urens* the flower-bearing portion of the spadix is pared in thin slices for the extraction of the juice. In *Arenga pinnata* and *Nypa fruticans*, it is the peduncle beneath the spike-bearing region of the

spadix that yields the neera. In *Corypha elata*, the gigantic spadix is severed at the point where the first ramification develops, and the toddy starts flowing. In the case of *Phoenix sylvestris*, a portion of the tender stem is pared, and the toddy trickles from the surface. Fresh sweet toddy contains twelve point five to seventeen point five sucrose, and sixteen to twenty per cent solids. Thus, apart from serving as a sweet or fermented beverage, toddy yields sucrose, alcohol, vinegar, treacle and sugar candy.'

'Do it! Just . . . pick it up!' exclaims one of the men, unhinged by the agony of anticipation. Hissing and groaning their disapproval, his fellows turn upon him, terrified that his misbehaviour at this crucial juncture may provoke Miss Soedhono to sweep disdainfully out of the room and leave them all unfulfilled. But, to their collective confusion and delight, she walks over to the table and, with a glimmer of a smile, enfolds the hilt of the machete in her hand.

'The honey in the male flower,' she purrs, 'is secreted by three inter-carpellary or septal glands of the pistillode. In the female flower, the corresponding stigma manifests itself outside the perianth lobes just a couple of days before its receptivity. When readiness is reached, the three fleshy lobes secrete a viscous nectar on their inner surface. Profuse quantities of this fluid pour out through three one-millimetre long orifices or slits.'

Without warning, Miss Soedhono swings the machete down onto the coconut, burying the edge of the blade deep in the hard, furry rind. The shock of impact jolts through each of the sixty-six men as if they were a single giant slab of flesh.

Miss Soedhono uncleaves the machete blade from the coconut's flesh with a deft twist of her wrist, and hacks a second time into the massive fruit. A neat wedge of shell is dislodged into the air and bounces onto the carpet at her feet.

'The solid sperm of the coconut,' she declares, each word enunciated with magisterial calm, 'whether desiccated or creamed, is approximately sixty-nine per cent fat.' She picks up the wounded fruit, cradling it gently in her palms, lifting it up to her breast. 'The liquid endosperm, popularly known as coconut milk, is approximately twenty-four per cent. It is rich in lauric acid, which is converted by the human or animal body into monolaurin, an antiviral, antibacterial and antiprotozoal monoglyceride. An invaluable substance, which has been demonstrated to destroy lipid-coated viruses and bacteria such as *Listeria monocytogenes, Helicobactor pylon*, cytomegalovirus, chlamydia, herpes and H.I.V. All of this, gentlemen, is here for the drinking.'

Solemnly, Miss Soedhono lifts the hairy globe to her mouth, aligns the white gash with her lips, and shuts her eyes. As she tilts the sphere upwards, her facial features are eclipsed, creating, to the delirious gaze of her audience, a grotesque substitute face, a fibrous, bulbous, hairy face with three blind eyes and a fearsome array of pink teeth capped in gleaming orange enamel, a nightmare head made all the more bizarre by the immaculately styled hairdo framing it.

Once, twice, three times Miss Soedhono's throat, exposed beneath this monstrous visage, pulsates in satisfaction, whereupon the sixty-six men groan and holler and whimper, each according to his nature. This is the moment of communal consummation they have all feared and resisted, and to which they now surrender themselves.

Miss Soedhono lowers the coconut, replaces it on the table. A single drop of milk twinkles on her chin as she surveys her audience.

'Thus concludes,' she says, 'my presentation. I hope that you will honour us with your presence again next year.'

She bows gravely, to raucous applause, and strolls out of

the room, past a phalanx of uniformed employees of the Hotel Magdalaya who stand ready with sixty-seven towels.

Sixty-seven? Yes, sixty-seven. One man, despite his best intentions, was unable to be here today. His flight was cancelled at the last minute, leaving him devastated at his misfortune. Vast merciless stretches of ocean have come between him and Indonesia – between him and Miss Soedhono. For longer than he can bear to think about, he'd been looking forward to his exquisite and shameful reward; now he wanders like a lost soul through the gift shops of his home city's airport. He buys worthless souvenirs for his wife, his wife who is sweet and kind but knows nothing of coconuts. The digital numbers on the overhead clocks change without regard for his yearning, queues of travellers disappear into their appointed slots, the sky discolours from blue to orange, until he knows it is over, Miss Soedhono's performance is over, it happened in front of other men and he missed it, and now he must wait another eternity to see it again.

FINESSE

Rumours that the dictator was ill were totally without foundation. He'd never been fitter, and anyone suggesting otherwise could expect to be forcibly corrected.

Nevertheless, the dictator considered it wise, from time to time, to confirm the robustness of his health by having X-rays made of his chest. And it was the fear of forcible correction that made his personal physician hesitate to speak when the great man asked if the X-rays showed anything unusual.

'You have a very big heart,' said the physician at last.

'I know that,' smiled the dictator. 'But how big?'

They were standing in the dictator's office; or rather, the dictator was sitting and the physician was standing. The physician hugged the folder of X-rays unhappily to his breast.

'Bigger than . . .' he began, looking to the open window for inspiration. 'Bigger than is perhaps totally consistent with

. . . with the size of heart that one might expect in a person who was . . . ah . . . in a state of health consistent with . . . with *remaining* in a state of health consistent with . . . um . . . sustained . . .'

The dictator sighed, impatient with this mealy-mouthedness. Sometimes it fell to a leader to rescue people from their own timidity.

'Bigger than is good for me, you mean?'

The physician's shoulders sank with relief.

'Yes.'

'I've often thought so,' the dictator smiled. 'But seriously, this big heart of mine: how much of a danger is it?'

'Danger?' The physician was nervous again, perspiring in a manner that the dictator found, frankly, irritating.

'Friend, we have known each other a long time,' he cautioned. 'Can we not speak freely?'

The physician gulped, grinning like an idiot. He and the dictator had known each other for twenty-three months, or say two years. Was this a long time? Certainly it was ten times longer than some people lasted before falling out of favour with a thud. On the other hand, knowing the dictator for a *very* long time didn't seem such a good idea, as his oldest friends and family members were mostly dead.

'It appears from the X-rays that you . . . that your heart . . . that you have cardiac myxoma.'

There, it was said. The physician waited for consequences, blinking behind his foggy glasses.

'Is that a cancer?' said the dictator.

'Yes, it's a cancer,' said the physician.

'Cancers can go away by themselves, can't they?' The dictator sounded doubtful; the notion went against everything he knew about politics.

'Not this one.'

'Deadly, is it?' said the dictator, confirming the strength of his enemy.

'Well, actually, the myxoma itself is benign. But what it does to the heart is ... ah ...'

'Fatal.'

'Yes.'

The dictator turned and walked to the window. He peered out, hands clasped behind his back.

'A cancer can be cut out,' he said.

'There are cancers of all sorts,' squirmed the physician. 'Some can simply be cut out. With others, the job is much more complicated.'

The dictator nodded. This distinction, too, conformed to his experience of politics.

'How soon can this kill me?'

'I am a humble all-rounder, no expert,' pleaded the physician. 'Books on the subject say that three months is usual. I don't know how they arrive at such a statistic. If it's an average, the figure of three months could be derived from one man surviving a week and another surviving ... um ... almost half a year.' The physician grimaced: half a year didn't sound like much. Maybe he should have taken greater liberties with arithmetic; the dictator, for all his honorary university degrees, was famously uneducated.

'Can you do the job?' he enquired.

The physician shook his head.

'I haven't the skill,' he said.

'Not if I gave you a fortnight off to practise and read the books thoroughly?'

The physician hugged the X-rays tightly, to keep from snickering.

'Not if I had a year,' he said. 'The affected blood vessels are very, very tiny. With these big peasant's hands of mine ...'

And he lifted one hand into the air, to show how miraculous it was, that the dictator's revolutionary regime had managed to fashion a half-decent doctor from such crude materials.

The dictator frowned, rotating his jaw. The physician began to wonder if he'd perhaps overdone the peasant stuff.

At last the dictator said,

'But I thought the problem was that my heart was too big.'

'Yes,' said the physician, 'but of course in a case like this, the problem can't be solved by simply yanking the heart out like . . . like a turnip from the soil. This is a job that requires great delicacy, great . . . finesse.'

The dictator leaned back in his chair. There was a loud creak. He was a man of seventy-two years old, overweight and moist-eyed, with thin hair the colour of hair-oil. On the wall behind him, a portrait hung in which he was ageless, in which he looked as if he could tear men apart with no help from anyone else.

'Find the doctor who can do the job,' he said.

Two days later, the physician was back in the dictator's office.

'Have you found the doctor?' demanded the old man.

'I believe so,' said the physician. 'According to all the surgeons I've consulted, there is one person who could possibly do it.'

'Excellent: what's his name?'

'It's a she, actually. A Mrs Sampras. You will remember, she was one of the fourteen surgeons who shamefully defected in 1992 to America, to perform unnecessary surgery on rich Jewish women.'

'But this is no use to me!' exclaimed the dictator. 'We must get her back!'

The physician bit his lip, nonplussed by the dictator's

apparent lapse of memory regarding the true circumstances of Mrs Sampras's disappearance.

'1992,' he repeated helpfully. 'You recall the incident, I'm sure, sir. Fourteen surgeons, all critical of you and your government. A cabal of Jewish businessmen organised the getaway plane ...'

'Yes, yes: filth and scum ...' hissed the dictator, fists clenched on the desk before him.

The physician had one more try at filling in the gaps.

' ...uh ... there was some suggestion, made in a subversive newspaper, that the surgeons never, in fact, left the country. That they were, in fact, being secretly detained in the Milleforte Labour Camp.'

The dictator raised his shoulders in indignation, spring-loaded to refute a vicious untruth. Then abruptly he relaxed, his eyelids drooping.

'Ah,' he said.

Having dismissed the physician, the dictator telephoned the chief administrator of the Milleforte Labour Camp.

'I don't suppose,' the dictator said after a few seconds of pleasantries, 'you know how Mrs Sampras is getting on in America? ... Mrs Sampras, the surgeon ...You don't say? That's *good*, that's *good*. You know, I was afraid she might have succumbed to the harsh weather of New York, or that maybe some drug-crazed nigger raped and killed her ... Ye-e-es. So she's in top form, is she? Fighting fit? Ha! Ha! Ha!' And his chair creaked again, with the sheer verve of his relief.

The following day, the dictator received a letter which had been dashed off to him by Mrs Sampras herself, delivered by fast car and motorcycle.

Dear Mr President, it said. *I understand you have been enquiring after my health. My health is fair: how's yours?*

Well, enough small talk. I seem to be forever making confessions: here is another. I haven't been at all happy in America. In fact, the experience has taken away all my zest for surgery. I wish I had never left my husband and children for this pampered existence.

But, I suppose we must all suffer the consequences of our bad decisions, and I am resigned to live out my life here, a traitor of no use to man or beast.

Regretfully, Gala Sampras

Pouting thoughtfully, the dictator folded the letter into his fist. A word was eluding him, a word he had heard for the first time only yesterday, although as an honorary doctor of literature he must have known it all along.

This, he thought, is going to require . . . finesse.

Before the security guards allowed Gala Sampras to see the dictator, they made sure she was not concealing any weapons. Her doctor's satchel was emptied out, even though it had been hastily supplied by the president's own physician and contained almost nothing. The slender rubber hose of the stethoscope was tugged experimentally between two strong fists, as if it might be used in an attempt to garrotte the nation's leader. A small disposable hypodermic was reluctantly left in its sterile wrapper, but a glass ampoule of antibiotic was confiscated, in case it contained poison.

A young man unzipped Gala's overcoat and frisked her from armpits to ankles, his fingers gentle and thorough, as if he had read in a book that a woman's erogenous zones could be hidden in the most unlikely places. He even lifted her skirt and passed his middle finger over her underpants, against her vulva. Perhaps he thought that one of his fellow soldiers

might have absentmindedly left a sharp object in there some-where, an electric cattle prod or a Swiss army knife, which she might whip out and attack the president with.

After a minute or two, the young man removed a ball-point pen from the breast pocket of Gala's jacket. He clicked the nib in and out, frowning, as if feeling himself required to make a complicated moral decision. Gala Sampras smiled despite herself, troubling the young man even more. It seemed so absurd that she'd been brought all the way here to slice the dictator's chest open with a scalpel, but here were his bodyguards trying to make sure she didn't stab him through the heart with a cheap plastic pen.

'Mightier than the sword, hm?' she mocked him as he handed the yellow Bic back.

The dictator welcomed Mrs Sampras graciously, extending his hand over the desk where he had signed the warrant for her arrest years previously. His handshake was firm but gentle. He was smiling, with lips that were ever-so-slightly cyanosed, from the cancer all around his heart. A subtle network of pale purple capillaries were showing on his nose.

'I'm honoured to have you here,' he said. It was true, in the sense that he'd investigated every alternative to Gala Sampras and failed to find anyone half as good. In future, more men would have to be encouraged to commit them-selves to a career in medicine.

Mrs Sampras said nothing as the dictator continued to pull at her wrist. Face impassive, she extracted her hand from his – extracted it matter-of-factly, as if his hand were a tool or a swab she was finished with.

There being nowhere for visitors to sit, she remained standing, transferring her doctor's satchel from her left hand

back to her right. While he looked her up and down, she avoided his gaze, instead taking stock of his office.

She was surprised to find that it looked exactly as she'd imagined it might, as a child might draw a dictator's office. There was a massive mahogany desk, strewn with leather-bound folders and the odd sheet of paper. There was an upholstered swivel chair for him to luxuriate in. There was an oil painting, or perhaps a giant colour photograph thinly disguised as an oil painting, of the dictator, installed on one of the walls. There was an uncurtained window looking out over the courtyard. And this was all. No other tables or chairs, no bookcases or display cabinets, no tools of any more complicated work than arbitrary approval and condemnation. Nothing to indicate any undictatorly quirks in the dictator's personality, nothing out of place. No caddy of golf clubs, no ornaments, no posters of Western film stars, no stag heads mounted on the walls or Virgin Marys dangling from the ceiling. Nothing. In speeches, the president liked to boast that he had no interests, no pastimes, other than overseeing the welfare of his country. Now Gala could see that this was true.

'Well, would you like to see my X-rays,' suggested the old man.

'Please,' she agreed briskly.

He handed the folder of silver-grey images over to her. She studied them one by one, holding them up to the sunlight streaming through the window behind his head. Surreptitiously, she cast her eyes downwards and examined his face through the transparent sheets of film. She fancied she could detect his fear.

'Well, what do you think?' he said, after clearing his throat.

'You are going to die very soon,' she said evenly, still shielding her face behind the last of the X-rays, 'unless you have a very complicated and risky operation.'

'I know that,' he sighed, with an edge of irritation to his voice. 'Do you have the skill to do it?'

'I have the skill,' she replied, lowering the sunlit negative of the dictator's cancer-speckled chest and shuffling it in with the others. 'But these are not the photographs I was hoping to see.'

'Those photographs are on their way. You will see them tomorrow.'

'Of all four?'

'Husband, two sons, daughter, yes,' the dictator reassured her.

Mrs Sampras replaced the folder of X-rays on the desk. She had a sudden yearning to stand at the window and look out, but didn't want to expose her back to the dictator.

'This operation,' said the old man, licking his blueish lips. 'Can it be done in our country, do you think?'

'There is no limit to what can be done in our country,' sighed Mrs Sampras. 'You yourself have proved that many times.'

'Yes, yes, but if you felt that a little trip to the United States might be desirable . . .'

'I've had my little trip to America, thank you,' said Gala.

The dictator stared hard into her eyes.

'You must have the best tools, you understand? Only the best.'

Gala looked down at her hands, as if checking the condition of her nails.

'I have the best here,' she assured the old man. 'In our own country.' She ignored his glare, contemplating her hands all the while. They were pale and finely-formed, with an angry scar here and there.

'All being well,' the dictator said at last, 'how soon can you perform the operation?'

She looked him straight in the chest.

'You need to lose some weight first, if possible.'

'A tall order,' he smirked. 'But I will stare the devil of temptation in the face.'

Mrs Sampras took hold of the handles of her borrowed satchel and clutched them, suddenly white-knuckled with fury. She breathed deep, and counted to ten or possibly twelve before replying.

'Which of your devils you stare in the face isn't my affair. You need to lose a quantity of fat, in order to have a better chance of recovery afterwards.'

The dictator appraised her through her overcoat, estimating her measure.

'As a woman, you have a favourite diet, no doubt?'

Gala flinched, white as a sheet, white as electrical flex.

'Anxiety about one's loved ones suppresses the appetite, I've found. If this is not a possibility for you, you might try being raped.'

An awful silence expanded to fill the room like methane gas, tainting every inch of air with terrifying speed. Mrs Sampras had overstepped the line; she knew it and the dictator knew it and Mrs Sampras knew the dictator knew it, and so on.

A foolish, reckless blow had been struck to a frail and delicate balance. Gala Sampras was nauseous with regret, as if she had, in a moment of hysteria, slashed a vital organ which should have been left alone at all costs. There was now a strong possibility that the dictator would have her tortured and shot, and that he himself would die under the knife of a lesser surgeon, or even give up on the idea of cure altogether, consoling himself with his revenge on her.

For a minute, both of them contemplated different kinds of death. The vision of a benign future in which the dictator lived to an Old Testament age and Mrs Sampras vacationed

with her family in the summer, trembled like a child's castle of blocks between them, ready to collapse at a single clumsy step.

At last the dictator spoke.

'Mrs Sampras. I am a rational man. I know that anxiety about loved ones is a very different thing from what is actually happening to them. The situation can be better than you fear – or much, much worse.'

Mrs Sampras replied immediately:

'You are right, I'm sure, Mr President. But much as we strive to be rational, anxiety can defeat us. Well, it defeats *me*, anyway. Sometimes I worry so much about my husband and children that I lose more than my appetite.' And she held up her hands, to show him that they were trembling. 'This is a terrible thing for a surgeon.'

He regarded her with pity and suspicion.

'You are tired,' he said. 'Let my staff show you to your quarters. When you've rested, we'll meet again.'

And with that, he pressed the button for the door to be opened. A young soldier glanced nervously into the room, confirming with a quick head count that both the president and the surgeon were, at this stage, still alive.

The dictator was not expecting to see Mrs Sampras again until the next day. Despite the cancer inside him, he was confident that he was not one of those weaklings who would die in seven days, but rather that he had the full half-year. He did not understand statistics and the law of averages, but he had often achieved what experts considered impossible and would no doubt do so again.

To help himself be patient, he visited those rooms within the government building where information was collated. Happily, he found an information collation session in progress, and urged the collators not to feel inhibited just

because he was watching. An hour passed, then it was time for a meal.

Late in the afternoon, the dictator was surprised to learn that Mrs Sampras was ready to see him again. She'd had plenty of rest, she said, and the sooner the preparations for the operation were underway, the better.

In the golden afternoon light, Mrs Sampras looked subtly different. She had changed her clothes, washed and groomed her hair. The overcoat was gone, and she looked every inch a woman.

'Of course,' she said, 'you understand there are grave risks in any surgical operation.'

'Of course,' the dictator said. 'For the surgeon no less than for the patient.'

'More for the patient, I would have thought,' suggested Mrs Sampras.

'Oh no, I'm sure the risk is equal,' the dictator begged to differ. 'A death affects not just the person him or herself, but spouses, children . . . It's a . . . what is the word I'm looking for? A knock-on effect.'

Mrs Sampras was tired of standing. She half-perched on one corner of the great desk, crossing her long legs over each other.

'What is your blood type?' she enquired coolly.

'Blood type?'

'Yes. A, B, B positive, O . . .'

'How complicated,' the dictator smiled. 'I have a man's blood.'

'Nevertheless I must know its clinical type.'

The dictator shrugged and spread his hands, open-palmed. Such knowledge was a luxury too rarefied for one whose only concern was the good of his nation.

Mrs Sampras opened her satchel and extracted the disposable hypodermic.

'I must take a sample of your blood from you,' she said, motioning him to bare his right arm.

He tried to push the sleeve of his suit jacket up, but it was too stiff. So, he removed the garment, hanging it carefully over the back of his armchair. Then he rolled up the sleeve of his shirt. Despite the unhurried deliberateness of his exertions, Mrs Sampras noted he was breathing heavily, his lips paler and bluer, his nose more purple.

Seated once more, the dictator extended his naked forearm across the desk towards her. She took hold of it with her warm, dry hands, testing the elasticity of his mottled flesh. She applied a leather tourniquet, and stroked a vein, encouraging it to swell up for her.

'You have a touch like velvet,' the dictator said. 'And beautiful fingers.'

Mrs Sampras removed the plastic sheath from the needle of the hypodermic.

'Just a little prick,' she said.

The next morning, the dictator's blood had been tested and the result made available for Mrs Sampras to peruse. She could not recall, in her days as a state surgeon, such speed and efficiency being possible. Either the country had modernised since she'd been removed from its mainstream, or heaven and earth had been moved for the great leader.

'You are B positive,' she informed him.

'Is that unusual?'

'Common, very common,' she said.

'Good,' the dictator beamed. 'That means the hospital will have it in plentiful supply, yes?'

'In our country,' said Mrs Sampras, 'blood of all kinds is in plentiful supply.'

She did not look at his face to note his reaction. Instead,

she stared at the vase of flowers standing on his desk, troubled by its presence there. Evidently the dictator had observed yesterday how the aridity of the office had struck her. So, today, he'd softened that aridity with flowers. Especially for her.

The vase was iridescent blue, as if kiln-glazed with toilet disinfectant. Red, white and pink carnations sprouted up from the neck. They looked so ghastly and ill-at-ease, Mrs Sampras wondered if they were real.

'You're wondering if they are real,' remarked the dictator.

'Yes,' she said.

'Of course they're real,' he purred. 'Touch them.'

'I believe you, Mr President,' said Mrs Sampras, motionless.

'Touch them.'

Mrs Sampras hesitated, spastic with distaste. She wondered if her future, the future of her husband and children, was somehow hanging in the balance at this moment. In the labour camp she had sunk to licking her tormentors' boots and worse, and yet she could not bring herself to touch these flowers.

'Brighten up the place no end, don't you think?' said the dictator, letting the challenge go.

'Yes,' she agreed. 'Shame to cut them, though, isn't it?'

The old man half-closed his eyes, as if weary of people with a poor grasp of realities.

'There are more,' he assured her, 'where those came from.' And, without warning, he leaned across the desk and handed Mrs Sampras an envelope.

Gala strove to remain calm as she examined the photographs of her family. She breathed deeply and blinked a few times. Her hands were steady as she shuffled the images over and over.

At last she said, 'The photographs of my children are very good. Very clear. One can see that they were taken very recently.'

The dictator leaned back in his chair, creaking with satisfaction.

'Well, they grow up so fast, don't they?' he said.

'Yes, by the grace of God they do,' said Mrs Sampras. 'But . . . the photograph of my husband seems less recent. In fact, it could have been taken years ago.'

There was another, even louder creak as the dictator leaned forward and interlocked his hands on the desk.

'I assure you it is recent.'

Mrs Sampras held the image close to her face, frowning.

'He doesn't look anywhere near as old,' she said, 'as I would expect him to look.'

The dictator laughed.

'Would that flatter him, I wonder – or cut him to the quick?'

'I don't know,' said Mrs Sampras. 'I will have to ask him myself.'

'I do hope you get your chance.'

'Ah, yes . . .' said Mrs Sampras doubtfully, as if she were in danger of losing focus in all sorts of matters. 'The question is when.'

'And the answer is,' the dictator assured her, 'as soon as possible. It would gladden the heart of an old man to witness such a reunion. In fact, I'm looking forward to it enormously. I'm sure it will be a high point of my convalescence.'

Gala licked her lips, swallowing, swallowing. After some effort, she succeeded in giving up – for the moment.

'You will still need to lose some weight,' she sighed.

Startlingly, the dictator sprang to his feet and swung his

arms vigorously, as if running a marathon. Hidden behind the desk, his legs moved feebly, if at all.

'See!' he teased, jovial and breathless. 'I've begun already!'

A week later, on the morning of the operation, Mrs Sampras and the dictator met in his office one more time. The dictator was identical in shape and appearance, but invited praise for having shed a number of pounds. Mrs Sampras praised him, solemn-faced. There was no point antagonising him about his flab; she was reserving the showdown for the arena where it really mattered.

'You cannot have men with guns inside an operating theatre,' she pointed out, when they were discussing the arrangements for the afternoon.

'They will stand well back,' argued the dictator. 'You will hardly notice they are there.'

Gala closed her eyes and pressed her lips tightly together. In her mind's eye, or the back of her retina, a negative image of sunlit flowers glowed. It was red roses today, far too many of them crammed into the vase, the stems ugly and thready from torn-off thorns.

'One speck of dust from a rifle,' she said, 'contains a million germs, more than enough to sweep through your body like a plague. A soldier's belt buckle can kill you – and not just in the way that is usual in our country.'

'Do you think I don't know that?' demanded the dictator. 'I have a university degree in these things. What I meant was, my men can watch you through the glass. It will be educational. They may be called upon to perform a bit of surgery themselves, one of these days.'

Gala Sampras looked the old man straight in the eyes.

'I hope they have not been instructed to shoot me if I appear to be in any way harming you,' she said, quietly and

reasonably. 'After all, I am going to cut a hole in your chest, open you up like a satchel, and put a stop to your heart. They know, I trust, that all this is as it should be?'

If the dictator was unnerved, he didn't show it.

'It is your . . . gentleness they will be watching for,' he said. 'Your thoroughness, your keen concentration, your . . . finesse. You see, they've heard that when you apply yourself to the task, you do it with love, as if your very own child was lying there.' His fat hand made tender stroking motions in the air between them, describing a crescent curve, like a half-moon, an infant's head, a woman's naked breast. 'And of course,' he continued, 'they will be watching at the end, to see me wake up.'

For the first time, Gala allowed herself to consider the possibility that for all her skill, the sheer force of nature, of statistics, might dictate the outcome.

'Mr President,' she pleaded. 'You understand that this operation has been rarely performed, and usually on much younger men.'

He laughed, throwing up one arm in the general direction of his portrait.

'Let's be optimistic!' he roared. 'This country was built on optimism, after all.'

Outside the window, a whistle blew. The dictator leapt to his feet, as if he'd already been granted a new lease of life. Enthusiastically, he motioned to Mrs Sampras to accompany him to the window. Rather than feel his hand grasping her arm, she hurried to comply.

Together, they looked down into courtyard. Foreshortened by the perspective of many storeys, a teenage girl was walking uncertainly between two phalanxes of soldiers, her gait stiff and artificial. Despite the fact that she had a young woman's figure, a fashionable haircut, and other features that

made her almost unrecognisable as the child she'd been only a few years ago, she was unmistakably Gala Sampras's daughter. She might have stepped straight out of the photograph in Gala's pocket. Eyes downcast, she negotiated the concrete paving as if walking on eggs, while two dozen men looked on impassively.

'Where are you . . .' whispered Mrs Sampras to the old man at her side. 'Where is she going?'

'She is on her way to meet you,' said the dictator. But, before Mrs Sampras could recover from her sharp intake of breath, he added: 'It's a shame she has arrived a little too early. I sometimes forget how fast our country's trains are nowadays.'

He led Mrs Sampras away from the window and signalled his readiness for the ordeal ahead. He escorted Mrs Sampras to the door, laying his palm gently on her shoulder, for she seemed discomposed, unsure of her balance.

'It's all right,' he reassured her. 'She'll be made most welcome. You and I won't be busy for long, will we? And if anything should delay us, I'm sure my staff will be able to find your daughter some companions of her own age. It's a young person's world, I've come to realise. We oldsters can only look on, eh?' And he smiled sadly, squeezing the surgeon's shoulder like an old, old friend.

In the operating theatre, everything was perfect and civilised and still. There wasn't a soldier to be seen. Four nurses and an anaesthetist stood waiting like nuns glowing under the tungsten light. The equipment and the furnishings were as modern as Dr Sampras might have expected from the most up-to-the-minute surgery in America. An assortment of silver instruments loosely wrapped in sterile green paper lay ready on two trolleys.

The dictator lay ready on what Dr Sampras and her fellow surgeons had, in the innocent days before the dictator's regime, jokingly referred to as 'the torture table'. The oil had been shampood out of his hair, and a few grey wisps stuck out from beneath his disposable cap. Freed from the restrictions of his uniform, his flesh lolled grossly under the thin sheet. Horizontal, his circulation was improved, and his lips were as pink as a baby's.

'Hello, Mrs Sampras,' he winked.

She approached him, not speaking. Her gloved hands were held in mid-air, hovering in limbo, postponing the moment. Her face was shrouded in gauzy paper, a veil which allowed only her dark eyes to show.

'Is it you behind that mask?' persisted the dictator.

'Yes, it's me,' she said emotionlessly.

'It covers your prettiest features.'

'It's necessary,' she said. Already the inside of her surgical mask was becoming damp with potentially lethal breath.

The anaesthetist, a woman too by the shape of her eyebows, looked to Gala and nodded. Colourless liquid began to trickle down a thin plastic tube into the cannula taped to the dictator's pale wrist.

The old man's face softened and grew infantile. Gala noticed for the first time that he had long soft eyelashes, like her own children. Those eyelashes were fluttering now, as if the old man were struggling against infant sleep at bedtime.

'If I should die before I wake . . .' he murmured.

'Don't worry about such things,' Gala advised him. 'We both have a long night ahead of us.'

FLESH REMAINS FLESH

Ashton Allan Clark was the richest man in Altchester; he had money on his breath and a sticky ooze of luxury clogging up his ears. If you had asked him what his fortune was founded on (assuming you were granted leave to speak to him, which few people were), he would have told you 'the finest tannery in all of England'. If you had asked his miserable employees the same question, they would have said 'maggots and misery' – unless they suspected you of being an informer. Are you an informer? No? Then let us begin our story.

Ashton Allan Clark was a small, meaty man, resembling nothing so much as a grossly overgrown otter. He habitually wore a black sable coat and doeskin trousers, and a top hat that was likewise furry. His hair, beard, moustache and side-boards were thick, dark and glistening with oil. They had been that way since he built the tannery in 1831, and it was now 1861, so it seemed likely that his hair colour was maintained

artificially. Clark's Tannery bought black dye by the gallon, giving rise to a folk tale among the workers' children – ragged, underfed illiterates, all of them – that Mr Clark dunked his head in a bucket of the stuff every Sunday. They also said he ate frog's legs, and fruitcake soaked in vinegar pickle.

This last allegation was a slander, but there was no shortage of truths about Ashton Allan Clark's private life that would have made the children gasp, were they not already gasping for air in the grey miasma that constituted Altchester's atmosphere, and were they not kept well segregated from his secrets by iron gates and guards. In fact, Clark's mansion, a villa that had been forcibly turned into a castle by the superimposition of turrets and imported gargoyles, was perched on a hillside far away from the tannery. The cab journey from the semi-rural outskirts of Altchester, where thrushes trilled in Mr Clark's trees, to the gloomy maze of cobbled streets and blackened buildings encircling Mr Clark's grim hive of industry, could take half an hour or more.

This was how long it had taken Mr Damien Hirsch to reach Mr Clark's mansion. It might have been quicker, but the horse had been sluggish in the summer heat, and a brief shower had turned the last mile of unpaved road into a slippery track of muck. The atmosphere here smelled healthier than those mephitic parts of the town where even newly-washed clothes reeked of the tannery, but still the air hung humid and Mr Hirsch wished the sky would tear itself open and unleash the rain in earnest.

It was late afternoon. He had been summoned to this house by a letter his employer had posted to him that morning. Mr Hirsch, who did not work in the tannery, preferred not to think of himself as an employee of Mr Clark; he preferred to think of himself as a gentleman whose expertise was

valuable enough to Mr Clark to warrant remuneration. Nevertheless, the tone of Mr Clark's letter had been nasty, and Mr Hirsch was coming to the conclusion that life would be altogether happier if he could tell Mr Clark to go to the devil. After all, as Altchester's only taxidermist, he was due a measure of respect.

'I put my trust in your competence, Hirsch,' complained Mr Clark, barely a minute after the servants had ushered the visitor into the house, 'and you let me down.'

'What do you mean, sir?' said Hirsch, following his host into the room known as Noah's Ark.

'You will see what I mean,' said Clark, speaking peevishly and walking stiffly.

Noah's Ark was a large parlour or a small ballroom, originally intended for piano recitals or intimate dances to amuse the country gentry. Or perhaps it had been a library? It was difficult to tell nowadays, as Mr Clark had no time for music, female company or books. The room had been stripped of whatever had been in it before, hung all about with red velvet drapes, and transformed into an exhibition of stuffed animals. But not the sorts of creatures one might expect in the homes of country gentry – not stags and foxes and wild boar. Nor were there any bodiless heads mounted neatly on burnished wooden plaques. No, what stood in the ballroom, intact and massive, was the following:

A huge cow, the size of – well, a cow – complete with monumental haunches and distended udders. A bullock, only slightly less gross, dark of hide, stupid of eye, with an iron ring through his nose. Three different breeds of sheep and ram, huddled together as if in fear of the colossal bovines, their fleeces varying from lush to newly-shorn, their mouths caught in a half-smile, except for one lamb frozen in mid-chew, its lips clamped on a realistic clump of grass, as though this

were the last shred of vegetation grazed from the polished wooden floor. Keeping them together, rearing immobile in an attitude of imperious attention, was a dog – a coal-black collie – whose ears were so erect that it was difficult to believe they could never tremble again.

'I see nothing out of order,' said Mr Hirsch. He was perspiring heavily; the room was warm from the setting sun and warmer still from the gaslights.

'Look closer,' said Mr Clark. 'At the nose of Albert.' Albert was Mr Clark's name for the bullock, just as Victoria was his name for the cow. 'Or study the ears of the lamb.'

Hirsch bent closer to his handiwork, these hulking brutes whose emptied interiors he had had to fill with elaborate metal architecture, sackfuls of plaster and miles of bandage. Victoria and Albert had almost killed him, in a manner of speaking. Lifting the flaccid hides was backbreaking work, the sort of labour that befitted those who toiled in Clark's tannery, not a qualified taxidermist. Sweating, puffing, staggering, Hirsch had heaved the cattle skins onto their fake skeletons, and had asked himself why he was doing this, when his slender fingers were more suited to scalpeling the tiny tarsal bones out of squirrels' feet.

He adjusted his spectacles as he peered at the bullock's nose. There were maggots crawling out of it. Likewise, the interior of the lamb's ears twinkled with some slight activity.

'This will not do,' said Mr Clark.

'I am sorry,' said Mr Hirsch. 'In my defence, flies will lay eggs wherever there is warmth and moisture. I had not anticipated you would keep the specimens in conditions of such humidity.'

'I think I need no reminding of the conditions under which flies breed in dead flesh. Nevertheless it was your task to render the hides perfectly dry.'

'Flesh remains flesh, unless it is largely replaced with the manufactured substances which you insisted be kept to a minimum in this display. Maggots have been known to breed in manuscripts of ancient vellum, when storage conditions fell below museum standards. Even so,' declared Hirsch, snapping open his satchel of phials and instruments, 'I can kill these pests with a simple injection of formaldehyde. Remember that their purchase is only superficial. There are no innards left to be corrupted.'

Ashton Allan Clark nodded. 'I should hope not.' Having scolded his visitor, he seemed to feel better. 'Your talents are very useful to me; I am sure I appreciate them better than anyone else in England. Indeed, I am about to offer you your biggest commission yet.'

Hirsch was kneeling in front of Albert, his spectacles fogging up. The hypodermic needle through which he had just squirted poison into the bullock's nostrils dripped clear liquid. 'I do not think I wish to mount anything larger than Victoria.'

'By 'biggest' I meant the amount of money I propose to give you,' Clark reassured him. 'The creature is significantly smaller than a cow.'

'Oh?'

This one small word was sufficient encouragement for Clark to stride out of the room and return, a few moments later, pulling a long serving-trolley such as might be used to transport tureens of soup from kitchen to dining-room. The top of it was veiled with a white sheet, and the entire burden was heavy enough for Hirsch to wonder why Mr Clark did not get a servant to pull it for him.

The mystery was not unexplained for long. As soon as the trolley was safely inside the room and the door had been shut behind it, Mr Clark whipped off the sheet and revealed

the supine body of an adolescent girl. She was clad only in a loose blouse and a threadbare skirt; her arms, legs and feet were bare. Her thick blonde hair had been pulled, by the force of Mr Clark's removal of the shroud, across her face. The fact that she did not brush it away from her open eyes spoke the truth of her condition.

'She is dead?' whispered Hirsch.

'Of course she is dead.'

'How did she come to be dead?'

'I don't know.'

'Then how did you come by her?'

'I found her.'

'Found her?'

'By the side of a road. Yesterday evening. I imagine she fell from a horse and broke her neck.'

Hirsch stepped forward and stroked the girl's hair off her face.

'Her neck looks intact to me.'

'Then perhaps her sweetheart took liberties with her, and afterwards strangled her.'

Hirsch began to feel giddy, as a memory percolated into his brain. The room's single elongated window flickered with a silent lightning flash.

'As I said, her neck looks –'

'What does it matter how she died?' thundered Ashton Allan Clark, at the same instant as the thunder rumbled through Heaven. 'Some humans live until their dotage, others die young. It's a melancholy truth, but there it is. My choice, when I saw her lying there by the road, was a stark one. Should I leave her to decompose, perhaps churned to a pulp by the wheels of passing carriages, or should I act?'

'Act?' With every passing second, Hirsch was remembering more clearly a phenomenon he had noticed only

half-consciously last night while drifting into sleep. Exhausted by the heat and the inhalation of denatured alcohol, he'd been unsure whether the wails and sobs echoing in his ears were coming (as he fancied) from the streets outside his window, or if they originated from the fevered dreams into which he was sinking. Recalling them now, with this poor dead girl in front of him, he was struck by how closely the cries had resembled the forlorn calls for an infant or a pet that has gone missing.

'To allow a beautiful creature like this to go to waste would be criminal,' declared Mr Clark with a quiet intensity that resembled passion. 'I want you to immortalise her, Hirsch. Let nothing corrupt her. She can be my shepherdess.' And he gestured towards his immobile menagerie, his Noah's Ark of farm animals, indicating how a shepherd lass might stand in relation to them. He even essayed a smile, as if this unusual facial contortion might help the taxidermist imagine the pretty picture of the girl and her beasts, as if a rare smile from Ashton Allan Clark might conjure into existence the tableau of a fresh-faced adolescent, clad fetchingly in a diaphanous dress, her hair spilling down her back, her pale white hand clutching a crozier such as might easily be supplied by a walking-stick manufacturer of Mr Clark's acquaintance.

'But . . . in the name of Heaven, Clark . . .' croaked Hirsch, perceiving in his employer's smile the sickening glint of madness. 'This is someone's daughter . . . !'

'Was, Hirsch, *was*,' corrected Mr Clark impatiently. 'She is meat now, and we must intervene at once, before the skin is spoiled.'

Mr Hirsch's spectacles were wholly fogged over now, in the unbearable heat of the gathering thunderstorm and his own distress. He dragged his sleeve across the lenses, and

noticed he was still holding the hypodermic. 'This . . . this girl,' he pleaded. 'I heard her friends and family calling for her, last night. She cannot simply disappear. Her loved ones will wish to bury her. Can you not un–?'

'Burial be damned!' shouted Mr Clark, and again the windows flashed with lightning. 'For a few precious days, her hide has value! Then it is a worthless shred of garbage, for parasites to feed on! Where is your pride, man? Where is your professional pride? Give me my shepherdess, and I'll give you more money that your miserable stags and foxes will ever make you!'

An appalling crash of thunder shook the walls of the house, at the same moment as Mr Hirsch lunged forward, with a cry of rage and terror, and stabbed his employer in the chest with the hypodermic, so wildly that the metal shaft of the instrument sank deep into the flesh, along with the noxious dregs of formaldehyde.

So, was Mr Clark dead? No, he was not dead. He awoke some time later, rearing up from the floor as if reanimated by a galvanic charge. His forehead, by now liberally smeared with sweat, hair-oil and an inky black substance, bumped against an obstruction hanging over him. It was the belly of Victoria, hard and unyielding like a full sack of flour. He crawled out from under it, and strove to gather up, as though they were the spilled contents of his pockets, the realities of his situation. It was night. Torrential rain was inundating the house. He had blood on his shirt-front. His head felt light and full of camphorous vapour, as if he had imbibed too much opium, cocaine and alcohol in unwise conjunction. The trolley which had borne the flawless corpse of the girl he had lured into his carriage was unencumbered. His shepherdess was gone.

Stumbling and cursing, as if his revived consciousness were an unwieldy burden he must balance on the framework of his soul, he burst out of his own front door, immediately drenched by the rain, and confirmed that Hirsch had fled, taking the girl with him. Had this been minutes or hours ago? On no account must the blackguard be permitted to find the girl's family, nor even wave the body under the noses of police or other meddlers. By the grace of God, no one had yet set eyes on his poor shepherdess – whose fate hung in the balance, entirely dependent on urgent rescue – except for the taxidermist and his driver, both of whom could be dispatched efficiently with the knife. The same curved, wooden-handled tanning knife with the ten-inch blade that had slid, with such buttery ease, into the soft flesh of his shepherdess, liberating her from her drab life as a tannery drudge and offering her an altogether cleaner, more cheerful future as the jewel in his grand display.

Within minutes he was seated in his carriage, rattling and skidding through the deluge towards the town, his knife nestled in his lap. He was still giddy and queasy, but the sound and the sensation of cobblestones under the wheels of his cabin gave him heart: he had reached the solid streets of Altchester already, and would surely draw abreast, any moment, with Hirsch's much meaner and slower vehicle. What's more, the farther he got, the less the elements seemed to resist him: the downpour thinned, the lightning ceased to flash, and the thunder kept its counsel.

Mr Clark peered out into the gloom. The streetlamps glimmered indistinct behind their veil of drizzle. A glimpse of peach-tinged light from a public house, and the sound of music, reassured Mr Clark that the world was carrying on much as usual, and that the prevailing hum of normalcy had yet to be disturbed by indignant alarms. Shabby street

vendors were emerging from shelter, sniffing out customers for their squalid wares. The warmth stored within the sewers and the dark brickwork of the buildings was escaping as steam.

'Faster!' yelled Mr Clark — with such vehemence that the wound in his chest throbbed. Nevertheless his annoyance was justified: the advance of the carriage had, with a sudden lurch, slackened off, pitching him forward. After scrabbling in his lap to check that the knife was still there, he slid open the cabin window and poked his head out into the darkness, squinting to determine what was obstructing progress.

He peered for no longer than a few moments, however, before uneasily sliding his window closed again and retracting his head into the raised lapels of his fur coat. In his nostrils and on his lips, he could taste an odour, familiar and yet monstrously intensified: dog dung and cured meat, both in immense quantities, as if a mist of liquefied ordure was drizzling from the skies and the street was paved with butchered flesh. Such was the smell borne by those who worked in the tannery; such was the perfume of those whose daily task was to chisel maggots out of what would soon be coats and gloves; such was the pungency of those who must rub bucketloads of canine filth into the festering hides of dead cattle.

Ashton Allan Clark huddled inside the vehicle which, by now, had come to a standstill. The horse snorted impatiently, and beat its hooves against the cobbles, but succeeded only in jingling its harness and agitating the contents of the cabin — that is, Mr Clark. It seemed to him that his carriage was being stealthily enveloped in a sea of shuffling, half-human forms, a noiseless horde of the walking dead.

In that moment of reconnaissance before pulling his head in, he had seen ghastly pale faces, listless staring eyes, grey flesh showing through torn and threadbare clothing. Now he fancied he could see, every few heartbeats, a naked

hand pawing at the rain-spattered windowpanes of his cabin — a different hand each time. Impossible, surely! Phantoms of an over-developed imagination. Yet wasn't that another ghostly palm? No sooner had the five gloveless fingers loomed into his vision than they had vanished. Mr Clark nerved himself to slide open the shutter once more.

'Can you not push through!' he shouted up at the invisible driver. No answer came, except the murmurous hubbub of a gathering crowd. The horse had stopped snorting and jingling its harness; indeed, there was no evidence that the carriage was any longer attached to the animal; it might have been unharnessed, abandoned, marooned in a moat of human refuse. Mr Clark slammed the window shut against the stink, cautioning himself to resist the fears that might unman him.

But there! There on the window-pane! That was *without doubt* a hand, a female hand, sliding its wet fingertips along the glass — and was that a cackle of laughter? Another hand! Another slide along the glass, another cackle! Did these women not understand that this intrusion was no joke? No wonder they could find no better work than the tannery, if their manners were as coarse as this!

Clark shut his eyes tightly, reassuring himself that the procession must be almost over; he could not believe that his employees, numerous though they were, had bred so profusely as to constitute a larger swarm than had yet passed. They were finite; they had their wretched little homes to go to and their wretched little children to feed; their work, if it was half as arduous as they were wont to plead to his foreman, ought to have given them an appetite for sleep. But no! To his horror, the cabin began to rock back and forth; the walls creaked and the floor swivelled beneath his feet. He opened his eyes, to see a face at the window: a girl's face, pale

and pretty, lips parted, breathing vapour. Her hair was plastered to her forehead with rain; her eyes were as dark as holes. For an instant only he saw her, and then she slipped below the range of his vision, as the entire carriage was lifted up like a vessel borne aloft by rising floodwaters.

'Set me down!' he shrieked. 'Set me down!' But they did not set him down.

Remembering his knife, he clutched it in his fist, swung open the door and leaned out into the gaseous, swirling dark, ready to slash without compunction at whatever flesh, bone or sinew squirmed beneath him. Before his blade could make its first incision, however, a powerful hand sprang out of the murk, pink and vicious like a stoat flayed alive, and seized hold of Mr Clark's oily black beard. One merciless tug sent him toppling into space.

The body of Ashton Allan Clark was not found until seventy years after his disappearance, by which time the descendents of the poor girl he'd murdered had long since given up hope of bringing him to justice, and his tannery had succumbed to arson, its unpeopled contents roasted to ash and fed into the sky above.

According to the testimony of the man who drove him through Altchester on his final ride, Mr Clark had begun the journey in a state of bloodless pallor, exhaling noxious chemicals with every panting breath; the cabman had presumed his destination was a doctor's surgery, with all possible urgency. But barely half-way, just as they were crossing the narrow bridge over the river Alt, Mr Clark flung open the door of his cabin and, evidently maddened by delusions, leapt into the inky waters.

His body (it was later determined) drifted into the mouth of a large cast-iron pipe, one of several such provided

to channel effluvia from the tannery direct into the River Alt. Mr Clark's corpulent physique allowed him to lodge as a sort of plug in the interior of the pipe, a plug which, as he swelled up in death, became unshiftably snug. The blockage was noted, but funds for public works were notoriously limited in Altchester, and it was some months before any action was taken, and this consisted merely of a man in a diving suit poking a primitive tool into the aperture, scraping and scooping out as much of the mysterious obstruction as he could before exhaustion overcame him.

Finally, in 1931, when the town of Altchester was being wholly rebuilt, renamed and refurbished, the Alt was diverted and all the land around the former tannery dug up. It was then that the cast-iron pipe was dredged up and spent some months drying in the sun. Upended by a crane, it disgorged a strange creature indeed: a perfectly cylindrical, otter-like beast, with vestigial legs and a wide-mouthed frog face, hollowed out like a lady's hand-muff. It was kept in the Natural History Museum until 1989, when an undetected flaw in its storage conditions resulted in its becoming, at long last, irredeemably corrupted.

LESS THAN PERFECT

Lachlan was a detective. Eighteen years old, no educational qualifications, two big bony fists. He'd tried stacking pallets, but it didn't suit his nature. So he was a detective. The pay wasn't great, the hours could be better, but he had no dependants and a sleek new car with automatic windows and a CD player. Criminals watch out: Lachlan's about.

Of course, criminals never suspected Lachlan was about. That was the whole point. They were always amazed when he caught them, as if they would've expected a detective to look like Columbo, with a raincoat and a cigarette. Which just proved how stupid they were. Smoking wasn't allowed, for a start.

The golden rule of being a detective was: Trust No One. Criminals came in all shapes, all ages, all sizes, all sexes. Both sexes, that is.

From a distance, through a dawdling cluster of other

bodies, Lachlan saw Mrs Weymouth coming towards him. She was immaculate as always, her dyed auburn hair held in place by spray and metal clips. She hadn't seen him yet; her attention was on a sheaf of papers she held in her hands as she walked. Despite his grudge against her, he had to admire the way she could move so confidently, even on high heels, with her legs constricted in a tight knee-length skirt and a matronly bosom that made her top-heavy. Her ugly square face was uglier for frowning as she read the papers in her hands, yet she moved like a model.

When she was close enough for him not to hit any innocent bystanders, he shot her in the chest with the Magnum. The impact lifted her out of her strapless black shoes, tossing her body through the air like a string bag of fruit. She landed with a smack on the polished floor, chest pumping blood, a burst container. He shot her once more to make sure, and her flaccid body slid along the floor on its own juice.

'I'd like a word with you, Lachlan,' said Mrs Weymouth, drawing abreast with him near the fresh fruit and vegetables.

'Yes?' Lachlan responded, his voice a discreet murmur. All around them in the supermarket aisle, the mass of humanity was shambling by, in weary pursuit of all the good things in life. Reluctantly Lachlan took his eyes off them, knowing that for some, the lure of low cost was not as attractive as no cost at all.

Mrs Weymouth seemed unconcerned by what evil misdeeds might be going on behind her back. Instead, she reached down into Lachlan's shopping trolley and fetched out a single banana, one of several he'd only just put in there. She held it up in the air between them and squeezed its yellow shaft with her hard, crimson-nailed fingertips.

'Yes?' he prompted her.

'It's soft,' she told him, squeezing the day-glo skin over and over. 'See? Soft inside.'

'I don't examine them,' Lachlan protested mildly. 'I just chuck 'em in.'

'That's exactly what I mean,' said Mrs Weymouth, her voice tight with irritation. 'You *throw* them into the trolley. I've seen you do it. Bananas. Apples. Peaches, even. Then later when you put them back, they're bruised. Next day, they're history.'

Lachlan wished she'd talk quieter. It would be just like her, unfair bitch, to blow his cover and then expect him to improve his detection rate.

'Are you saying,' he dared to challenge, 'that all the fruit here is perfect until I touch it?'

Mrs Weymouth sighed ostentatiously, her eyes half-closed. Her eyelids had about a hundred wrinkles on them: she was as old as his foster-mum – older, even.

'We do our best,' she said.

'So do I, Mrs Weymouth,' said Lachlan, turning his face away from her, in a gesture he hoped might remind her of the unsupervised multitudes overrunning the store. 'I've got to keep my eyes on everybody. Sometimes maybe I'm looking so hard, what I'm putting in the trolley gets a bit of a bump.'

But Mrs Weymouth wasn't finished with him yet.

'I saw a packet of chocolate rollettes you put back on the shelf yesterday,' she said, 'half-squashed. The damage was caused by the sharp edge of a tin or suchlike while in your trolley. No customer is going to buy those rollettes now. They'll choose a packet that's perfect. The damaged one will end up in the clearance racks, and we'll lose money on it.'

Lachlan leaned on the cross-bar of his trolley and stared her straight in the eye.

'So sue me,' he said. Then, aloud: 'Sorry. It won't happen again.'

She nodded and turned on her ridiculous heels. He let her go; she wasn't worth the ammo. He had work to do.

All day, Lachlan walked the aisles of the supermarket, taking items off the shelves, loading them into his trolley, moving on; then, one by one, he would put the items back, as if he'd changed his mind or discovered he couldn't afford them. All day, as he played this mindless game of selection and deselection, he watched the shoppers, appraising their clothing, scrutinising their hands, reading their faces. In this fluorescent fairyland of unbeatable offers, friendly service and loyalty schemes, hordes of would-be thieves were in constant motion, sniffing for their opportunity. Lachlan couldn't hope to catch them all, but he could catch some.

As soon as he had a suspect, he would follow at a discreet distance. It was easier to spot someone who was thinking of stealing something than someone who'd already done it, so usually when he followed someone, he could expect to catch them in the act.

He'd been in this game a long time now, and he knew a thing or two. No one ever stole suddenly, on impulse, innocent up until the moment temptation whispered. They all came into the store intending to steal, it was just a matter of what and when. You could see it on their faces. Guilty as sin, from the word go.

Like any detective, Lachlan found the wiles of his quarry both impressive and pathetic. There really was no limit to what people would try. He'd had a guy with half a watermelon dangling between his legs, in a special sling pinned to his trousers and hidden by a long overcoat. He'd had an old lady with a pair of raw trout in her handbag. He'd had plenty of women hugely pregnant with disposable nappies, rustling as they moved. He'd had a guy with combat trousers, all the

pockets bulging so hard with Pilsner cans he could barely walk. He'd had a guy nudging a frozen Christmas turkey along the floor to the cigarette kiosk, then kicking it like a football towards the exit.

Mostly, people would attempt smaller thefts with subtler gestures: a tin of herrings slipped into a coat pocket, a tiny bottle of vanilla essence hidden in a palm, a chocolate bar up the sleeve. There were signs everywhere saying DETEC-TIVES PATROL THIS STORE but it didn't seem to make any difference.

Maybe no-one read those signs, the same way they didn't seem to read anything else in the store – prices, labels, instructions, opening hours, the lot. People never seemed to have a clue where anything was even if they were right underneath a sign telling them. They would stand for ages next to a sign saying BUY TWO GET ONE FREE, and then they'd put two into their trolley anyway. At the check-outs, they'd offer loyalty cards from other supermarkets. Or they'd say, 'I'm sorry, I've just realised I don't have any money.'

Thickos. Liars. Trust No One.

There was a girl in his sights now, and she was going to steal something for sure. She was only young, with a thick mop of unkempt golden hair and tight jeans. Her grey polyester top was loose though, ideal for concealment. She had big eyes and lips, no make-up. Like him, she had a few pimples here and there.

She was roaming all around the store, pushing her trolley down the middle of the aisles. She wasn't examining the products on the shelves, she was examining the aisles and the people. Was she looking for someone? No way. There was a look people got on their faces when they were searching for someone they knew, someone they'd agreed to meet up

with. This girl didn't have that look. She didn't care who any of the other shoppers were, he could see that. She was looking for an empty aisle.

Round and round the store she went, like a rat in a maze. He followed her, half-a-dozen steps behind. Despite his awkward gait, which used to trip him up when he'd been younger and less experienced, he pushed his trolley swiftly and smoothly. The girl was never out of his sight for longer than a few seconds. Sometimes she entered an aisle, sometimes she just glanced into it and passed it by for the next one along. The aisles she didn't bother with were always the ones that had several other shoppers in them.

She came to rest at last in toiletries. Lots of people stole stuff here, mostly the more expensive brands of toothpaste, deodorants, lip salves. Lachlan used lip salve himself, because his top lip was prone to cracking, and his choice of brand was the same one that he'd caught several people stealing. Thieves went for quality. But quality cost them dear, if Lachlan was on the case.

This girl wasn't interested in toiletries, however. She already had what she wanted, in her trolley. It was a long narrow refrigerated dessert, some sort of blueberry or apple Danish packaged in a silver tinfoil tray. She fetched it out, holding it vertically in her fingers. Held like that, side-on to his gaze, it looked like a musical instrument – like one of those recorders he'd been excused from playing at school.

The girl looked right and left, slowly enough for him to melt out of eyeshot at the crucial instant. Then she leaned close to the shelves, as if straining to read the minuscule guarantees printed on a packet of something-or-other. *If not completely satisfied,* blah blah blah. *This does not affect your statutory rights.* What were statutory rights? The right to remain silent,

the right to one phone call . . . Yes! She was doing it now – a gyration of both elbows and a backward thrust of her pear-shaped buttocks.

Lachlan pushed his trolley round the corner, letting it squeak all it liked. The girl turned to face him, her face blank and arrogant, like a Hollywood movie actress.

She'd done a good job with the Danish, he had to admit. It wasn't poking out through the fabric of her top, although her breasts certainly were. He'd seen plenty of people with products falling out of their clothing as they walked, smack onto the floor at their feet. That wouldn't happen to this girl. She'd stowed the Danish inside her jeans, inside the waistband, right next to her flesh probably. Her sex parts were liable to go numb if she didn't make her getaway pronto.

'Excuse me, miss,' he said. 'Would you mind coming with me for a minute?'

She stiffened, folding her arms across her front.

'Why?' she said.

'I think you know why,' he said, without emotion.

Leaving her trolley, she walked beside him along the aisle, her face ghastly pale. He took her to the storage bay behind the delicatessen, and into a little windowless room. There was a desk, a chair, a telephone, a filing cabinet, and a fire extinguisher. The bare essentials. Lachlan closed the door.

'OK,' he said. 'I think we both know what you've got inside your trousers.'

Sullenly, the girl reached inside her clothing and pulled out the Danish.

'Have a seat,' said Lachlan, indicating the desk, 'while I phone the police.'

'Please, no,' she begged in a small voice.

Lachlan looked her up and down. She had the classic

gun-to-the-head expression, and sweat glistened on her clasped hands.

'There's one thing you can do to make me forget the whole thing,' he said. 'I think you can guess what that is.'

In silence she undressed, pulling her top over her head, exposing her white midriff slightly marked in red by the sharp tinfoil edges of the Danish. Her breasts, barely contained in a faded flesh-coloured bra, were as big as Mrs Weymouth's, a strange sight on such a young body. She left the bra on, but took her jeans and panties off in one motion, hooking her thumbs into the two sets of waistbands. Her pubic hair was golden.

'The bra too,' he said.

'Please,' she said.

'Do it,' he said.

She unhooked her bra, and finally her breasts were revealed, round and perfect like pale pink melons.

'Turn around,' he said, 'and put your hands against the wall.'

He grabbed the cheeks of her bottom and exposed her slit. His erect penis slid in easily, and he ejaculated in about two seconds.

The girl was wheeling her trolley towards the checkouts now; he'd better close in fast or she would get away. It was company policy not to apprehend shoplifters at the checkouts, to save other customers embarrassment.

'Excuse me, miss,' he said.

'What for?' she challenged him, sullen like in his vision of her.

'Would you mind accompanying me,' he said.

She frowned and bit down hard on her lower lip. She was much better-looking than he'd thought. She had long blonde eyelashes which were only visible at close quarters. Her eyes

weren't a standard colour, and they shone with feelings he couldn't identify. Then, suddenly, awkwardly, she smiled, and reached inside her clothing. The stolen Danish was yanked forth, momentarily distending the fabric of her top like that alien baby bursting out of somebody's stomach in that *Alien* movie.

'Here,' she said, holding the somewhat buckled package out to him. 'Sorry.'

Nonplussed, he took hold of it. The tinfoil part was chilly and damp, but the cardboard lid was already warm. Warm from the heat of her flesh.

'Look, I've given it back, OK?' she said, nervously, tossing her hair off her forehead. 'Let's just forget all about it. I can't afford it anyway.'

Lachlan examined the Danish at a glance.

'No one will want to buy this now,' he informed her. 'Its edges are all crumpled. It's as good as wrecked. We'll lose money on it.'

Anger and anxiety flashed across the girl's face.

'Jesus, what does a crappy frozen dessert mean to *you*?'

Lachlan tossed it back into her trolley, unmoved.

'It's for sale. You didn't pay for it. That's theft. My job is to hand you on to the police. I'm just doing my job.'

She stared him straight in the eyes, defiantly at first, then with a slow flush of fear as she glimpsed the impenetrable, steely sureness in him.

'Please,' she said then, licking her lips in naked distress. 'I've been done for this twice already. Once more, and they'll put me away for sure. I just got hungry for something sweet, that's all. I don't have much money.' She gestured limply. 'It's hard sometimes.'

He drew a deep breath. How to explain to her that life was tough for everyone, everyone in the whole wide dirty

world? A bit of slack in one place resulted in a tightening of the screws further down the line. If he let her go, Mrs Weymouth would probably find out about it, and he'd lose his job. Then before you knew it he'd be no better off than this girl was now. He'd lose his car and everything. Conceivably he and this girl would end up standing next to each other at the Job Centre, looking lost and hopeless. There'd be a position going as a store detective and she'd probably get it, because women got everything nowadays.

'I've got a job to do,' was how he summed up these complexities. 'Come with me please.'

'Wait a minute,' she said, her hands trembling as she stepped closer to him. 'I– I could let you have sex with me.'

'What?' said Lachlan. 'I beg your pardon?'

Her eyes were shiny, darting back and forth like fish. Against the odds, though, no one had steered into their aisle yet; they were still alone. And she – so close to him that he could see the pores in her skin and the frightened pulse-beat in her pale throat – she raised her whisper loud above the Muzak, deadly serious:

'I could let you fuck me. In the car park. In your car. I know you've got one. I've seen you driving around the town. Your sound system must be about two million watts.'

'Look . . .' he said, his voice hoarse all of a sudden.

'I could take all my clothes off,' she hissed urgently. 'You'd see everything. I'd do whatever you wanted.'

He cleared his throat, blushing hot.

'I can't just walk out of the store,' he said. 'It's not allowed.'

'Jesus, don't you have tea breaks or something?' she squeaked, almost hysterical, then got hold of herself. 'Whenever,' she assured him. 'Just come out whenever you can, and I'll meet you there.'

He gaped at her in disbelief, and she stared back at him imploringly. An old lady trundled round the corner, took one look at them, and passed by, embarrassed. Supermarket life was circling them, waiting for their aisle to be cleared of intimacy and return to normal.

'You must think I'm stupid,' said Lachlan.

'No, look,' she said in desperation. 'Look: I'll give you this . . .' She delved a small pink hand into a pocket of her jeans, and pulled out a key-ring with several keys jingling off it.

'It's all my keys,' she assured him breathlessly, holding them up by the plastic Bart Simpson trinket that linked them. 'The keys to everything . . . my front door, my back door, everything . . . this little one's for my bike — it's parked just outside — you can see it through the window, there, look!'

With his narrowed eyes he followed where she was pointing, and, sure enough, there was a bicycle blurrily visible through the wall of plate glass, just under the giant affiched letters saying FOR ALL YOUR NEEDS

'I can't do without these keys, do you understand?' she pleaded. 'I can't even get home. I *have* to have them.' She pressed the keys against his dangling hand, and let them go. Instinctively he grabbed them rather than let them fall to the ground; it was a reflex action.

She put both her soft palms on his right shoulder and lifted herself up on tiptoes to murmur in his ear. 'You've got me right where you want me. I'll be waiting.'

And she ran off, leaving her trolley behind.

Lachlan steadied himself for a few moments, aware that inside his clothes he was soaked with perspiration. He wiped his forehead and mouth, inspected his sleeve. The news was not good. God knows what the customers would think, seeing him in this state.

The first thing to do was get rid of the Danish – if Mrs Weymouth saw it she would go ballistic. Furtively, heart pounding, he rushed the damp and damaged specimen to the frozen goods section, fearing the old woman's eyes on him with every step. He hid the Danish under others of its kind, piling the straight and perfect ones on top of it three layers deep.

This done, undetected, he relaxed a little. The light in the supermarket seemed less harsh, the central heating less high. Mrs Weymouth was at the far end of the store, pretending to care about a disabled shopper. The clock above the community noticeboard said six thirty-eight. Another hour-and-a-half and he was a free man.

For the next little while he walked the girl's trolley around the supermarket, putting items back on the shelves. Spaghetti. Bread. Peanut butter. Sugar Puffs. Milk. Sanitary pads.

This last one made him wonder. He wasn't sure if he could cope with a vagina that was bleeding, even if it was the only one he'd ever get hold of. It wasn't clean, somehow.

At eight o'clock, as the last shoppers were being ushered out of the supermarket into the summer dusk, Lachlan was already outside, standing right next to the girl's bicycle, waiting.

Not born yesterday, he had a sick feeling she wouldn't show up, but still he hoped she might. He ran his sharp eyes back and forth across all the cars parked in neat rows, in case she was hiding amongst them. He remembered her very well, physically. A single glimpse of her face or her behind would have been enough to identify her, if she'd been anywhere about.

As more and more cars pulled away, there were fewer places where a girl could be hiding. Lachlan consulted the watch on his big bony wrist. Eight minutes had passed in

what had felt like twenty seconds. Nothing sexual was going to happen now. Golden rule: Trust No One.

He tried to imagine some way he could get revenge. God, how she must despise him, if she was willing to lose her bike just to avoid a few seconds of unwanted attention. Maybe she was scared of him. That would be tragic, if that was all it was. It could have been a fantastic experience. She would have got her keys back; he would have found out what intercourse was like. She might even have enjoyed it. There was nothing wrong with his sex organs, that was for sure.

What was he going to do with her bike? He could take it away with him, sell it maybe. As long as he didn't get in trouble with the police. Like all private detectives, he had an uneasy relationship with the boys in blue. One of them had stopped him once, on one of those long sleepless nights when he'd taken the car out for a drive, CDs belting out into the lonely dark. The cop had told him it was a mystery how a moron like Lachlan had ever been judged fit for a car license. That was the sort of crack you didn't forget in a hurry.

Lachlan looked at the girl's bicycle again. His car, he suddenly remembered, didn't have a roof rack. Never mind the bike, then: he could maybe use the chain and the padlock for something. Keep something of his own safe from theft, something he hadn't thought of yet. Also, without the chain, her bike would most likely get stolen during the night, which would serve her right.

He slipped the smallest of the keys into the bike's padlock, and twisted. Through his fingers he could sense something wasn't right. Nothing clicked or fell open.

'Hey!' a male voice shouted from not far away. '*Hey!*'

Lachlan tried to pull the key out, but it was gripped tight in the lock. An athletic-looking man with grey hair and paint-spattered training clothes had set two evenly-weighted

shopping bags down on the asphalt and began to stride towards Lachlan from the vaulted entrance of the supermarket. Panicking, Lachlan let the keys go and ran to his own car. It was instantly identifiable by the silver demister strips on the back window, the little Celtic flag on the aerial, and the big warning stickers about what would happen if anyone tried to break in and steal the potent black metallic speakers within. A new addition to the vehicle's distinguishing features, however, was one that Lachlan noticed only as he was struggling to unlock the door. All along the driver's side, gouged deeply into the paintwork with a sharp implement, was the word WANKER.

Finally bursting into the car, he slammed the door behind him and started the motor. With scarcely a second's pause he began to reverse the car, dizzily relieved to find that the bicycle's owner had given up the pursuit and was returning to his shopping bags. Not worth it.

Lachlan pulled on the brake and sat tight, loath to be pushed now that the heat was off. The bicycle man cycled away; Lachlan memorised his distinguishing features for future reference.

After a few more minutes the carpark lights, synchronised with the sunset, glowed all around him. Mrs Weymouth and the big boss were locking the supermarket's entrance inside a big trellis of iron bars. The big boss pointed a device at a hidden alarm and pressed the trigger. Then he and Mrs Weymouth walked to the same car.

When they'd driven off, Lachlan reversed fully into the empty expanse of tarmac. The keys to everything lay discarded near the bike stands, for the girl to retrieve if she was still out there somewhere, spying on the scene, waiting for him to make his move.

Blinking away tears, Lachlan edged his precious injured

vehicle towards the exit, conscious that if he allowed his anger and his hurt to get on top of him, he might crash the car in the dangerous traffic beyond the supermarket, and lose more than he'd lost already. In the rear-view mirror, his own face was reflected back at him undisguised, the hare-lip vivid and glistening above his malformed teeth.

Looking right and left, forwards and backwards, he indicated to the world where he was meaning to go. Then, gunning the engine, he followed through and left them all for dead.

A HOLE WITH TWO ENDS

'It was nice of us to come, wasn't it?' said Sandra to Neil, as they were walking back to their car. She kept her voice low, so as not to be overheard by the woman whose horrid little cottage they'd just left.

'Of course it was,' sighed Neil. 'It's this little anti-English game they play – making you feel like a complete bastard even when you're bending over backwards for them.'

'Can one refer to a woman as a "bastard", I wonder?' mused Sandra as they stepped up to the Daewo. 'I mean, in the pejorative sense?'

'Don't see why not.'

Neither of them needed to voice what had been obvious to them as soon as they'd arrived for the interview: that this latest candidate for the job was yet another Highlands loser, a waste of their valuable time.

Neil pointed his electronic key at the car and its doors

obediently unlocked themselves. As he and Sandra swung into their seats, they got a clear view of the vehicle parked in front of the cottage – a junkheap of uncertain pedigree, speckled with rust. When Sandra, right at the beginning of the interview, had reminded the woman that anyone working at Loch Eye Pottery would need their own transport, the woman had waved her cigarette at her 'motor'. In fact, she'd pushed for a petrol allowance on top of the wage. Then later she'd admitted that the car 'needed serviced' (ugh! illiterate expression!) and in any case it belonged to 'Hughie' and Hughie was 'down the road' just now and it would surely be easier all round if Neil and Sandra could just bring the pottery here and then pick it up again when it was painted?

That was the problem with making anything entrepreneurial happen up here. Your workforce had to be drawn from people who were stuck in the stagnant shallows of self-deception: the long term unemployed, the nervous-breakdown survivors, counterculture failures, alcoholics, benefit scroungers, small-time dope dealers . . . a whole countryside full of perpetual losers stranded in decrepit cottages that stank of cigarette smoke and baby shit and booze.

Neil noticed, as he was revving the engine, that the folio of (really quite good) watercolours the woman had originally sent them was still lying on the dashboard.

'Damn,' he said. 'Shall we . . . ?'

'No, I *couldn't*,' groaned Sandra. 'We'll post them back.'

There wasn't an SAE, of course, but then, equipping the back rooms of Loch Eye Pottery with a few half-way reliable workers had cost them so much hassle already, another 58 pence wouldn't make much difference.

They pulled out of the farm road, wincing in unison as the potholes rattled the Daewo's suspension. Between the two strips of crumbling concrete, a furrow of grass had been

allowed to grow so thick that it bashed and scraped against the underbelly of the chassis. In their quest for a couple more recruits to copy Sandra's elegant Loch Eye designs onto bowls and jugs in a serene and beautiful workplace for a very reasonable £3.75 an hour, they might be rewarded with a puncture.

Thankfully, they cruised onto the bitumen road unscathed. The drive between here and their home in Loandhu would be a smooth, pleasant one now, through drowsy farmlands and forests turning gold and emerald in the late afternoon sun.

'We shouldn't have let that blonde girl go – that Alison,' said Neil, slipping his Ray-Bans on. 'She was the most talented we had. Reliable too.'

'Yes,' murmured Sandra coolly, tidying her fringe in the sunvisor mirror. 'I know you liked her.' She frowned as she flicked a stray lock of hair back and forth: perspiration had got to it, and the more she tried to fluff it out the lanker it looked. Her big brown eyes were, she noted, a little bloodshot, and the flesh around them was finely wrinkled. For forty-eight, though, she was in pretty good shape – better than *him*, if honest truth were told – and her sacred principle never to go to a hairdresser north of Edinburgh was still paying dividends.

'It has nothing to do with *liking* her,' said Neil, accelerating. 'It's just that she didn't have the usual drawbacks.'

'Oh, I'd love to know what those are,' she volleyed back. 'Perhaps something to do with—? *Look out!*'

Her shrill cry focused him on the road ahead, but it was too late. A flash of grey passed in front of the car, and was swept under the wheels with a sickening jolt, a muffled soft collision of steel and rubber with flesh and bone. Sandra spun round in her seat and saw the creature leaping through the

scrub at the side of the road, then wriggling frantically through the barbed wire fence of the field beyond.

Neil slowed the car and brought it to a stop as close to the road's edge as he could manage.

'It's dead for sure,' he cautioned her, as she wrenched her door open and sprang out.

'It was still running,' she called over her shoulder.

He hurried to catch up to her, squinting in the fierce sunlight, following her silhouette with its windblown halo of honey-and-grey hair. 'It's a nervous system reflex,' he said. 'The animal's had it, but it keeps going for a few seconds. Like a chicken with its head cut off.'

'We ran over its back legs,' she said. 'I saw it dragging them. It's injured, that's all.'

Farther back than they thought possible, they found the accident site. An unspectacular smear of blood, lightly garnished with fur, glistened on the grey tar. Sandra was already leaning against the barbed wire, peering into the empty field. It was an unkempt expanse, stubble in parts, churned-up mud in others, engraved with the dried footprints of cows long moved elsewhere. The farmhouse appeared to be half a mile away, barricaded with a phalanx of hay-bales sheathed in black plastic. In the desolate middle distance, nothing moved.

'We can't leave it to die,' she said.

Neil was about to argue, realised he didn't know what they would be arguing about. 'What do you think it was?'

'A wildcat. Scottish wildcat. Rare. Only three thousand left in all of Britain.' She began to climb over the barbed wire. 'Hold this down for me.'

He lowered the tense cable of steel as far as he could push it while she swung her legs over. The flesh of her buttocks bulged against the delicate beige cotton of her trousers as she strained to keep a safe channel of vacancy between her

crotch and the snarly metal spikes. Coming down on the other side, she yelped, not because she'd been snagged by the barbed wire – she hadn't – but because there was an unexpected drop through insubstantial scrub.

'You'll have to be careful,' she called up at him, annoying him with her presumption that he'd follow. She was already stretching her arms high, grabbing hold of the barbed wire so she could hang on it with all her weight. Her breasts looked good that way, pressing out through the yellow cashmere of her pullover; her sharply upturned face smoothed the wrinkles out of her bare neck, stripping years off her age. He hesitated, then climbed over the wire himself, landing rather gracelessly beside her.

'Come on,' she said. 'It must be hiding in this verge somewhere. It would hide in the closest available spot.' Already she was visualising the magic moment of discovery: a shivering, cowering creature yanked rudely out of legend, blinking up at her from a nest of grass. A tabby the size of an ocelot, golden-eyed and panting with fright.

She stumped off, peering into the tangled embankment as she moved along the field's perimeter. There wasn't much grass at ground level; most of it was bristling sideways out of the earthy barricade, lushest near the top as if nourished by the fence-stakes. Beneath this furzy mane of vegetation, the bulwark of clay was crumbly and embedded with stones and lumps of concrete. It was also riddled with rabbit holes.

'It'll have crawled into one of these,' decided Sandra. Spot judgements were her *forte*; in matters of instinct she was rarely wrong.

'If so,' said Neil, 'it's probably dead by now. Or vicious as hell. What are we supposed to do, call "Here, pussy?" '

'We ran it down,' she reminded him. 'It's our responsibility.'

Neil breathed deep and counted to three. If any single

factor had inhibited the growth of their business, it was Sandra's occasional attacks of sentimental scruple, which could flare up, like hormonal flushes, at the strangest times.

'Jesus,' he said, visualising the wildcat from memories of infra-red pictures he'd seen in newspapers. 'This isn't some old lady's beloved moggy, you know.'

Sandra didn't reply. She was already making her way along the line of the barricade, no longer expecting the cat to be revealed entire, but straining for a fugitive glimpse of gleaming eyes, striped flank, twitching tail. Already she could imagine, inside the snug-fitting lid of a Loch Eye Pottery sugar-bowl, a tiny painting of a cat's face, staring out as if from a hole, hidden there to surprise the customer. Did any of her staff have the skill to paint such an image? Alison might have, if she hadn't minxed herself out of a job.

Sandra snatched up a lone birch twig from the ground, briskly denuded it by tearing off its sprigs and leaves, and poked it into the nearest rabbithole. A few steps farther on, she poked it into the next, and the next, each time testing how far the stick would go. Most of the passages were narrow, too narrow to fit a large feline; some of them had been collapsed by erosion or were clogged, like dead arteries, with ossified debris.

'Hey, I just remembered I didn't lock the car,' said Neil, when they'd moved fifty yards or so from where they'd begun.

'Forget the car for a minute, can't you?' she said. 'This thing's still alive, I know it.'

He squared his shoulders, preparing to argue the point, but there was a hint of pleading in her eyes, a flustered lick of her lips, letting him know she didn't want to fight. He smiled, let his shoulders fall.

'I hope you don't have your heart set on having it stuffed,' he sighed. 'If it's badly mangled . . .'

'It's going to be fine,' she insisted, pressing onwards, stick in hand, Neil following on.

Only a few moments later, her hunch was proved right. A rabbithole she'd poked her stick into emitted a dull scrabbling noise, and Neil, six feet behind her, was startled to see the furry tip of a big striped tail trembling out of the nearest hole to him. He uttered an involuntary shout, causing the creature to jerk back inside with a puff of loose soil. Neil and Sandra, a man's span apart, realised they were standing at opposite ends of a horizontal tunnel through the curved embankment, a simple sinus in the soil.

Without a word, Sandra lowered herself to the ground and squatted in front of her aperture. Neil did the same at his.

It was late afternoon by now, almost dusk. They were too low down now to see the road, but they knew it was unlit and potentially dangerous. The sun was disappearing behind trees, casting a flickering glow over the fields. All around Neil and Sandra, the picture quality of the world was being adjusted as if by contrast and brightness knobs on God's remote control: the sharper contours of grass and scarred earth were sharpened further, almost luminescent, while the duller stretches were retreating into darkness.

'The car . . .' said Neil.

'Forget the car,' hissed Sandra through clenched teeth. She leaned closer to the hole in the embankment, squinting into its horribly pregnant shaft.

'Your trousers . . .' he warned her softly, as she shuffled forwards on her knees across the dirt.

'I can see its eyes,' she said. 'It's frightened.' Neil watched her settle onto all fours, her palms balancing gingerly on the ground. Her bosom was pressed between her arms, bulging forward, a soft glow of cashmere in the twilight. He suddenly wanted her more intensely than he'd

wanted her for years; he felt like mounting her here and now in the field.

'Of course it's bloody frightened,' he said. 'But what can we do?'

'I'll poke the stick in,' she said. 'That'll make it move backwards, towards your end. Once its tail pokes out, you grab it and pull.'

He snorted in disbelief. Trust her to leave that part to him . . . Raise the finance for the pottery, give the troublesome employees the sack, grab the wildcat by the tail: Neil'll fix it!

'What if it tears me to shreds?'

She groaned in exasperation.

'We ran over its legs! It's just dragging its hindquarters back and forth.'

'So you say.' But he kneeled forward, bracing himself. The sound of the animal's anxious breathing was having a weird effect on him, as if it were a drug he'd sniffed into his bloodstream. Imagining himself a broken animal trapped in a claustrophobic shaft, he was almost intoxicated with pity. Or not quite pity, more a craving for the thing to be all right, despite what had happened.

Sandra inserted the stick carefully, almost tenderly, into the hole. On her face was an expression of intent curiosity, an ardent childlike wish for the desired outcome. Her lips were parted, her eyes half-closed.

From inside the tunnel came a fierce hiss and the sound of scrabbling. But no sign of the animal at Neil's end: no hide nor hair, so to speak. Sandra leaned further into the hole, her arm disappearing inside it, her cheek brushing against the earth, her hair mingling with the rough grass.

'I need a longer stick,' she breathed.

'Well, find one,' he urged her, his voice shaking with anticipation. 'You're liable to get your fingers bitten off.'

She withdrew her arm. Her sleeve was covered in soil, dark brown against the luxurious yellow. She glanced all around, but didn't get up off her knees.

'I can't see anything better than what I've got,' she said, studiously examining the end of her stick as if for blood or saliva. 'And I'm not leaving this hole.'

For another few minutes they squatted there, while the world grew darker all around them. Their eyes were well adjusted to the fading light, and they could still see each other and, of course, the holes in the embankment, perfectly well. But the rest of the environs – the empty field behind them, the long lampless road, the treetops of the hidden forest – was inexorably merging with the deepening mauve of the evening sky.

'The car's parking lights aren't on,' said Neil.

Sandra turned her face to him, stared directly into his eyes through the gathering chill of dusk. Her left cheek was smeared with dirt, her white teeth were bare.

'Forget – the fucking – car.' Her tone was savage but her diction was crystal.

She turned away from him and started to claw at the edges of the hole with her fingers.

'Dig,' she said.

He watched her, mesmerised. Her red fingernails were replaced by grimy black ones. Damp earth flurried over her trousers.

'Dig, you bastard,' she hissed.

He dug at his own hole. There were skiing gloves in the boot of the car, which would've made the task more comfortable, not to mention more efficient, but he knew better than to suggest this. Instead, he jabbed at the soil with his fingers, fumbling for purchase on larger clumps and stones, grunting with effort. It was penance, he knew; a more potent offering than denials and red roses.

They worked doggedly as the light was extinguished all around them. They burrowed in rhythm, panted in unison, swaying on their knees. Their flushed, contorted faces looked bone-pale under the rise of a colossal moon. From inside the earth before them, an anxious, inhuman moan made itself heard, growing steadily louder and more despairing.

At last, when they'd excavated so much soil that there was only about a metre of tunnel left undisclosed, the moment came. The wildcat's striped tail, bristling electrically, convulsed into view, and Neil grabbed it in his filthy hands and yanked. A grotesquely loud shriek of terror registered on him first, then the fact that bestial teeth were clamped into his fist – as though a mallet had slammed a bunch of iron nails right through his flesh. The massive creature was a squirming chaos of fur and muscle on the end of his arm, its claws ripping at his thighs and elbows as it flailed through the air.

Unthinkingly, he ran towards Sandra and, even as he released his hold, she lunged at the creature herself, arms thrust forward in a fearless, angry embrace. For a split-second she had it clutched tight to her – it might, in that instant, have been an ordinary cat after all – but then its huge yellow eyes blazed with fury, and in an eruption of brute force it clawed its way up her breast, onto her face. Its crushed hind limbs swung crazily as it clung to her head for a nightmarish instant, then it tumbled down her back and hit the ground. With a slithering of skewed bone, it heaved itself away, hyper-ventilating, into the darkness.

'Don't stop! Don't *stop*!' shrieked Sandra, as Neil fell back in horror at the damage to his hands, the blood running down her face. 'Useless fucking coward!'

A deep claw-gouge from forehead to brow to cheek – missing her eye by a miracle – was bubbling and spattering blood all over her chest and shoulders. Yet she ignored it, and

instead whirled around and stumbled into the gloom, hunching down like some sort of primate, her arms swinging low through the air, brushing the inky vegetation.

Suddenly there was a screech, not of a living being this time, but of tyres on a road surface – a short, surreally musical screech, and then a loud crash of metal on metal.

'Jesus Christ, the car . . . !' barked Neil.

'Come *on*!' yelled Sandra, still pursuing her prey.

'But don't you understand—?'

'I understand everything!' she raged, fetching up a stick – a much larger and heavier stick than before. 'Whatever's happened has happened. Who gives a fuck? It's over! It's over!'

Cudgel dangling from her fist, she pushed on into the darkness, her hunched form a piebald pelt of yellow and black. He wanted to follow her, to restrain her, to enfold her in his arms, to carry her home, but he was half-blinded by the pain in his hand, a nauseous mixture of numbness and agony, a greasy mess of bloody fingers. He heard his own voice grunting and whimpering as he strained to get his legs to move, but he just stood there shivering on the churned earth.

He knew this was all lunacy now, that they couldn't hope to save this creature, this half-crushed, fear-crazed demon of pure instinct. But it seemed his wife understood this too, and that it didn't make any difference. She was swinging the stick into the undergrowth, not in a tentative, exploratory way, but with all her might. Earth and grass exploded into the air, gobs of raw clay flying around like flesh, as she flailed viciously, over and over, her weapon now clutched in both black fists.

'I see its eyes!' she kept screaming, hoarse with feral longing as the whole countryside was falling into blackness around her and all the tiny stars came out of Heaven to bear witness. 'I see its eyes!'

THE SMALLNESS
OF THE ACTION

One Wednesday morning, in a moment of carelessness, Christine dropped her baby on the floor and broke him. She was lifting him from his cot to the changing table, and he just sort of slipped out of her hands.

The house was carpeted, but only very thinly over solid concrete. There was no mistaking the snap of bone as the heavy little body hit the floor: a collision of two hard objects disguised in soft covering. The more brittle of the two caved in.

Christine bent down at once and picked her baby up again. The total time he had spent asserting his freedom, making his own way through the challenges of space and gravity, couldn't have been more than a second. Yet, in that single clock tick, he had managed to become unstuck.

At least he was not dead. As she lifted him up, he was crying furiously – shrieking, really. Who knows, maybe he

wasn't seriously injured: he often shrieked, after all. Shrieking was his way of telling her that he wasn't asleep. That was all he ever had to tell her, ever.

Flinching from the ferocity of the noise, Christine laid her baby on the changing table and checked him for damage. It was immediately obvious what had happened. There was no blood, but one of her baby's arms swivelled loosely inside its jumpsuit sleeve, like a sausage in a stocking. Christine could tell, even at a glance, that there was no longer any connection at the shoulder.

While she was wondering what to do next, she unfastened the press-studs on the crotch of the jumpsuit and exposed the soiled nappy. Her baby's legs, kicking convulsively, were obviously unbroken – which must mean that his back was OK as well. His voice was louder than ever, as if the accident had triggered a growth spurt in his vocal cords.

Christine changed her baby's nappy, as she'd done countless times before. She washed and powdered the flesh carefully, as if it might be needed for some special meal or artistic creation, then wrapped it up again, out of sight. Dodging her baby's kicks, she wrestled his tiny legs back into the jumpsuit. Outside, the sun emerged from behind a cloud and beamed in on both of them through the bay window. A bright vista of suburbia stretched from her street's gentle incline all the way to infinity. No event of any dramatic importance could possibly happen here. All the contents, both human and architectural, of this little corner of the universe were fixed firmly in place.

Christine lifted her baby off the changing table and back into his cot. She arranged the loose, floppy arm neatly by his side so that it resembled the other one. She arranged the pale blue blanket over his squirming body and tucked it gently up to his spittly chin. Every time he kicked the blanket away she

replaced it, while the window-shaped rectangle of sunlight inched across the floor almost imperceptibly and motes of dust loitered in the overbreathed air.

After a long time the baby stopped shrieking, then his noise subsided to a gulping, gasping yawn. His face began to unswell, gradually losing its resemblance to a punnet of squashed tomato and settling back into an image of a human infant. But for his ugliness and the drool on his perpetually inflamed chin, he might almost be a baby from the cover of a baby magazine. Almost.

Looking at him sometimes, she couldn't actually see him as an infant at all. He seemed unconvincing as a new arrival to the world. There was a darkness in his brow, a slyness in his eyes, a set to his mouth, which made him look like he was a man already, as if her womb had been some kind of public bar where he'd already spent half a lifetime sipping beer, swapping grievances with his mates, and staring at women's breasts.

Christine sat down gingerly in the softest armchair, easing herself into it for fear of making the pains from her still-unhealed episiotomy worse. It had been several months now since she'd been cut open, and the wound was refusing to go away. Bending down so recklessly to pick up her fallen baby had really yanked at the scars. She took a deep breath, held it for a long time, and let it go. Then she settled in, next to the cot and the changing table, and watched the sun move across the carpet for the rest of the day.

At twilight, her husband came home.

'How's my little man, then?' he said.

'He's fine,' Christine replied.

'Have a good day, then?'

'Me?' she said.

'Yeah,' he said.

As always, she felt like shoving him into a chair, standing over him, and telling him exactly what her day had been like. She wanted to let him know that her day had been an outrage, a mockery, an insult. All those minutes joined end to end, yet endless; an eternity of useless minutes spent either waiting for nothing to happen, or of waiting for something to stop; of longing for someone else's sleep (never your own) to go on and on, of being bored and anxious knowing it wouldn't. She wanted to rail against all the hands-on fussery, the brainless drudgery, the interminable succession of soft interventions, pathetically small triumphs erased by repetition, washed away by piss and tears and lukewarm water, all to achieve an illusion of normality. Every morning at 8:15, her husband would leave her alone in the house with an infant gurgling in a bed of clean fluffy cotton; at 5:45 he would return and find her alone in the house with an infant gurgling in a bed of clean fluffy cotton; nothing, apparently, had happened. She had, apparently, lain around the house like a trusted pet, luxuriating in the quiet and the central heating. No one could begin to understand the violence that was done to her mind and spirit every day, the way her soul was tenderised by a thousand hammer blows delivered with instinctive accuracy and force by a furious little fist.

'Fine thanks,' she said.

He switched on the television and, before the picture even materialised, walked away to the kitchen to make them both a cup of tea. He had a few minutes to kill, waiting for a domestic soap opera to finish and for the news to begin.

'Here you are, love,' he said, handing her a steaming mug as the strident music announced the roundup of the day's important events.

News no longer made sense to Christine. She wondered

whether it made any sense to anybody really, beyond giving them something to discuss at work. A glimpse of a man in a grey suit, strenuously denying the 'findings' of a 'commission'. What commission? What findings? What man? In a moment he was gone, replaced by some new war in a faraway country. What country? What war?

'Shhh,' her husband would say, if she ever asked. 'I've missed some.'

Numb, she would leave the battleground to its soldiers and journalists, and prepare dinner. She vaguely wished to be sympathetic to the people suffering in the war, but everyone who appeared on camera seemed so wonderfully free to her, so alive; not one of them was confined to a baby's cot-side, unavailable to comment on important matters. They gesticulated angrily at the camera, stating their opinions with passion, and the world listened. These war people were exotic creatures, like cheetahs or antelopes, filmed in the wild. Even when covered with blood, stumbling down a bombed street, they inhabited a wider and airier sphere than hers.

A baby's explosive cry sped through the house and found her where she stood in the kitchen. It impacted against its natural target, her brain, for what must have been the thousandth time.

By chance (for he rarely touched their baby) her husband had made some overture to the infant during an advertisement. In doing so, he evidently nudged the baby's broken shoulder, well-swaddled though it was in the bedding, and the infant began to scream, as suddenly and loudly as a car alarm.

Christine pulled a bubbling saucepan off the flame, covered it with a lid, and hurried out of the kitchen to the front room.

'I just tickled him,' her husband protested, helpless by the crib, his hands twitching at his sides.

'It's all right,' she reassured him, displacing him at the epicentre of trouble. 'He's ... touchy just now.'

'Teething, maybe,' he suggested, straining manfully to meet her somewhere near where he guessed she lived.

'Could be,' she sighed, her eyes squinting shut against the electric proximity of the baby's shrieking as she lifted him, swaddling clothes and all, to her breast. 'Could be.'

In a couple of minutes she had him quiet, sucking at her. His mouthings were like soft rainfall heard above the low distant thunder of the tumbledryer. Everything was as it always was, by this time of evening. The accident was already fading in her memory, like yesterday's news, yesterday's grey-suited men.

Next day, Christine dropped her baby again.

This time it was not exactly an accident, although it was certainly not premeditated either. She was changing him, again, and had just got to the part where she was holding him aloft, blowing gently on his freshly powdered groin. His disjointed arm was strapped with a ribbon of gauze to his stocky torso, and tied with a bow at the back. His free arm punched the air as he yelled. She blew at a distance, taking deep breaths, keeping her face well clear of his lunging feet.

She wondered what would happen if she let him fall.

Her grip was firm; she had no intention of loosening it. Yet she was entranced by the hugeness of the responsibility she carried, and the smallness of the action that might cast a spotlight on her. A single loosening of her fingers would be enough. Even if she was startled into loosening them by the ring of a telephone or a knock at the door, she might still be dragged into the glare of public condemnation. How strange! Her own life had been pummelled into unrecognizability by her baby, she had been hacked mercilessly adrift from the life she'd constructed for herself before falling pregnant, yet no-one was

investigating this enormity; there was no public outcry, no police interest, no social worker sniffing around the door. No-one seemed to think that anything untoward had occurred, despite the fact that a confident young woman with a keen wit had been brutalised into a shuffling automaton.

One of the reasons she couldn't understand newspapers nowadays was that, even from the occasional headline she had time and energy to read, she got the impression that more and more children were being awarded large sums of money to compensate them for any unhappiness they may have suffered while in the care of grownups. The grievances ranged from sexual abuse to misdiagnosis of learning difficulties, and Christine had no doubt that some of them were awful enough to bother the courts with. But she couldn't understand why no one ever mentioned the suffering of the carers. Tortured to insanity, they ended up with their picture in the paper, captioned THE FACE OF EVIL.

Christine was about to replace her baby in his cot when, without warning, he started peeing. His hard nub of a penis squirted scalding urine onto her breast. In a paroxysm of disgust, she let him fall.

Again, he landed on the thinly carpeted floor; again there was a snap of bone. Again, she picked him up immediately and checked the damage. There was a good deal more of it this time. He had landed bottom-first.

However, calming him down didn't take quite as long this time. It was as though he himself could tell how badly broken he was, and was scared to make it worse. Tucked up in flannelette, he looked up at her in brute bewilderment.

'Meh,' he said.

Next day, Christine left her baby alone in the house while she went to the local police station. It wasn't far away, a squat

ugly prefab opposite the veterinary surgery and the Red Cross charity shop.

Christine walked in through a glass door decorated with leaflets about solvent abuse and prohibited penknives. She identified a policeman and said she needed help.

The policeman was a beetle-browed young man with greased white hair and shoulders the shape of a Pepsi bottle. There were puckered holes in his big earlobes where studs or ear-rings had once dangled. Apart from the official frills on his short-sleeved shirt, he might have been a shop assistant in a clothing store for teenagers.

Pushing her misgivings under, Christine tried to explain the problem. She was alone in the house with a baby, she said, and she was losing her mind. Could the Law help?

'Are you afraid you might harm your baby?' asked the policeman.

'My baby is fine,' said Christine. 'It's *me* who's in danger.'

'In danger of what?'

'In danger of ceasing to exist.'

There was a pause while the policeman considered this.

'Do you want to see a WPC?' he said at last.

'A what?'

'A woman police constable.'

'What difference would that make?'

He picked up a telephone and pressed one button. Within sixty seconds Christine was led into a claustrophobically small room, like a bathroom but with two chairs and a desk instead of a tub and toilet. The walls were papered with posters about domestic violence. Christine took a seat, already regretting coming. She wanted to make the police understand that if they wanted to help her they shouldn't be going about it this way, they should be bringing her somewhere nice, they shouldn't be enclosing her in smaller and smaller spaces. But

somebody else had already started talking. A thirtysomething female in a police uniform was asking questions.

'Are you afraid you might harm your baby?'

'My baby isn't the one in danger. *I'm* in danger,' said Christine.

'What makes you think so?'

'I used to be human being. I'm turning into a machine.'

The policewoman smiled wryly.

'I'm sure we all feel that way sometimes.'

'I feel that way *all* the time,' retorted Christine.

'So what would you like us to do?'

'I want you to take my baby away.'

'You don't feel you can care for your baby anymore?'

'I can care for him perfectly well. It's the only thing I *can* do nowadays.'

'So what are you hoping the police department could do with your baby?'

'I thought you might be able to organise giving him to a female prisoner in a gaol. They're stuck in a cell all day and night anyway. I'm sure it would work out fine, with the right person.'

The policewoman chewed on this for a while, then leaned forward and looked straight into Christine's eyes.

'Look,' she urged, in a compassionate tone. 'Let's forget the sarcasm ...What are you *really* trying to say to me?'

Christine's heart sank. She had done her best to explain. Trying over and over again was so exhausting; surely there must be *one* thing in her life that didn't have to be repeated for endless futility.

'I used to have a life ...' she sighed.

'The first year can be very difficult,' agreed the policewoman. It was as if she was agreeing that the first year of being strangled could be very difficult, or the first year of drowning.

'I need it to stop now.'

'What do you think will happen if it doesn't stop?'

'It's already happening.'

'What's already happening?'

'I'm ceasing to exist.'

'You look real to me.'

The conversation went round and round like this for three or four minutes. The urgent message Christine had wanted to put into the policewoman's mind kept being deflected, as if by an instinct of avoidance, like an infant turning away from a spoon.

'But I'm in *danger*,' she kept insisting.

'You think you might harm yourself?'

'The harm's already *done*.'

'You feel you're not coping?'

'Coping is *all* I'm doing.'

'You mean you're *barely* coping.'

'I'm coping perfectly *well*.'

'Well . . . that's *good*.'

'You don't *understand*,' pleaded Christine. 'Look at *you*. You're *here*. You're not sitting next to a baby's cot all day.'

The policewoman grinned.

'Been there, done that,' she said. Noting the look of aggrieved incomprehension on Christine's face, she went all sincere again. 'My babies grew up, that's all,' she summarised gently. 'They're at school now.'

It was incredible. It was like going to the police when you'd been burgled or attacked or raped, and them telling you to forget it, because life goes on and in a few years from now, what will it matter?

'I think you might benefit from seeing a counsellor,' suggested the policewoman.

'Will a counsellor take my baby away?'

'No, no, don't worry about that.'

Christine smiled. It seemed the only possible way to handle such a lunatic situation.

'Where's your baby now?' asked the policewoman.

'At home.'

'Who's looking after him?'

Christine thought for a moment.

'The neighbours,' she replied. In truth, she hardly knew the neighbours, couldn't have picked them out of a police line-up.

The policewoman noticed her momentary hesitation, and sat back formally, to signal the end of the interview.

'Well, you'd better go and rescue your neighbours then.'

'Yes,' said Christine.

When Christine returned home, the sound of the baby's screaming was leaking through the four walls of the house like a muted fire siren. She looked at her neighbours' houses on either side; there was no sign of life. Perhaps there were women in those houses; perhaps not. Perhaps there were even women with babies. The curtains were drawn, opaque as the ozone layer separating earth from space.

Christine opened the door of her own little house and let herself in. The screaming was instantly much louder, of course: there were different acoustic principles operating on this side of the threshold.

She walked straight over to her baby's cot. He was purple from shrieking, and smelled of sewage. It was not his normal bad smell, but something aggressively more evil.

Christine began to undress him, but the stink pierced her sinuses like a needle-thin skewer. Her baby's eyes bulged as he screamed, as if in outrage at her idiocy in imagining she could make things better for him. Christine refastened the

press-studs on his jumpsuit, sealing up the poisonous nappy while she considered what to do.

She picked her baby up and held him above her head, high above her head. She stared up at him.

His body was a black mass against the electric light bulb, a squirming eclipse of this indoor sun. She held him there for a long time, staring up at his dark howling face and his loose broken limbs dangling so close to her face.

Then, with all her strength, she threw him across the room, bouncing him off the wall with a plasticene thud.

As before, she immediately went to retrieve her baby. It was important that there should be no delay between action and reaction. As long as you responded at once, things would always be OK. In a flash, she crossed the room to where her baby's body lay and scooped it up in her arms. But there was something missing, she could tell.

Her baby's head had come off from his body. Christine dropped to her knees, still hugging the loose-limbed torso to her breast with one arm, and scanned the carpeted floor from wall to wall. She spied the head at once: it had rolled underneath a table.

Gently Christine laid her baby's body down on the carpet and crawled over to the table in question. She retrieved the head (too big for one hand: she had to use both) and squatted to examine it. She flipped it over, exchanging the hairy back for the fleshy front. Cradling the baby's face in her hands, she turned it clockwise until its knitted brows were parallel to hers.

Her baby looked at her as though for the first time. He uttered no sound. An expression of dawning human intelligence replaced his customary look of animal cunning. His lips twitched, as if he might have something to say to her at last.

Then, after two languorous blinks, his eyes fell shut like a porcelain doll's. Drained of the ruddiness of fury, his skin was pale, like the skin of the glossy babies in glossy baby magazines.

Careful to move smoothly, Christine carried the sleeping head to the sleeping body and reunited the two.

From this day on, Christine's baby was never any trouble. He kept to himself in his cot, making no demands. Nature had taken over, as the policewoman had hinted that it would.

A window opened in Christine's existence, inviting her to look through. She hesitated, unsure. Her soul was so tiny, a shrivelled little thing which trembled inside her massive swollen body like an escaped laboratory mouse in an abandoned, echoing research institute.

Experimentally, Christine at last resumed doing something she'd done habitually in a previous life: she began reading a book. It was a hardback novel from the bestseller lists, brought home to her by her husband several days before. Since taking shy possession of it, she had read only a few pages, tiring quickly of the unaccustomed mental exercise. But it seemed good so far. It was what her fellow grownups were reading, right now, everywhere across the country, perhaps even the world.

Her husband stood at their baby's cot as she turned the pages.

'How's my little man, then?' he murmured, not daring to touch. 'Very quiet today.'

'Yes, he's a good boy,' agreed Christine. 'Isn't it time for the news?'

ALL BLACK

'Are we there yet?'

My daughter's head stirs on my shoulder. Lulled by the thrum-da-dum-dum of the train, I have been dozing too. Daydreaming of John stroking the small of my naked back, his middle finger straying into the cleft of my bottom. I blink against the reality of this long journey away from him.

'Let me see my watch,' I say, shrugging at my right arm under the weight of her warm little body. She moves just enough for me to get my wrist into view.

'Ages to go yet,' I say.

'But it's dark.'

'It just looks that way, 'cause the lights are on and the train windows are tinted.' It's an authoritative, grown-up explanation, but inside me I have my doubts. It really does look quite dark out there. I wonder if my watch is wrong.

'Are you hungry?'

She doesn't reply. Asleep again. My forearm has pins and needles now; I flex my hand, but carefully. If I move too much, my daughter will get irritable and shift her head from my shoulder to my lap. I can't afford to be seen with my daughter's head in my lap, even by total strangers on a train. If my wife heard about it, she'd accuse me of paedophilia, incest, child abuse, whatever. My access rights are hanging by a thread as it is.

Looking sideways, across the aisle, at the man flicking through the free railway magazine, I manage to read the digital numbers on his wristwatch. They're the same as on mine. Yet outside, it looks like sunset.

I rub my eyes with my left hand. My eyelids are still sore from all the crying. I am in transit between two people who are furious with me. I am travelling two hundred miles only to exchange one tantrum of hysterical jealousy for another.

My wife can't talk to me for two minutes without letting me know how much it hurts her to live on the same planet as me. We'll start off talking about Tess, what our daughter has or hasn't had to eat or drink, and almost immediately my wife will be shrieking, weeping, threatening, invoking the name of her lawyer. Weeks pass without me seeing Tess, and I have to get the woman at legal aid to write a letter for me, so that my wife doesn't bin it unread. Then finally we come to some arrangement. I can take Tess to McDonalds. Or the zoo. Or the movies. Two hundred miles' journey, and I pay to sit in a dark cinema with my daughter as she watches sentimental heterosexual garbage from the Walt Disney corporation.

When Tess is with her mother, which is almost every minute of my life, my partner John is happy. He doesn't mention her, pretends she doesn't exist. He sucks my cock as if it's never had any biological purpose except to give him pleasure. He revels in the freedom of unsafe sex with me, secure in

the knowledge that I'm no risk. It's as if he's encoded my ten years of faithful marriage as some kind of pre-sexual state, a miraculous virginity preparing me for him. All we have to do is be inseparable from each other, and the plagues of the world can't touch us.

But when I talk about how much I miss my daughter, his face darkens. In a manner of speaking. John being black.

This visit, the first time Tessa came to stay a weekend with me in my new home, has been hell. Hell for me, hell for John. I don't know what Tessa thought of it all. John didn't mention her name when he was shouting abuse and recriminations at me, as I was leaving. He was at least mature enough not to do that. He's growing older too, little by little. Soon – if we can get over this – the age difference between us will matter less and less.

Something is wrong with the train. It's slowing to a halt. The sky outside is grey, as if overcast, even though it's cloudless. The train stops.

'Are we there yet?'

'Nowhere near.'

'What's happening?'

'I don't know.'

The train starts moving backwards, smoothly and quietly. Tess sits up and presses her face and palms against the window, watching the trees and electricity poles going the wrong way.

An announcement comes over the PA. There is signalling failure up ahead, and the train is going back a few stops, to Perth. From there, passengers for Edinburgh and beyond will be conveyed by coach. Apologies, unavoidable, every effort being made, make sure you have all your personal belongings with you, don't lumber us with your luggage.

'Are we going back to John's house?' Tessa asks, frowning.

'It's not John's house,' I retort without thinking. 'It's my house.'

She is silent. My claim is nonsense to her: how can a house that doesn't have her and Mummy in it be mine? I am sick with misery. The greatest victory my wife can win is for every truly happy memory I have of our daughter and me to be locked in the past – the straight years. I'm not allowed to have any happy parenting memories that don't have my wife in them, as if all the wonderful moments (chasing the squealing toddler Tess around the garden with the watering can, balancing her on her tricycle, teaching her how to put new laces in her trainers) were only possible because Heather was standing by, approving.

'No, we're not going back,' I sigh. 'The train has to drop us off at a station. The special lights it needs to see the safe way home aren't working properly. We're going on a coach instead.'

'With horses?'

'No, coaches are . . . well, they're buses, basically.'

I know she's going to ask me what the difference is, and I'm racking my brains in the few seconds' grace.

'What's the difference between a coach and a bus?'

'I don't think there is one. It's like the difference between films and movies.'

John wouldn't like that, theatre director that he is. For him, films are uncompromising arty projects made by *auteurs*. Movies are Hollywood hamburgers made by homophobic corporations. But there is a bigger world of language outside John's narrow queer one. It's not my world anymore, but it exists. And most people live in it.

'Has John got a job?' my daughter asks, as fearlessly as if she were asking if he owned a bicycle.

'I told you: he's a playwright. He writes plays.'

'Like *Peter Pan*?'

'No. For grown-ups. One of his plays was being per-formed at a special festival just before we came up to visit.'

'What was it about?'

My mind goes blank when I think of John's play. At first I think this is because I'm stressed with grief at the memory of him telling me we can't go on together, then I think it's because of how difficult it is to explain a gay play to a child so as not to make her mother go ballistic.

After a few more seconds, I realise it's neither of those things. In the lurid electric light of the train interior, travel-ling backwards with my eight-year-old daughter at my side, I suddenly realise that my gorgeous talented award-winning partner's play wasn't about anything really, except being gay. Judged next to any children's story, it had no plot to speak of.

I take a deep breath.

'It was about . . . Somebody tries to get a person to give up being a politician.'

'How?'

'By telling a secret about him.'

'What secret?'

I snigger playfully, caught between fatherly tease and infantile embarrassment.

'It's a secret,' I wink.

'Can I see the play?' she says, rising to the challenge.

'It's over,' I tell her.

'Over?'

'It was on for a while,' I say, recalling the passions, the intrigues, the arguments, the complicated negotiations, that were poured into those ten long days. 'Then it closed.'

There is a pause while Tess chews this over.

'So everybody knows the secret except me,' she says at last.

'Yeah,' I grin, feeling dirty, as ashamed of my cowardice and my compromise as Tessa's mother would like me to feel of my sexuality itself.

The train is stopping at Perth station: more PA messages about not leaving anything behind. Tessa peers through the window at the descending gloom.

'Is it night time?' she says, as she gathers her things together.

'No, it's only afternoon. Four thirty.'

'Is it going to rain, then?'

I'm preoccupied with checking we have everything while people jostle past us through the aisle.

'I don't know. Maybe.'

'My carry bag is open at the top,' she reminds me. 'I don't want my new book to get wet.'

I am shocked by this concern of hers. Her new book is *Great People Through The Ages*, given her as a present by John when she first arrived – when he was still able to keep his feelings under control. I would've thought she'd want to dump the book in the nearest rubbish bin as soon as I wasn't looking. But she is frowning, trying to figure out a way of folding the top of her carry bag so the rain can't get in.

'It's all right, Tess, if it starts raining I'll shelter it inside my coat.' I am almost weeping again. This is what it's come to: tears I would once have shed over momentous events like the birth of a child or the death of a close relative I now want to shed when it looks as though there's some hope that my daughter will accept the gift of a crappy politically correct book from my lover.

We step out onto the platform. All the lights are on. But then they always are, aren't they, in railway stations? I look beyond the concrete carapace of the glorified shed we've been stranded in. The sky is mauve now, even though it's the

middle of summer. I am unsettled to discover that I can't tell whether the luminous orb near the horizon is the sun or the moon.

A uniformed employee of the railway is beckoning us towards the overpass stairs. He is holding a hastily felt-tipped sign that reads *Edinburgh and The South*, as if Edinburgh and The South were a rhythm & blues band struggling to draw a crowd at the local pub.

'This way,' I say, still choking on my hopes for a brighter future.

In the station car park, there are three coaches, or buses, waiting. One for Glasgow/Carlisle, one for Edinburgh/Newcastle, one for London. My daughter and I stand in the correct queue, along with about thirty other people. Immediately behind us, a young man and woman make the best of the circumstances by snogging. The sound of their lips sucking on each other is comically erotic and a bit surreal under the darkening sky. A middle-aged lady in front of us remarks on the strange weather.

'Not natural, is it?' she sniffs.

I feel perversely tempted to defend the rights of the sky to go dark whenever it pleases, but say nothing. I am on my way back to the straight world. There are rules to be obeyed. By the time I get to my wife's place in Keswick, I'll be so straight-acting someone's liable to try and sign me up to the local football team.

'John's a nice colour,' says Tessa all of a sudden. 'Nicer than I thought.'

I blush from my ears down to my shoulders. I wish we were alone in a room together, my daughter and I. Then I could sit back in an armchair while she said these things, and allow myself to go faint with pleasure at hearing them, without this sick fear of having to shush her any moment.

'Your mum already told you he was black, didn't she?' I remind her gently. The memory of Heather hissing at me, in front of Tess, that it must be a nice change for me to play with a big black dick instead of my own limp little excuse, is still raw in my mind.

'He doesn't look black to me,' says Tessa. 'He's brown'.

I smile. Black people are a rarity in my wife's town. Invisible, almost. Like homosexuals.

'We say he's black, though,' I inform her. 'That's just the way it is.'

Tess is not to be fobbed off in this way.

'But he's *not*,' she insists. 'He's . . . he's the colour of chocolate blancmange.'

I burst out laughing. The thought of John as a sculpture of chocolate blancmange makes him ridiculous and benign. A little less like a fearsome, formless chaos of emotions, capable of sweeping me out of his life like a natural disaster. I think of the surface of refrigerated blancmange as it returns to room temperature: the silky dusting of condensation slowly starting to twinkle. I think of John's skin. But Tessa is still waiting for a satisfactory explanation.

'We use the word black because he's not white like us,' I offer.

'We're not white,' she says, as if any fool could see this.

'Well, close enough,' I sigh.

'You're *pink*,' she tells me, pointing up at my face. 'With red spots. And in the dark, you're black. We're all black.'

We are finally allowed to board the bus, coach, whatever. It's five o'clock by now, but just about all the light in the sky is gone. There are no stars, and the moon – yes, it definitely must have been the moon I saw – is pale.

As soon as we've taken our seats, Tess switches on the overhead light, the little directional one next to the ventilation

nub. She extracts John's book from her carry bag and opens it at page one.

The bus driver apologises on behalf of the train company for the delay, and reminds us that there is to be no smoking anywhere on the vehicle. He will drive us to each of the rail-way stations the train would have stopped at, but he'd prefer to bypass some of the 'really out-of-the-way ones'. Anyone from such a station is invited to come forward and make a special request. No one comes forward. We are all normal, no trouble.

The bus pulls out of the car park, its headlights sweeping across the gloomy tarmac. On our way to the main road, a few drunken-looking young men wave, but by and large the streets of Perth seem deserted. It's as if people have hurried home in anticipation of the downpour or the snowstorm or whatever it is that is threatening in the skies.

On the seat next to me, Tess is reading about the great men and women of history. A very butch-looking Sappho is on the same page as Shakespeare, but little Tess isn't quite ready for poetry yet. She turns pages until she finds Cleopatra, who is as black-skinned as, well, a chocolate blanc-mange. The Queen of the Nile sits in a throne flanked by handmaidens and exotic pets. The demographics of this par-ticular nook of ancient Egypt suggest a happy fusion of female gospel choir and zoo.

I wonder why I'm so irritated by this book, given that these people did exist, and were most likely as black and/or as gay as they're painted here. Isn't this better than the history books I grew up with, full of macho white men fighting wars? At random, I read a bit of the text. It says that Cleopatra was a wise and resourceful ruler who did all she could to pre-vent her peaceable civilisation falling into the hands of greedy Roman plunderers. I somehow suspect that in this

book, Cleopatra is not going to spread her legs for any hunky man in armour.

'What does Mummy say about John and me?' I ask Tess once the bus has been travelling for a while.

'Nothing,' says Tess.

'Nothing at all?'

'She's busy.'

'Busy taking care of you?'

'Just busy.'

Defeated, I look out the window. Even allowing for the tinted windows, it's bizarrely dark out there. At a time of evening when, only yesterday, it wasn't even dusk. Car headlights flash past us monotonously. The bus driver murmurs into a mobile phone. I don't catch the words, but the tone of his voice has a halo of anxiety.

I become aware that the people travelling in the bus with us are very quiet. I hear a couple of them whisper to each other from time to time, but otherwise nobody says anything. I swivel around in my seat, to take stock of my fellow passengers. They glance back at me, startled, white-faced. No, *really* white-faced. They are afraid. They, too, remember yesterday. They, too, can't see any reason why today should be so different.

As we drive on, we go slower and slower. The driver frequently flashes his headlights in warning to approaching cars. It seems some motorists haven't accepted the freakish weather conditions and are driving without lights, as though there's no visibility problem. As though they refuse to be bullied by what they regard as an unreasonable change in the prevailing conditions. Alarmingly, the darker the sky gets, the more motorists seem to be in the grip of this wishful thinking.

'Jesus, wake up, will you?' mutters our driver loudly, as another unlit car hurtles past us.

Pretty soon we are travelling at thirty miles an hour. Every fourth or fifth vehicle we pass has no lights on. Some of them hoot their horns mournfully, most just drive by in silence.

With so little illumination outside, the windows of the bus become mirrors. Each of us stares uneasily at his or her reflected *chiaroscuro* face. Except Tess, who keeps reading her new book. The great 'woman of color' Harriet Tubman is freeing the slaves, with a little help from an unpictured president.

'Interesting book?' I ask, clearing my throat first.

'Uh-huh,' she replies. She reaches up to the air-conditioning nozzle and fiddles with it. I can tell she's mistaken this nozzle for a dimmer, and is trying to make her light shine stronger.

'That's for air,' I tell her gently. 'The light isn't adjustable. It's either on or off.'

'It's getting darker,' she complains.

'Yes,' I say, squinting out of the window.

'No,' she says, 'not out there. In *here*. The *light* is getting darker.'

She points to the book on her lap. A female astronaut is smiling for a photograph taken shortly before she's blown to atoms in the *Challenger*. I can barely make out the text. My daughter is right.

Before long the light inside the bus has faded to a submarine luminescence. The engine still purrs obediently, but it's as if all the cabin bulbs are connected to their own little batteries, batteries that all happen to be running down at the same time. The overhead lights, the light above the first-aid compartment, the light for whether the closet toilet is occupied or not: all dimming to yellow. It occurs to me that the provision of a toilet is probably what makes a coach different

from a bus, but now is not the time to raise this educational fact with Tessa. I'm glad she's engrossed in her book of great people, oblivious to the mounting tension.

A woman makes her way up the aisle and alerts the driver to what he can see perfectly well for himself. He answers her irritably. She returns to her seat, and passes on the message to her husband in a tense whimper. He mutters bluff reassurances to her, like 'Bollocks', 'We'll see about that', and so on.

'Get a fuckin' move on!' someone shouts from the very back.

The driver speaks tersely to someone on his little telephone. Then, cursing under his breath, he rotates the steering wheel vigorously and veers us off the road.

The coach cruises on a bay of smooth bitumen, finally coming to rest in front of a petrol station. At least I *think* it's a petrol station. Yes: I can just make out the filling pumps standing in shadow, like denuded tree stumps. There is a pale rectangle of light further on, emanating from the glass front of the station building itself. I can see several people standing close together in there, huddled behind the counter, illuminated by a single flickering phosphorescent tube.

The coach door swings open with a hiss. As soon as our driver rears up from his seat and steps out of the coach, I know, deep in my guts, right inside my bone marrow, that my daughter and I have to get out too. All around us, our heavy-breathing, shadowy fellow-passengers are seething with panic, hesitating on the nightmare brink between passivity and mania.

'Come on, Tess, we're going.'

Amazingly, she doesn't protest that we're not there yet, or ask questions. She just dumps her book in her carry bag and scrambles out into the aisle. I don't even bother with my own

bag, which has my underwear and dressing gown in it, my dressing gown which always smells of the man I love. I push Tessa along with both hands, and we jump out of the bus like we're leaping off a spinning merry-go-round.

, The driver is already arguing heatedly with the people through the locked glass door of the service station, but whatever he's arguing with them about becomes irrelevant when the engine of his bus suddenly roars. One of the panicking passengers has taken over the driver's seat. Gears squealing, the vehicle lurches out of the parking bay. Its head and tail lights die as it speeds onto the road, making it look less like a bus than a trailer-load of dark metal being towed by an invisible force.

I scoop Tess up in my arms and run clumsily after it. Not to catch up with the bus, just to get back to the road. I must reach the open road, I don't know why, I just must. My daughter weighs a ton, struggling and squirming, trying to evade the sharpness of my fingers against her ribs.

'I can run, Daddy,' she pants, so I put her down. Behind us at the service station, a crash of glass is followed by shouts and screams. Tess and I sprint through the darkness, through a miasma of diesel fumes.

A few minutes later, we're standing by the side of a motorway. Not on a slip road: on the fine-gravelled edge of the actual motorway itself. There are large signs warning that this is illegal, but those signs are shrouded in shadow. Only about a third of the motorway lamps have any light coming out of them at all, and the glow is so feeble that it's affected by insects flying round the glass. The sky is inky black, without stars. A sinking moon is diffused like an acid burn against the horizon, subtly outlining the edges of city buildings – an extinguished city.

'I'll get you home, Tess,' I promise, as three dark cars whizz past us.

Tessa takes no interest in the traffic; she's looking at me, chewing at her lips. There's something she needs to say, some vital piece of information she feels I can no longer be expected to cope without.

'Mummy sleeps with all the lights on,' she says, staring at me as if this knowledge is sure to knock me flat. 'Every room in the house. All lit up. I switch mine off when she's gone to sleep.'

Of course I haven't the faintest idea how to take this. I smile gravely and nod as if I understand, just like I do with John when he's raging against enemies who seem quite harmless to me, just like I used to do with my wife when she'd try to tell me what it is that a woman needs.

A car with blazing headlights speeds into view. I stick my thumb out, then wave frantically with my whole hand. The car doesn't even slow down, and I almost get my arm slammed off by its passenger mirror.

'Don't get run over, Daddy!' pleads my daughter. Actually, it's more of a command, and I feel her fist seizing the fabric of my coat.

I stand well back, and wait for the next lighted car. Twenty, thirty dark ones pass. Some of them are badly dented, some have unidentifiable smears and splatters on their bodywork. One driver winds down a window and yells something we cannot hear, but other than this the cars might as well be empty shells.

In between rejections, the motorway is as still and lonely as a canyon. I wonder how long all this is taking, and look at my watch. The electronic numbers have disappeared, reducing my watch to a useless bracelet.

Time can now only be measured in the gradual dimming

of the motorway lamps. A huge articulated lorry looms out of the distance, slows down, and stops for us just as the last of the motorway lights is petering out. We can't quite believe it as the lorry approaches, a monstrous filthy thing crawling along in the slow lane with its grid of headlights on dazzling full beam. It comes to a standstill right next to us, a balm of heat and diesel radiating from its greasy undercarriage. The driver's cabin is so high off the ground we can't see anyone inside. For a few moments we stand staring.

'Well, do you want a fucking lift or not?' a hoarse male voice calls out.

I jolt into action, wresting the cabin door open, trying to lift Tess up onto a metal rung. She slips out of my grasp, climbing like a monkey, leaving me holding her carry bag. I scramble after her, banging a shin in my haste, in my fear that some unknown man is going to drive my daughter away into the dark.

As soon as we're inside, before I've even slammed the door shut, we're on the move.

'Thanks,' I say, suppressing a coughing fit in the thick haze of cigarette smoke.

'No probs,' says the driver. He is a giant of a man, like a bodybuilder gone to seed, ugly but mesmerising. His grey hair is slicked with oil, his shovel-shaped face is ruddy and bristled. He keeps his bloodshot eyes on the road as he speaks.

'Get off of my gear stick,' he says. Tessa moves her legs closer to mine. We squash together, father and daughter.

'Where you going?' he says, as he overtakes two unlit cars. I note that he flips on his indicators while doing this, as if light were in plentiful supply.

'I . . . my daughter's going home to her mother's. In Keswick.'

'Where the fuck's that?'

'It's in Cumbria.'

'I ain't going to fucking Cumbria. I'm going to the depot.'

'Where's the depot?'

'Carlisle.'

I don't know what to say, so I say, 'Fine.' Carlisle is not a million miles away from where I'm trying to get to, except that I have no idea anymore where I should be heading for. My wife's house may be hidden in pitch darkness by now. John's house – my house – may be the same. All I want is to find a little oasis of light where I can get my daughter safely settled.

'Do you think there'll be light at the depot?'

'There fucking better be.'

'And if there's not?'

'I'll soon get it sorted.'

His self-possession is inspirational, annoying, terrifying, sexy. I want to grab him by the sleeve and ask him to explain please, please, what the hell does he think is happening. But I'm afraid to ask, even politely, in case he says he doesn't know, in case he suddenly starts weeping and wailing, this big strong man with his arms like Arnold Schwarzenegger. I want to leave his confidence unchallenged, surrender myself to his agenda, cling to the light he trusts in so blindly.

A wave of nausea passes over me and I realise that I haven't slept in a long time. Instead, I've spent the weekend nights arguing in my lover's bed, defending the right of humankind to propagate itself. Instead of snoozing the nights away, I've been propping my eyes open, begging for a forgiving kiss, inventing preposterous conspiracy theories as to why a perfectly good and popular play should be pulled off the stage after ten performances. If I make it as far as Heather's

house, she's hardly likely to greet me with pillows and blankets. I tilt my head back and count to ten and beyond.

The driver seems more interested in Tessa than in me. Possibly he has a little daughter too, or happy memories of one.

'Past your bedtime, eh?' he smirks out of the side of his mouth.

'It's still early,' says Tess. She is quite capable of reading the time on the glowing dashboard clock.

'Right enough, right enough,' says the driver. 'Where you been, then?'

'Visiting.'

'Very good.'

'My dad's friend gave me a book.'

'Very nice.'

'Can I have the light on?' she asks, pointing to the switch for the cabin bulb.

He shakes his head.

'Not while I'm driving. It's against the law. I could get done for it.'

She folds her arms across her chest, miffed. The three of us sit not speaking for a while, perched on top of the giant motor growling and vibrating through the floor. I look out the window. From my high vantage point, I have a good view of the countryside, especially now that the motorway lamps are all off. To my bewilderment, I can see that there are still houses and buildings, dotted here and there across the benighted landscape, in which lights are glowing just like normal. Every now and then, we drive close by a village or a town, and I can see beacons – a single functioning street light, an illuminated church clock, even a shop sign – shining mysteriously in the almost universal gloom. There seems no logic to it, no reason why.

Our driver is ready for another cigarette. He holds the steering wheel with his elbows while he attempts, unsuccessfully, to strike a match. I reach out my hand, offering to help him, and he shrugs me away. Three matches fall dead on the floor before he gives up and tosses the box over his shoulder. But there is a cigarette lighter in his dashboard, and he uses that. His cigarette tip glows fierce and bright as he sucks hard on the filter.

Tess is fidgeting, slumping, shoring herself up again, sinking towards unconsciousness. Gingerly she rests her cheek on the back of the seat and blinks into the invisible cargo hidden behind a veil of steel mesh.

'What's in the back?' she says.

'Stuff,' the driver replies.

'What stuff?'

'It's a secret.'

She sighs and goes to sleep. The driver catches my eye and winks. Then he stretches his back, gyrates his massive shoulders, cracks his knuckles, and settles down to drive us through the night.

MOUSE

He had just leapt through a burning inferno of fire, guns blazing, when the screen went blue. Not funny. Not funny at all. This game was mega difficult, and what it did not need was computer failure.

Manny threw himself backwards in his swivel chair, making it creak. He was hyped-up, sweaty. Playing *Runner* was a high-octane experience. And what was so frustrating about getting ejected like this was that you couldn't re-start where you'd left off; the entire quest had to begin all over again.

The action figure in this game – the one you animated with your mouse-clicking fingers – was Lena, a beautiful girl trying to escape from a nameless hell-hole in the former Soviet bloc. Hordes of secret police, guard dogs, soldiers and freelance psychopaths did their utmost to stop her reaching freedom. If you took your eyes off the screen for just one second, BLAM! The programmers were total sadists, definitely

on the side of evil. Not one of the 60,000 guys playing the game, from Canada to Korea, had ever managed to get Lena across the border.

The extra incentive of *Runner* was that every time Lena got attacked her skimpy clothing got more threadbare. Rips appeared in her T-shirt, shreds were stripped off her trousers. A close shave with a grenade could blow her outer layers right off, reducing her to bra and panties. Obviously, the holy grail was to see Lena butt-naked.

But this was where things got hard. *Runner* was not completely divorced from reality. Lena was athletic, sure, but not superhuman. She got tired, ran slower, got injured. If her brush with an ex-Commie commando or a flame-thrower was too close, she might lose her underwear, but she would also be dead. The challenge was to allow Lena to undergo enough mayhem to get seriously unclothed, but not so much that she was toast and a message came on the screen asking if you wanted to start again.

The best part of *Runner* for Manny was actually those rare quiet moments when Lena was having a rest. You laid her down and kept watch while she recouped energy points. A digital counter at the bottom of the screen would keep track of her robustifying health. She would breathe deep, her bosom rising and falling, her cleavage shiny with realistic sweat. Her big dark eyes would half-close ... And then some mad fucker would jump out of nowhere with a bazooka. It was a good thing Lena was equipped with automatic weapons, knives, kung fu skills, and whatever else an Eastern European lassie needs to survive. Manny was getting the hang of her, the way she responded, how far she could leap, how to make her kick and jab. He was determined to get her to the border one day, because that would be the ultimate thrill, plus he would finally be free to do something else.

Manny focused on the blue screen. It was decorated with the ugly white typewriting characteristic of error messages. Some of it said: 'Generic host processes for win32 services encountered a problem and needed to close. BCCode : d5 BCP1 : 00802edo BCP2 : 00000002 BCP3 : 00804edo OSVer : 5_1_2700 SP : 1_0 Product : 623_1'. Down the bottom there was a cryptic 'detailed report' consisting only of: 'C:\WINDOWS\ Minidump\ Mini017304-01.dmp'. Manny rebooted, and a little box told him that the system had 'recovered from a serious error'. He jabbed *Runner's* icon irritably. This was happening far too often. Serious errors fifty times a day. If the system had really 'recovered', why couldn't it just play the damn game?

The *Runner* menu blossomed onto his screen like the opening shot of a movie. Lena stood immobile, all alone in an Eastern-European-style street with cathedrals and monuments silhouetted against the polluted sky. Her Slavic features were impassive. A computerised loop of breeze fluttered the pixels of her glossy brown hair. She had all her clothes on: a bomber jacket, a simple olive-green T-shirt, a short leather skirt. He hadn't seen her in a skirt before. Each time you played the game, she had different gear on. Her enemies were always different, too. One day you'd get a pack of ravenous wolves, the next a bunch of lesbian-looking stormtroopers with whips and acetylene torches.

READY 2 PLAY? winked the option panel. He considered it, but was too worried about being interrupted again. Instead, he closed down the game and opened his email program. He dashed off an email to one of his gaming pals in Duluth, Minnesota, whom he'd never met.

hi varez (he wrote)

help! im having pormblems with minidumps. ive got a 900mhz amd cpu with 128 ram thats running win xp pro. my virus scanner is

up2date but last week my firewall was off and i got the msblast.exe virus. ive manged to get rid of the virus but its fucked up my xp. it does a minidump 4 no reason, usaully right in the middle of runner. one second im flying, next second with no warnming the screen goes blue. i dont know what to do or how to fix it, ive re installed xp 3 times now but no joy. any ideas?

Manny suddenly felt very tired. It was only nine o'clock at night. He had eaten too much pizza maybe. There was no Coke left except the carbonless dregs in about a zillion bottles lying around the flat. An ambulance dragged its lonely siren through the streets outside his tenement building. He walked over to the living room window and looked down three storeys to the grocery store across the road. A Pakistani woman was putting more oranges on a display crate already piled high with oranges. The whole shopfront was like an art exhibition of fruits and vegetables. Manny liked to look at all the exotic colours and shapes, although he wouldn't dream of buying anything that wasn't in a packet or a take-away carton.

Manny went for a piss – in the dark, because the light-bulb in the bathroom had blown a while back. While he was standing in the mirrored gloom, hoping that his pee was landing inside the vague white blur of ceramic, he heard a scream.

It came from below, one of the flats on the lower floors. It didn't sound like a horror movie scream, an axe-murderer-is-gonna-get-me scream. It was more like kind of a yelp. It was definitely female, though. Or maybe it was a child. He hadn't thought there were any kids in the building.

He went and sat down in front of the computer again. Only a few minutes had passed, too few for Varez to have replied to his email. Even so, he checked. A fresh bunch of spammers offered him cheap meds, hot singles in his area, the

latest war games, a surgically enhanced penis, a credit record wiped clean. There was one legitimate email, from Mike, a gaming pal somewhere in Asia. Mike was a dipshit, and 'Mike' wasn't his real name. He pretended to be a serious gamer, but all he wanted was company, the loser. Midget spotty Korean with thick glasses, most likely. '*Greetings!*' Greetings to you too, you sad wanker.

A weird ringing sound jolted Manny half out of his skin. He peered at the PC, wondering what new outrage Bill Gates had sprung on him. But the ringing sound was coming from the hallway. It was the doorbell, a sound he couldn't recall ever hearing before.

He checked the front of his track suit pants to make sure there weren't any damp patches, wiped his fuzzy jaw in case the pizza had left traces. Then he walked over and opened the door.

'Hi,' said a young woman with big blue eyes and masses of blonde hair.

'Hi,' he said.

'I'm from downstairs,' she said. She wasn't wearing lipstick but apart from that she was kind of almost the spitting image of Courtney Love. She had a cardigan on, but it wasn't too mumsy, more like alternative clothing for students. Her hair was dyed and damaged from the chemicals but you can't have everything. She had a great figure, great tits.

'Yeah? I'm from upstairs,' he quipped.

The woman wasn't amused. She had a stressed look on her face. She wanted to get down to business. 'I could use some help,' she said.

'Yeah?' he said noncommittally.

'There's a mouse in my flat,' she said. 'I can't stand mice.'

'Hit it over the head with a whatsaname . . . a frypan,' he advised her.

'I don't want him killed. But he's got to go,' she said.

'So . . .'

'So can you come and help me.'

'What can *I* do?'

'Are you scared of mice?'

'No.'

'Well, I am, so that makes you more qualified, doesn't it?'

He fidgeted against the door jamb. He had no shoes on, his armpits were sweaty, he was aware that his Pixies T-shirt was tight around the belly.

'Couldn't you just buy a cat?'

She put her hands on her hips, and her bosom kind of poked out of the cardigan all by itself. 'Look, I would like to be able to go to sleep tonight. Do you have a problem with that?'

The woman's name was Gee or maybe G, he couldn't tell which. Her flat was directly below his. Much cleaner than his, grime-wise, although just as messy, stuff-wise. Shoes, crumpled T-shirts and scrunched-up tights were scattered all over. Empty mugs in various pastel colours sat on the carpeted floor. A crappy sound system, balanced on a coffee-table rather than in a proper home entertainment cabinet, was piled high with the plastic cases of CDs by artists he didn't recognise. A couple of loose discs lay on an angora sweater, reflecting the light from a ricepaper-shrouded lamp. The whole place smelled of Indian food.

'OK, so where is your intruder?' said Manny, balling his fists, as if about to engage in a bit of hand-to-hand.

'I don't know,' said Gee. 'He could be anywhere.'

'He's probably interested in nibbles,' said Manny. 'Let's try the kitchen.'

The kitchen was tidier than the rest of the place; maybe

Gee had already cleaned it up, to dissuade the rodent. All sorts of weird alternative food was standing around on the worktops: herbal tea, burgul, tamarind paste, goat's milk. If the mouse had any fucking sense, he would have moved on to another flat by now.

'What am I supposed to do if he's hiding?' said Manny.

'He comes out frequently,' said Gee. 'He's amazingly brazen about it.'

They stood together in the kitchen. The refrigerator hummed. There was a fridge magnet on the freezer compartment that said 'UPLIFTMENT THROUGHOUT YOUR DAY'. There was also a reminder about a credit card payment and a half-disintegrated Bugs Bunny sticker.

'Let's sit down,' said Gee. 'He'll come out if we sit down. Would you like a drink?'

'A beer would be good.'

'I don't have any alcohol. I've got orange juice. Ribena. Goat's milk . . .'

'Coke?'

'I could make you fresh lemonade, with sugar and lemons. Or if you want something fizzy, there's a delicious Vitamin B supplement that comes in effervescent form. It's even brown.'

He looked her straight in the face, to judge if she was taking the piss. Her expression was inscrutable.

'Just orange juice, thanks,' he said. 'With ice. Have you got ice?'

'I think so.'

She opened the fridge door, and immediately a mouse ran out from under the chassis.

'Aaaaahhh!' screamed Gee.

'Aaaah!' yelled Manny. They both jumped as the creature scurried near their shoes. Manny stamped his foot onto the

parquet flooring but it was more a nervous gesture than a serious attempt to squash the mouse, which darted, unharmed, into the next room.

'Don't *do* that!' cried Gee. 'I told you I didn't want him killed!'

'Well, how do expect . . . ?'

'Catch him, what do you think?'

He was about to argue with her, but on second thoughts he was too squeamish to squash a mouse's body under his foot. Besides, it would make a mess and this woman was so damn pushy she might expect him to clean her carpet afterwards.

'OK,' he said. 'Have you got a plastic container? Like, a container with a lid, the kind that take-away chinky food comes in?'

She frowned at the word 'chinky' but within a couple of seconds she had found exactly the sort of container he meant. It was transparent, with a very faint yellow discolouration from the Indian curry that had once been in it. She handed it over.

'Thanks,' he said.

'I thought you said you weren't scared of mice,' she said.

'It was the sh – shurprise,' he said. 'I wasn't ready for it.'

'But I *told* you there was a mouse here.'

'I thought . . . I thought it might have left by now.'

She gave him a funny look. He wondered if she suspected him of suspecting her to be a nutter, some kind of sex pest who lured guys into her flat on a mouse-hunting pretext.

'Orange juice, yes?' she said.

They went and sat in the living room, on a flaccid green velour couch. He had the plastic food container in one hand and a glass of orange juice in the other. He drank the juice

faster than he would've liked to, so that he could put the glass down and not look like such a pillock. She got settled next to him on the couch. There was a faint halo of milk on her upper lip from a gulp she'd taken in the kitchen; she had her hands free. What did she need her hands free for? He leaned away from her, as casually as he could. It was a small couch, sagging in the middle, and her body was inches away from his.

She picked up a CD from its angora nest and fed it into the CD player. She pressed a couple of buttons with her slender fingers. A sound like the oldfashioned Microsoft bootup 'wave' came on, the pleasingly abstract sound that Windows used to have before they changed it to the current annoying little tune. But then the sound from the CD didn't die off, it went on and on and on, the same tone, like a choir stuck on one note with no need to breathe. Gee handed him the CD cover. *HU*, it said.

'HU,' he murmured. 'Never heard of them. Electronica?'

'It's lots of people singing together, maybe a hundred. Somewhere in America, I think. It's the Sound of Sounds.'

'Very nice,' he said. 'Does anything else happen?'

'No, it's like this all the way. You just have to sort of sink into it.'

He slumped back into the couch, demonstrating goodwill. The voices from the sound system went 'huuuuuuuuuuu-uuuuuuuuuuuuu.'

'Where'd you get it?' he asked, casting his gaze around the room in search of small grey rodents.

'I bought it,' she said. 'It's part of my training.'

'Massage?' As soon as he'd said it he blushed, in case she thought he meant sexual massage, like in a massage parlour.

'No, it's a spiritual thing.'

'Right.'

'Its part of Eckankar,' she said. 'My religion.'

'Right.'

They sat together in silence, apart from the Americans going 'hu'. Gee's flat was warm and cosy and smelled good. Everything a mouse could want, probably. But the mouse was nowhere to be seen.

Eventually, Gee said: 'I hear you sometimes.'

'Yeah?'

'Through the ceiling.'

'Yeah?'

'I hear you when you get angry. You yell "fuck".'

He blushed again. 'It's my computer. It's playing up. I'm having loads of problems with minidumps.'

'Minidumps?'

He grimaced. 'They're . . . uh . . . when there's a serious error, and . . . It's a sort of default thing. The system dumps itself into a swap file for later retrieval. But sometimes . . . ah . . . It's too complicated to explain.' He stared at his hands, holding the plastic food container. The odd thing was, he could've been a lot more articulate if he'd made the effort. He could've spoken like a computer instruction manual written by experts. It's just that Gee's femaleness put him off. It was as if the equation they made, his gender and hers put together, could only add up to a certain kind of conversational result. A negative number.

'You shouldn't have to get so mad at a machine, ever,' she said. 'It's just a heap of wires and printed circuits. You're a soul. A spark of God.'

'Uh-huh.' He wondered if he had what it took to wait around until the mouse decided to show itself. The longer he stayed here, the more chance there was that this freaky woman would try to sell him on her whacko religion. 'Have you considered rat poison?' he asked.

'I told you, I don't want the mouse killed.'

'It's a soul, right?'

'It could be a person,' she agreed, 'on their spiritual journey towards divinity.'

'But right now it's taking a cheese break, right?'

She smiled. The goat's milk traces were still on her upper lip. He wanted to wipe them off, not because they disgusted him but because he thought she probably wouldn't want to be sitting around with goat's milk on her face and she couldn't see it herself and he was too shy to tell her.

'Can I tell you a bit about Eckankar?' she said.

He gave it a few seconds' thought. 'I'm not much into religion,' he warned her. 'I probably wouldn't get it.'

'Oh, I don't mind,' she said. The room was warmer than it needed to be. She took off her cardigan and tossed it behind the couch. She had the most beautiful skin on her arms. It was lightly tanned, and in the lamplight he could see a very subtle down of pale golden hair on the tops of her forearms. She had thin wrists, exquisite. That was the word that came into his head, exquisite. Not a word that occurred to him often.

'ECK is the Divine Spirit, the current of life that flows through all living things,' she said, not particularly dramatically, more as if she was telling him about a great restaurant she'd discovered. 'Eckankar unifies a person's soul with Light and Sound, which are twin aspects of the Holy or Divine Spirit. Our souls are eternal and on a spiritual journey of reincarnation to discover our true selves.'

'I'm with you so far,' he said, gazing around the room.

'The Light of God,' she said, 'appears in many ways. Sometimes it manifests as a sound. Sometimes it's like a flash of white or blue light.'

'Um . . . That must be brilliant.'

She laughed, a giggly, bronchial laugh. He wondered if she was high on something.

'It *is* brilliant,' she said. 'Through ECK teachings, people can learn from their past lives and understand their Karma. There's not really any such thing as sin, but we can be in error, and error can hold us back from the next level. The Spiritual Eye aids us on our soul journeys and in understanding our dreams. Do you have dreams, Manny?'

'Uh . . . Yeah. Sometimes.'

'What was the last dream you had? Can you remember it?'

'Uh . . .' He blushed. 'I can't remember.'

'Dreams can be a kind of astral projection,' Gee went on, raking her fingers through her hair. 'We leave our bodies and travel to different places and meet different spiritual beings. These beings help us escape the cycle of error and realise ourselves. Dreams are journeys of discovery. And dreams are windows.'

He turned to her, glum. 'Look, I . . . I think this is all . . . It doesn't mean anything to me.'

'It didn't mean anything to me, either, six months ago. I was just like you.'

He snorted. A creature less like him was impossible to imagine. She was sitting so close to him he could smell her femaleness. The brocaded texture of her bra and the swell of her breasts were both visible through her T-shirt. Her wrists were maybe two-thirds the size of his. Her neck was smooth and delicate. He wanted to lie in her arms and come between her legs. He wanted to smash the jewel case of her damn 'HU' CD over her head. If there was a God, He would definitely be instructing the mouse to chew right through the electrical cord of the sound system, just to make those annoying Americans shut the fuck up.

'It's an American religion, right?' said Manny, after a deep breath.

'The spiritual home of Eckankar is the Temple of ECK in Chanhassen, Minnesota.'

'I could've guessed.' Manny thought of his internet buddy Varez, also located in Minnesota. How close was Duluth to Chanwhatsit, he wondered? Maybe Varez knew some of these Ecky people in his neighbourhood. Maybe the whole area was crawling with them, singing 'hu' in the checkout queues at the supermarket, at the chip shop, the bus stop, everywhere. Although maybe Minnesota didn't have buses. Or chip shops.

'It's all about spiritual unfoldment,' Gee was saying. 'As you unfold spiritually, you learn to express the love of God through doing things for others.'

'Well, I'm here to do something for you,' he reminded her. 'And I'm not interested in ECK.'

'Sorry,' she said, lowering her eyes. 'I didn't mean to hassle you. ECK's not like that. It's for people who are ready.'

'Well, I'm ready for—' He was about to make a wise-crack about a mouse, when lo and fucking behold, the mouse himself walked out from behind a stack of books and just sat there, in plain view, right in the middle of the room. Manny and Gee both froze.

The mouse seemed cool with this. He was the calmest mouse Manny had ever seen. His tiny eyes focused first on the man, then on the woman. He wasn't even panting. Other than that, he was a standard, unexceptional mouse, with grey fur, pink feet and a tail. He was maybe five inches long, tail included. Gee was hyperventilating at the sight of him. Her bosom shook from the thud of her heartbeat.

Slowly, without taking his eyes off the rodent, Manny lowered himself to the floor. On his knees, he crawled across the carpet, holding the upside-down plastic container aloft in one hand. The mouse turned away from him, apparently

unconcerned. Maybe the daft little fucker was stoned on some weird herbal tea he'd made the mistake of nibbling at.

With a swift, smooth motion, Manny brought the plastic container down. The mouse was trapped neatly underneath, with just a bit of tail sticking out.

'The lid, gimme the lid,' said Manny. Gee handed it to him. Careful not to lift the tub more than he absolutely had to, Manny began to slide the lid under. The mouse huddled in one corner until the last possible instant and then hopped onto the interior of the lid, allowing Manny to slide it the last few inches into place. He snapped the container shut. Mission accomplished. One Mouse Jalfrezi.

'What do you want me to do with it?' he asked Gee. His voice shook a little from the excitement of having done so well. His hand wanted to tremble but he kept it still.

'Throw it out the window, I guess,' she said.

'Out the *window*?' He was disappointed in her. She had been so concerned for the animal's welfare. His image of her was all bound up with kindness.

'Sure,' she said. 'I'm only on the second floor. There's grass in the back yard. Mice are built different from humans; they're light, with different bones. You could throw one off a skyscraper and as long as there was grass below, it would survive. Second floor is nothing to a mouse.'

She had her arms folded across her chest, a bit defensive. He tried to decide if she was trying to hide the fact that she knew bugger-all about the aerodynamic properties of mice, or if she was just scared the rodent might jump out of its plastic prison and nip into her clothing.

'OK,' he said. 'Which window?'

She led him into her bedroom, which was a duplicate of his: exactly the same dimensions, layout, everything. Well, not everything. The bed was a double, leaving very little room to

manoeuvre. Piles of clothes lay on the floor, handbags, super-market bags, hairbrushes, books. He trod gingerly, afraid to step on fragile things, embarrassed to be here at all.

'My bedroom window is directly above the thickest part of the garden,' she explained. She drew the blinds, opened the shutter.

'Don't drop it back in here, whatever you do,' she said, as he lifted the container up. He stretched his arm out into the night air. The rear façade of another apartment building, on the far side of the communal garden, had lights on in several of its windows. In one of these windows, a young man and woman stood watching. They waved to Manny as he un-clasped the plastic container and let its furry little burden fall out into the dark.

'Done,' he said, and drew his arm back in. She pulled on a sash and the blinds closed again, giving them privacy in the bedroom.

'Thank you,' she said.

'No problem,' he said.

Adrenalin was still flowing through him. He felt the need to do something masculine and demonstrative, something additional to what he'd already done. With a casual flick of the wrist, he tossed the plastic container onto the bed. The bed was a rumpled, exotic affair with three or four quilts in clashing colours and textures. It looked very comfortable. A cotton nightdress was draped over one of the pillows. The other pillow had an open book laid on it, half-finished and face down.

'Well, thanks again,' said Gee, and walked out of the room. She waited until he'd followed her out before reaching her hand back inside to switch off the light.

In the living room, the Americans were still chanting 'HU'.

'You don't find it a wee bit annoying?' he asked her. 'I mean, after a while?'

'Find what annoying?' She seemed deeply pensive all of a sudden, focused on some deeply private part of herself.

'The Yanks singing "HU".'

'I've got it programmed to repeat, actually.'

'Oh.' He hadn't picked her as the sort of person who could program a CD player.

'HU is an ancient name for God,' she explained, and yawned, showing all her grey fillings and a cute pink tongue. 'Sorry, I'm really sleepy. I start work at six in the morning, so this is way past my bedtime.'

'Don't let me keep you up,' he said.

'It's OK, I'll crash soon.' She pottered around the living room, collecting empty mugs and glasses. She had a way of clasping them with her fingers so she could hold three in each hand. 'Excuse the mess,' she said.

'You should see *my* flat,' he said.

'Maybe I will one day,' she said. 'As long as there's no mice in it.' And with a touch of her big toe she turned the sound system off. The worshipful voices disappeared abruptly.

'Thank God for that,' said Manny.

Gee fronted up to him one last time, her expression darkened by disappointment. Or anger, maybe. There was a hefty weight of stoneware and glass dangling in her hands, and if she lost her rag and smashed the lot against his skull, he would be in big trouble.

'Singing HU,' she said wearily, 'lifts you into a higher state of awareness. But only if you're open to it. I have days when I'm not, and then I can't stand to hear it. Which lets me know I'm in a dangerously bad state, and I should be singing HU even more. But sometimes . . . sleep's important too.'

'Right,' he said. 'Goodnight, then.' And he got the hell

out of there before she had a chance to pull anything else
on him.

Back in his own flat, Manny found it difficult to calm down.
The front door was shut behind him, but he didn't feel private. After all, anybody could ring his doorbell any time they
liked; they could knock at his door if they were so inclined;
this had never occurred to Manny before. He was used to
feeling the building around him like a suit of armour or a
giant phone cubicle or something – a structure that contained only him inside it. Now he was forced to reconsider it
as a network of dwellings, a honeycomb of competing lives.

Also, because his place was architecturally identical to
Gee's, he had a hallucinatory sensation that he was still down
there. As though he were wandering around in her flat but it
had been filled with his stuff, or as though his own flat had
been subtly altered, Photoshopped, Micrografixed, to resemble hers. His computer table, with the PC equipment stacked
on top of it, seemed insubstantial, as if all this stuff had been
beamed in from another galaxy and was just a glowing illusion, a hologram. He reached out to touch his monitor. It was
solid and warm.

He sat down on his swivel chair. He took his accustomed
position in front of the screen, whose glassy surface had gone
black from lack of intervention. He touched the mouse
gently and the screen sprang back to life, a gallery of icons.

He checked for emails. More offers of penis enlarge-
ment, miraculous credit, cheap drugs. Oh yes, and a response
from Varez. Very detailed instructions as to how to fix the
minidumps. The guy clearly had an ultra-methodical mind.
'Follow the instructions in the first section. If the problem is not
resolved, proceed to the next section.' Not exactly a buddy-buddy
tone, but lucid.

Manny followed the instructions faithfully, resizing the swap file to a smaller amount of RAM, rebooting, then restoring the swap file's original RAM. Time would tell if this made any difference. If it didn't, there were the more radical options of deleting the Minidump Files, deleting the Sysdata.xml File, or even disabling the Automatic Restart.

'*Any more questions, just ask,*' said Varez.

OK, thought Manny, *How about: Can a mouse really be chucked off a skyscraper without being hurt when it hits the ground?*

He clicked and clicked, feeling horny and irritable and bloated and hungry. The *Runner* menu blossomed onto his screen like the opening shot of a movie. Lena stood immobile, all alone in an Eastern-European-style street with cathedrals and monuments silhouetted against the polluted sky. Her Slavic features were impassive. She had all her clothes on: a long red raincoat, shiny like PVC, a black roll-neck sweater, knee-length boots. Winter had come to Lena-land.

READY 2 PLAY?

He closed his eyes, pinched them with his forefingers. In his mind's visual display, a tiny mouse was falling through space, gathering speed as it fell. Splat. Mouse brains on a slab of concrete. A star-shaped pattern of blood surrounding a little furry body. What else could you expect, for fuck's sake?

He clicked to indicate he was ready to play. He tried to visualise the ground underneath Gee's window, under his own window. He couldn't recall ever having seen any grass down there. On his PC screen, a sudden flash of motion alerted him to danger. Lena had been run over by a tank. She was fully clothed, with realistic tyre-marks on her raincoat. Her current health status was, according to the digital counter, zero.

In disgust, he pressed the exit icon and got up. He rummaged around in the kitchen cabinet for a torch. Amazingly,

in amongst the useless crap – the spare bags for vacuum cleaners, the candles, spare bits of sink – he found a small torch complete with batteries. Providence of this kind seemed beyond rational explanation.

He put on some shoes and a windcheater, gripped his torch like a weapon, and went out into the night.

It was true what Gee had said. The area behind the flats, under his window and hers, was covered in grass. Mown not that long ago (God knows by who) but still soft and springy, and smelling damply green in the dark. A lush vegetal carpet, an organic mouse mattress. He could go back inside now.

But he didn't. He had come this far and he wasn't going back until he'd made sure. A falling body wasn't like a leaf fluttering to the ground, it was flesh and bone. Manny had felt the weight of that little creature when he'd let it go.

He squinted into the cold. Besides his narrow torch beam, there was precious little light. The inhabitants of the ground floor flat had gone to bed, as had Gee, if her darkened window was anything to go by. His own window was a feeble square of light in a monumental edifice of gloom. At this upwards angle, he could see the lightbulb in his kitchen and the ceiling cornices, but nothing else. The block of flats on the opposite side of the gardens was almost totally lost in the blackness; just two windows had lights on, right near the bottom, as if the whole apartment block were a gigantic stack of electronic equipment on standby. He pointed his torch at it, wielding it like a remote control. The beam didn't reach. It didn't even get as far as the fences which he knew, from memory, kept one garden bordered off from the next.

The area of ground to be examined was maybe twenty foot square. Logically, if the mouse was dead it would be lying directly underneath where it had been tossed out. If it

was horribly injured it might have dragged its broken body a few steps before perishing in agony. If it was OK, it would be nowhere to be found. He shone the torch into the grass, but could only see inside a small circumference, not the cinematic sweep he'd imagined. The batteries weren't as robust as he'd thought. The beam of light had started off white, then turned pale yellow almost at once. He would have to be methodical, strafing the designated area in a strictly geometrical, non-overlapping pattern.

After a couple of minutes traipsing back and forth, his batteries were almost dead. He blinked hard and wide, willing his eyes to function better than they naturally wanted to. He should've started in the centre of the rectangle, not the edge. He should've had the guts to test out if Gee was just playing hard to get. He should have put a warmer jumper on. He should never have left home.

Stumbling in the dimness, he almost stepped on something small and grey. It was the mouse. He went down on his knees before it, and the fabric of his track pants was instantly soaked with moisture.

'Jesus,' he muttered. The torch beam illuminated the mouse quite neatly; the scant circle of light and the tiny rodent were just right for each other. The animal was alive, unconcerned, just sitting there in the grass.

'What are you doing here, you dumb bastard?' Manny whispered.

The mouse looked up at him, chewing on nothing. Manny wondered if a certain percentage of mice were born totally lacking a scamper reflex, or if this particular specimen was brain-damaged.

'Get moving, you loser,' he muttered, feinting an attack on the furry body with the tip of his torch. The mouse turned around, one leg at a time, and walked off into the

darkness. Manny kept the torch beam on the tail, tracking the mouse's progress. Within seconds he'd lost sight of it and was left with nothing but a few watts of battery-powered torch-light, a patch of damp grass and an invisible world.

Manny switched the torch off. Everything went black. He was shivering. He was blind. Then, tinge by tinge, the colours started coming through.

SOMEONE TO KISS IT BETTER

When Dougie got home, *she* was there, as per usual. Sitting on the sofa, as per usual, with no housework done. Watching television, as per usual. Except . . . Except this time there wasn't a television for her to be watching.

'Where's the TV, then?' he asked.

'It's gone,' she said.

'What do you mean it's gone?'

'It's been stolen.'

'Stolen? What the fuck you playin at?' It was impossible the television had been stolen. She had sold it, broken it, lost it, lent it out, given it away to the fucken Red Cross.

'I went out shoppin,' she said. 'When I got back, our stuff was gone.'

'Stuff? What stuff?' Christ! The way she never told him what he needed to know right away!

'All the electronic gear, what do you think?' she sighed.

'TV. DVD player. CD player. Um . . . radio.' She sighed again, in a shivery kind of way. 'Is that everything?' She looked him straight in the eyes, so he could see she'd been crying.

'Ever thought of lockin the door behind you, you dumb cunt?'

'I did lock it,' she said, blinking hard as she looked down at her fingernails.

'So how did they get in? It's a fucken security flat, int it?'

'They must have had keys. The keys you lost last week. When you were drunk and got carried home from the pub.'

She spoke without accusatory emphasis, as she had learned to, but she'd still not learned to not speak at all. Her words were like little spoonfuls of spinach going into Popeye the Sailor-Man; his temper pumped up like a cartoon muscle.

'I told you I dint lose those fucken keys!' he yelled, thrusting two fingers right near her face. She winced momentarily, but because he hadn't hit her, she didn't manage to bite her tongue.

'So where are they, then?'

'I told you before!' he screamed, smacking her across the cheeks with alternating sides of his big right hand. 'You bloody took them, dint you? Put them in your big fucken handbag and lost them, dint you?' His left hand reined her in as she tried to struggle away from the blows. 'That handbag of yours is like a fucken Black Hole! There's a whole fucken universe gets sucked in there, and what the fuck happens to it then eh? What the fuck happens to it then?'

'You're totally fucken mad,' she squealed through a whirl of hair and fingers as he kept the blows raining down. 'You belong in a fucken home.'

She wrenched away the arm he was holding her by, so he grabbed her by the throat and squeezed hard. He hunched

his shoulders up in case she tried to get at his eyes; instead she tried to punch him in the ribs, but couldn't do much at such close range. Then, as he kept the pressure on, she tried to . . . to *tickle* him on the chest. Fuck! That's where he was most ticklish, too – which nobody else would have known except his mother. That's what happened when you let a woman get too intimate with your body: she found out about things no-one but your Mum should know.

Anyway, all of a sudden she seemed to get a surge of strength, and started tickling him so hard he had to take his hands off her throat. She even got an involuntary braying sound out of him, almost a laugh, which was her big mistake. 'Fucken funny, is it?!' he shrieked, and shoved her to the floor.

At least, most of her got shoved to the floor. Her head only went down as far as the little wooden table the TV used to stand on, and smashed right through the top of it with an explosive crack. It was the most spectacular thing, like a special effect in a movie. It gave Dougie the shock of his life, that was for sure.

Immediately he knelt down to get her out.

It was complicated, though, because the broken table had turned into a sort of cage around her head. The shards of wood were still bolted to the tubular frame, and the springiness of the metal had pulled the splintered edges back up into a V-shaped wedge which couldn't be opened outwards. Only her nose and some hair were showing. He tried pushing the splintered wood inwards, but her face was stuck right underneath, stuck like in a vice. If he tried to drag her out sideways, that wouldn't be any good either: her face would get all torn up. Maybe he'd even blind her.

So, he squatted, waiting for his rage to pass over so he could think what to do.

After a minute or two, he realized there was no point worrying about blinding her, no point trying to get her head out.

In fact, he'd probably interfered too much with her already, and now he had better leave her exactly where she was.

He hadn't meant to kill her. At least not permanently. That is, he *had* meant to kill her, because what she'd done deserved killing, and nothing less than her death could have satisfied him, but if he could've had things just as he wanted them, he would have killed her, and then when she'd been lying there for a while, dead, she would have suddenly started coughing and gurgling and would be alive again. Then he would have said,

'So just remember: that's what you get.'

But she wasn't dead like that. She was dead like a tray of meat under cellophane.

He tried to remember if fingerprints got left on skin, or only on doorknobs and walls and guns and things like that. He'd watched a lot of crime shows, but not concentrating that hard, you know, not like there was going to be a fucken exam at the end.

Fucked if he could remember.

In the kitchen, the plastic bags of shopping were still standing around: fucked if he was going to put them away. Outside, it was dark already.

Back in the living room, Dougie snapped out of it and got serious. With a tea-towel he wiped the caved-in table-top where he'd tried to prise the broken pieces apart. Then, groping into the narrow space where her head was wedged between the splintered wood and the *TV TIMES*, he managed to wrap the tea-towel around her neck and rub it back and forth until he was satisfied.

The hardest part was already taken care of: if he'd tried to fake that, and make it *look* like the flat had been burgled, he'd have to've taken all the stuff out himself, and where would he have dumped it? Someplace where the police would find it in about two minutes, probably, and then he'd be fucked. But this way, it was all done for him: his flat really *had* been broken into, his stuff really *was* stolen, the cunts really *had* killed his girlfriend. His de facto.

His Gemma.

Dougie made a quick inspection of the flat to make sure he knew everything that was missing, and then tackled the final problem.

Too many people in this town knew he had a temper. Gemma's parents for starters, Gemma's GP no fucken doubt, Christ knows what other busybody. He couldn't just walk into the police station and say he'd found his girlfriend murdered. If he'd been born the sort of middle-class ponce who could make a claim like that and expect tea and sympathy from the law instead of the fucken third degree, he wouldn't have had a fucken temper to begin with, would he?

No, he'd stay right here, and this is how it would appear: burglars had done the place over, and they'd done Dougie's girlfriend over, and they'd fucken done Dougie over, too. The police would find them both lying here next to each other, cart them both away in an ambulance, her dead, him a mess but alive.

All he had to do was inflict the injuries.

He held his fist up in front of his face, clenched it until it trembled. Tentatively he bounced his knuckles against his brow, softly then harder, but not hard enough to hurt much.

He punched himself in the stomach, doing it suddenly as if to catch himself unaware, but of course he wasn't unaware at all and didn't even get winded. Besides, being winded was

fuck-all use, because an outsider couldn't see it. He needed bruises, cuts, broken ribs maybe, teeth knocked out. Yes! – fucken teeth knocked out! What were a few fucken teeth in exchange for a lifetime of freedom? Shit, what was a month in hospital compared to twenty years in jail?

He looked at his fist again, and realised that even if he could bring himself to hit himself as hard as he was able, he still couldn't do the sort of damage he needed to. Attached to himself, he couldn't get enough swing into the punches – it was a simple case of leverage.

He had another idea, though, and this one might work.

He'd go out, drive to the housing estate at the edge of town, pick a fight with some drunk bastard in a back street, get done over, drive home, lie down next to Gemma on the floor.

As long as he didn't get himself killed, he could manage all that no bother: he'd done it before, hadn't he? Crawled in next to Gemma in the bed – 'What happened to *you?*' 'Got a beating, dint I?' 'Who did it?' 'Fucken hell – somebody – anybody – Who fucken cares? You want some yourself?'

'Oi! Shithead!' yelled Dougie. 'Have a go if you're hard enough!'

The stranger stopped, peered squinting into the darkness. 'Who you talken to, pal?'

Dougie stepped forward, but not so far up the alley as to get in the lights of the High Street. Whoever was going to do the business would have to be motivated enough to step into the dark.

'Scrape the shit out your ears, you might hear better!'

The youth hesitated, took a step closer. He was a suede-head, pale as a dollop of mash, dressed up in fleecy jogging gear like a fucken idiot.

'Fucken idiot!'

But the youth didn't bite.

'Mad bastard,' he snorted, and walked away.

Dougie considered going somewhere else, though this was the place most notorious for aggro. The cops left it alone, too, until much later at night when the rich people in the trendier parts of town had all safely found their cars and gone home.

'Oi!'

Another fucken suedehead – no, it was the same one, coming back with a mate.

'Who's your boyfriend, shithead?' called Dougie. 'Has he got a big dick then?'

This did the trick, apart from a couple of feints and shoves to get things properly physical. The two lads weren't heavyweights but they were wiry and vicious and not too drunk. Dougie landed a few good blows to their faces at the very start, but after that it was their game. They fucken murdered him – in a manner of speaking. He certainly went unconscious for a minute, and by the time they'd put the last boot (well, trainer) in before running away, he was coughing up blood and vomit.

All in all he felt his beating had gone on longer than necessary: he could probably have got by with less. Clasping his arms around his abdomen where he lay, he tried to raise himself up using his knees and left shoulder as a lever; succeeded. Breathing was painful: broken ribs, probably, but nothing that would stop him driving home. His nose was broken, maybe, his lips felt split wide open in a couple of places, his knuckles were already blue . . . Underneath his clothes, he must be all the colours of the fucken rainbow. He cackled hysterically, then retched again, his forehead bouncing off the ground.

'Oh my God – what have they *done* to you?'

A female voice – female legs running over to him – female arms reaching down to him.

'I'm all right – leave me alone,' he barked, turning his face away, into the hunch of his shoulders as he struggled to stand.

'Let me help you!'

'I'm all right, *really*,' he groaned, lurching on his knees, into the dark. 'It's nothing to do with you.'

'I know it isn't,' she said. 'Just let me help you up.'

She steadied him as he got to his feet, then grabbed him by the shoulders as he tried to walk away. 'Listen: I'm a nurse. I saw them kicking you. You've had a lot of blows to the head. You need to go to a hospital for observation in case you have a brain haemorrhage. You can't just go home.'

'Let go of me.'

'Listen: calm down. They're gone. You're safe now. You don't need to run away.'

'Fuck *off*!' Again he tore free of her, again she grabbed him by the shoulders, and this time she pulled him around to face her.

'You might still *die*,' she announced six inches from his nose, a blonde woman in her late twenties, no lipstick, big blue eyes, quite shaggable. 'Do you understand that?'

'I'm fine,' he sighed, shoulders slumping, as she looked him over. 'If you're a nurse, why don't you go back to the hospital?'

'I'm off duty,' she said.

'You don't act like it.'

She smiled ruefully, as though he was pointing out something that everyone else pointed out too. 'I've got a pencil-torch in my car,' she said. 'I want to look at your pupils.'

'Got nice eyes, have I?' he smirked, giving in, falling into step with her.

'No comment,' she said. 'I'm just hoping they're reacting to light still.'

She led him to her car, which was parked only fifty yards or so behind his, and opened both its front doors. He collapsed into the passenger's seat, surprised at his own frailty. She swung into the driver's seat like she was sailboarding, easily manoeuvring her long legs under the steering-wheel clamp.

'You play sport?' It would be best if she wasn't too athletic.

'I keep fit,' she murmured, rummaging through the glove compartment. 'I don't drink . . . stay out of fights . . .'

'Hey, I'm not drunk,' he objected. 'Smell my breath.'

She leaned close, took a sniff. Her own breath, or perhaps her skin, smelled of restaurant food: no particular dish, just stuff you don't get at home or at the chip shop.

'You're right,' she said, with new respect. 'So why did they beat you up? Were you robbed?'

His first thought was to say yes, but then he thought she'd want to take him straight to the police. 'I was just in the wrong place at the wrong time,' he shrugged.

She'd found the pencil-torch and shone it into her lap to test the batteries. She told him to look up at the car's ceiling. She pulled her door shut to kill the overhead light. Then with a deft motion she flicked the little torch beam at each of his pupils in turn.

'No problems yet,' she said. 'But a bleed can happen fast. You should still go to hospital, get this done every fifteen minutes. I'm not joking.'

'How 'bout you take me home and I lie down?' he said wearily. 'I don't fancy sitting in a Casualty ward half the fucken night waiting for a doctor to see me.'

She mistook him to mean that he wanted her to stay with him, at his place or hers, shining lights into his eyes until she was fully satisfied.

'Look,' she said. 'If you don't want to go to a hospital, I can't force you.'

'No, no,' he hastened to assure her. 'I'll go. It's just ... I've got my girlfriend waiting at home ...'

She glanced skeptically at him, caught his eye, saw that it was true after all. After a flicker of misgiving, she made a decision.

'I'll drive you to the hospital I work at,' she said. 'You might get seen quicker there.'

She unlocked and unshackled the steering-wheel clamp and leaned down, her cheek pressed against the steering-wheel, as she shoved the clamp away under the seat. For an instant she closed her eyes with effort.

That was the instant he used. He threw himself at her, bringing his body whudding down on her head and the steering-wheel. With a couple of fierce jerks of his torso he got her neck wedged against the upholstered arc of steel and pressed and pressed and pressed, grunting in fear and desperation. She was strong but had no room to move. The most she could do was scratch frantically at his trousers; she had no hope of getting near where he was ticklish, or where he could be hurt.

When she stopped struggling, he let her slide off the wheel; she slumped first onto the seat and then as much of her as there was room for fell lower. Crying out at the pain in his ribs and back, he heaved her sideways away from the pedals and gears, into the space under the passenger seat, mostly. Then he started the car.

There was a model of a Husky dog dangling on the ignition key ring, a fluffy one in realistic colours. He'd always had a thing about key ring figures. His own key ring figure collection was lost in the past, gone the way of all football card albums and cornflake trinkets, but this Husky was a beautiful thing, something special.

'Don't be fucken daft,' he said aloud.

He drove to the railway bridge at the edge of the estate, and parked in a lay-by. He dragged the woman's body down the steeply-sloped embankment to the river's cemented rim and began to undress her there. He'd decided that if she was found naked, the police would think something sexual had happened to her, and go out looking for the sorts of guys who did stuff like that.

Dougie's bruised and swollen fingers fumbled with the fastenings of her clothes; a nauseating pain was starting up behind his eyes. He couldn't figure out how the bra worked, its clasp was like one of those childproof things on medicine bottles, and he couldn't tear the fabric with his hands either. But he got the rest of her naked, and launched her into the water, as beautiful as a boat. He didn't hang around to see if she would sink or float, though, but stumbled back up the slope to the car. He drove that car straight back into the estate and parked it in the same spot where it had come from.

Finding his own car took longer than he expected. He seemed to have mental block on what kind of car it was – was it white or blue, a Ford or something Jap or what. But he did find it in the end and it did start and finally he was on the home stretch.

As he drove, he wondered if there were any painkillers at home.

The police would note the damage done to him on the outside, but what he felt on the inside was invisible, so was it really necessary for him to be in so much pain? A bit of fucken paracetamol wouldn't do any harm, surely. Especially if he was going to be lying on the floor, with broken ribs probably, and no pillow for his head. Jesus! Life didn't believe

in making things easy for him, did it? Maybe he could rest his head on something soft, something that was already on the floor?

Shit! All this weakling stuff had taken his mind off the road, and he'd taken a wrong turn. Where the fuck . . . ? He squinted at the street signs, losing focus sickeningly, getting it back, losing it again.

'You'll lie on the fucken floor and you'll fucken like it!' he exclaimed abruptly, bashing his palms against the steering-wheel for emphasis. A spike of pain shot up through his hands to his head, but he'd won the argument. He would do this thing properly. The police would be impressed. He would be the most wretched-looking fucker they'd ever seen outside of a morgue.

He saw the road he should have taken first time round, turned down it with a screech of tyres. This one connected with . . . with . . . He couldn't remember the name of the fucken road, but he would know it when he saw it, he knew it like the back of his fucken hand. What the fuck did anything need a name for, anyway?

He noticed that as he turned the steering-wheel, something sharp was clicking around inside his left wrist like a loose chicken bone or something. Had he maybe broken that as well? Christ!

This was about where the turn-off should be, but there wasn't any turn-off there. There just wasn't. Politicians were always changing the roads, paid good money to sit on their arses changing the maps of the city. He would have to back up, take the first left he could find, drive west until he hit the water again, then start afresh.

The pain behind his eyes was growing. Maybe there wouldn't even be any para.. what was it?.. paradol.. in the

fucken house. *She* was always getting pains, woman pains. With a woman swallowing the pain killers all the fucken time, he'd be lucky if there was any left for him.

'Keep the fuck out of it!' he bawled, impulsively veering around a corner. To lie down anywhere, even on a hard floor, would be bliss. It would be an effort not to tell the police to fuck off and let him sleep.

For an instant he blacked out, but pulled himself back into consciousness with a wrench at the steering-wheel. He was drenched with sweat.

'I want to get home!' he pleaded, then felt ashamed, clearing his throat, pretending the childish tone had been caused by something stuck there.

At last, however, the streets sorted themselves out and looked familiar. He slowed to stop at an intersection, and everything he saw there was what ought to be there. He took the right turn and was rewarded with the houses he expected to see.

He should've taken that Husky key ring, though, Christ! Not the keys themselves, of course, but that little furry model of the dog. He could see it in front of him now: it was the most beautiful, the most valuable thing he would have ever owned, except he would never own it now. What an idiot he'd been! Who'd have known he got it from someone else? Fuck! His only chance to have it, and he'd left it behind. The fucken story of his life.

All of a sudden the pain behind his eyes got so bad he knew he couldn't drive any longer, so he skidded to a stop. But like magic, he looked up and saw that he was there after all, parked in front of home.

Sobbing uncontrollably, he stumbled out of the car, synchronising his shallow breaths with each second he had to endure before he could lie down. *She* would be there, he

would lie down next to her, and when he woke up everything would be all right.

In the doorway he swayed, half-blind. The pocket of his trousers seemed to have grown much smaller, and his battered fingers groping into the denim slit sent cold thrills of pain up his arms and down his spine. The keys came out at last, but he couldn't make them fit into the lock.

He thought of calling out for her to let him in, then laughed and was racked by a spasm of coughing. The pain behind his eyes was beyond belief; he lurched forward and hit the top of his head against the door, which gave a moment's relief, so he did it again, and again.

He must have got a bit carried away, because eventually the door opened and he fell forward into the passageway. There was carpet there which hadn't been there before, and yet he recognized that carpet. It was the carpet he had known all through his childhood — the carpet of his *real* home, his family home.

'Oh God, Douglas, what's happened to you?'

He rolled over on the floor to find her leaning over him: his mother. He had found her. Driving blind through the spiralling streets of his pain, he had found her. She knelt down to him now, and lifted his head up from the floor, cradling it in her lap. Weeping, she wiped his own tears from his face. 'I'm in trouble, Mum,' he tried to say, but he could only open and close his lips, open and close, without words.

She spoke to him in return, but a roaring in his ears kept the sound of her voice from him. He knew what she was saying, though: he didn't even need to read her lips, nor even her eyes: he understood it from the way she was there for him and him alone, surviving only for his survival, existing only so that he might exist. He knew what she was offering

as the light failed inside him: 'Come back and stay with me. I'll hide you. Have another chance. Have all the chances in the world.'

The tunnel was already opening. He curled up, knees against his chest, fists clenched, ready.

BEYOND PAIN

Morpheus, drummer of North Ayrshire's foremost death metal group Corpse Grinder, was defending himself against the sunshine. The sunshine was out to get him, and he must vanquish it, repel it back to its accursed dominion, and restore the supremacy of night. In the final minutes of his sleep, he'd flung his muscular, tattooed arms across his face, shielding his eyes. It was no use. The dark was gone.

Morpheus sat up, aware of two things simultaneously: his band's Eastern European tour was due to start that evening, and he had a strange sensation in his head. He blinked and squinted in the surfeit of winter light beaming into the tiny flat through its uncurtained bay window. The cars parked on the street outside were white with a night's worth of snow, dazzlingly, belligerently white. Snow-covered cars had never worried Morpheus before, but they worried him now.

'I feel funny,' he said to his girlfriend Ildiko – in

Hungarian. This in itself wasn't strange. The bed in which they lay together was in Budapest.

'Well, you're a funny guy,' said Ildiko, nuzzling her head against his shoulder, pushing him back down onto the bed. Wisps of her abundant mane tickled his brow, or maybe the wisps were his own. Between them, they had enough hair for half a dozen people.

'You've got a great sense of rhythm, too,' she murmured into his ear, humping his thigh playfully.

He stroked her under the sheets, expecting her to be still naked, but she was snugly wrapped in warm cotton. His palms, callused by years of drumming 240 beats per minute on such songs as 'Inferno Express', 'Pestilential Maelstrom' and 'Meet You In Gomorrah', lingered over the strange scab-like textures on her garment.

'What have you got on?' he said. She sat up, displaying his own black Corpse Grinder T-shirt. She turned to show him the embossed silver letters on the back: European Tour 2000 – Budapest, Bratislava, Prague, Wrocław, Warsaw, and other places whose names had already been half-disintegrated by the washing machine, even though the shirts had yet to go on sale to the general public. 'Hand-wash only' the merchandise said, but let's face it, who hand-washes T-shirts?

'Looks good on you,' said Morpheus. It was a relief to be eyeballing something dark.

'I thought it might be nice to do a swap. I have a nice pink nightie you can wear.'

'Ha ha ha,' he groaned, wondering if the Hungarian for 'ha ha ha' was something subtly different.

Ildiko was the wittiest girlfriend he'd ever had. She wasn't a groupie; in fact she wasn't even particularly fond of Corpse Grinder. Ambient was more her thing, cool electronic noises that hung around the room like a whiff of

air-freshener. Corpse Grinder's clamorous epics about disem-
bowelment, tortured souls, teeming maggots and impaled
Christs weren't very useful, she said, when she was trying to
concentrate on her university textbooks. But she liked
Corpse Grinder's drummer. She liked him a lot.

'I've got a strange feeling in my head,' he said.

'A pain?' she suggested, getting out of bed, her bottom
amply covered by the hem of the XXL T-shirt. 'PREPARE
YE!' said the slogan under the list of tour dates.

'Yeah, a pain,' he conceded, frowning.

'A . . . headache, then?' she said, pulling her toasty warm
tights off the old cast-iron heating duct.

'I don't get headaches,' said Morpheus, wincing as she
stepped in front of the window and his eyes were blasted by
an aura of fierce sunshine all around her silhouette.

'Well, you seem to have one now.'

'Maybe it's a . . . a . . .' He didn't know the Hungarian
word for brain tumour. 'Maybe I'm going to die.'

She tossed his T-shirt back to him in order to put on a bra.

'Start with an aspirin,' she advised him.

'You know I don't believe in drugs,' he chided her,
shielding his face with his massive sunlit hands.

It was true that Morpheus never got headaches. Even when
he was a teenager in Maybole, just plain Nicky Wilkie then,
he'd never felt pain in any part of his body, except the blisters
on his hands when he first joined The Unbelievably Uglies
(later The U.U., then Judas Kiss, then finally Corpse
Grinder.) 'Pain is an illusion,' he used to say. 'Power of the
mind, mate!'

It was true, too, that Morpheus didn't believe in drugs.
Not many of their fans knew it, but Corpse Grinder were an
unusually straight bunch of guys, having long ago ejected and

replaced members whose bad habits made them incapable of rehearsing the tricky time signatures of the band's music, or enduring the punishing pace of their concerts. When Corpse Grinder were still based in Scotland, Neil the guitarist (Cerberus) used to get drunk occasionally, and Charlie the bass player (Janus) might drop an E on his nights off, but now that they were older, and based in Budapest, they were as clean as Cliff Richard.

'Funny the way things have turned out,' Cerb would say. 'Ayrshire to Hungary. Back home, nobody wanted to know us: we'd still be playing in the local pub. Here, we're a stadium act.'

Morpheus tended to excuse himself when Cerb got started in this vein; at twenty-two, he was a bit young for dewy-eyed reminiscence. Besides, it wasn't quite true that Corpse Grinder were a stadium act; they only toured stadiums when they landed a support slot to a bigger group, like Pantera or Metallica. That's what this tour of Eastern Europe was all about, despite the exclusive billing on the Corpse Grinder T-shirt: they were one of several warm-up acts for that hoary old heavy metal warhorse, Slayer. Thousands and thousands of Eastern European adolescents were primed to crawl out of the woodwork to see Slayer, and with any luck they would spare a cheer for Corpse Grinder too, and buy a CD or a T-shirt ('Hand-wash only!').

'Maybe your neck is stiff, Morph,' suggested Ildiko. 'Maybe you slept in a bad position.'

'Yeah, next to *you*,' he grimaced, rubbing his temples experimentally.

'Stop grouching,' she said, fully dressed and efficient by now. 'I've brought you a coffee.'

'Not that Portuguese garbage in the blue and yellow packet?'

'No, it's Dutch. Top brand. Inferno Expresso.' She stared down at him, poker-faced until he twigged she was joking.

'Ha ha ha,' he said.

A little while later, she convinced him to go for a walk in the fresh air. His 'bad head', as she diplomatically called it, might respond to oxygen and exercise. So, the pair of them dressed up in their anoraks and gloves and fur-lined Polish boots, and took to the streets outside Ildiko's apartment. Morpheus wore dark sunglasses, a mainstream rock star affectation he usually avoided, but the sun on the snow was still fearsomely bright.

'Fantastic day, Ildiko!' called Hajnalka, the florist.

'Sure is!' she called back.

'That's all people talk about in Scotland, too,' muttered Morpheus, keeping his eyes on the footpath, where the footprints of pedestrians had scuffed the snow into a more tolerable mud-grey. 'The weather.'

'Must be a human trait, then, I'd reckon,' she said, leading him under the tarpaulin canopies of a street market.

The traders were out in force today. As well as the usual stalls of mobile phones, outmoded Italian leather jackets, counterfeit Gap and Adidas gear, bootleg Hollywood videos, blue-and-yellow packets of Portuguese coffee, Britney Spears calendars and discount confectionery, there were more traditional wares on offer: home-made strawberry jam, fat headless chickens, stamp albums from the Communist era, reams of stolen office paper, gigantic mouldy salamis.

'Would you like a Bounty bar?' said Ildiko, casting her eye over a trestle table loaded with chocolates from America via the Arab Emirates.

'I feel . . . there's a strange feeling in my stomach,' said Morpheus.

'You feel sick, in other words?' said Ildiko, buying a Mars for herself.

'I'm never sick,' insisted Morpeus, shoving his sunglasses up under his hood as he rummaged through some pirated CDs. There was a Slayer greatest hits compilation, called *The Biggest Hist of Slayer*, as well as the most recent album by (of all people) Cradle of Filth. No Corpse Grinder, of course.

'You wouldn't want there to be, would you?' said Ildiko, noting his disappointment. 'You don't get any money from illegal copies.'

'We've never seen any money from the official releases, either,' he grumbled. 'At least the pirates pay their own costs.'

Ildiko zipped her unopened chocolate bar into a jacket pocket. 'I want something nourishing first,' she said. 'Let's go to Café Kalvin and have a Halaszle.'

'I'm not hungry.'

'You'll need something inside you for tonight.'

It was the first time she'd alluded to the fact that tonight was showtime: the first gig of twenty-two, the firing-on-all-cylinders start to Corpse Grinder's highest-profile tour ever.

'Plenty of time, plenty of time,' said Morpheus, his eye caught by a glossy magazine that looked as though it might be about thrash metal. It proved to be pornography for leather fetishists.

'Have some of my soup, Morph,' Ildiko urged him, stirring some cream into her Halaszle.

'It's too early in the day for anything fishy,' he said. The lights inside the Café Kalvin were nice and subdued, though the sight of the pale cream revolving in the dark soup around Ildiko's twirling spoon was making him slightly dizzy.

'It's one o'clock,' she reminded him. The gig at the castle was due to kick off at seven thirty, with Corpse Grinder following Ferfiak (the homegrown pretenders) at eight fifteen. Morpheus, still helplessly staring at the swirling cream in the

Halaszle, had a sudden pre-vision of his band's ideal light show — flickering red strobes and sweeping white lariats of dervish luminescence.

'Gonna blow everyone away tonight,' he declared, picking up a fork and teaspoon, and drumming a high-speed fanfare on the edge of the table. Even through the tablecloth, his power and skill were unmistakable.

'Are you ready to order or what?' called the waitress.

Morph walked through the door under the sign that said GYOGYSZERTAR. It could have been the name of an Eastern European thrash metal or Goth group, but it meant 'pharmacy'.

'I have a headache,' he told the old uniformed lady behind the counter.

'Speak up,' she said, cupping one gnarled hand behind her ear.

'Headache,' he repeated, shame-faced.

'What have you tried?'

'Nothing. What have you got?'

She gestured behind her, at a wall bristling with little cardboard boxes. Analgesia for every man, woman and child in Budapest, by the looks. Was there really enough pain inside a sufficient number of skulls to justify the existence of all these pills?

'I've heard aspirin's pretty good,' said Morpheus, wishing the old woman would take charge.

'In that case, you don't need to pay through the nose for a fancy brand name.' She seemed to be warming to him, showing a motherly side. 'We have mounds of no-name aspirin out the back. You can get a hundred of them for the same price as twenty Bayer.'

'I only need a couple,' pleaded Morph, wondering what

he'd done to deserve a run-in with Hungary's only surviving pre-capitalist.

'I'll get you fifty,' she smiled, already moving towards the store-room, as if he were a cheeky little boy at the baker's and she was about to sneak him a bag of yesterday's donuts.

A minute later she stood in front of him with a plastic bottle and a glass of water.

'What, here?' said Morpheus, alarmed.

'Certainly. No time like the present.'

He shook two pills out of the bottle and threw them into his mouth, quickly chasing them with a swallow of water.

'You've never done this before?' she said, as he half-choked and grimaced and drank more water.

'Arghhh,' he replied, shaking his head.

'Are you working in Budapest?' She could tell he was a foreigner, of course.

'I'm a musician.'

'Really? What's your name?'

'Uh . . . Nicky.'

'English?'

'Scottish.'

'Beautiful place. What brings you to this den of thieves?'

Not enough demand for Corpse Grinder in Scotland, he thought. 'My girlfriend lives here,' he said.

'That's nice,' she said, the corners of her eyes wrinkling benignly. 'That'll be a hundred forint.'

'How's the head?' said Ildiko as they walked back towards the flat. Drizzle was eating into the snow like a mist of acid. The parked cars were emerging from their white canopies like giant metal mushrooms.

'Worse,' said Morph. 'I shouldn't have taken those pills. Power of the mind, that's what's needed.'

Indoors once more, he allowed Ildiko to massage his neck and shoulders while he watched TV. With the remote control he turned the brightness down so far that the faces went negroid.

'Maybe you should let the other guys know,' said Ildiko.

'Know what?'

'That you may not be well enough to play.'

'Of course I'll be well enough. Mind over matter.'

She kissed his head. Her fingers were tired from kneading his tense musculature.

'Hey, look!' he said. 'It's the lead singer of Ferfiak!' On the TV, a heavily tattooed young man was telling a journalist that his band was going to blow Slayer off the stage all the way across Europe. Then the bass player pushed forward, middle fingers raised in defiance, and shouted in English: 'We're gonna kick some asses!'

Morph and Ildiko cackled gleefully.

At six, Morpheus was on his way to the castle, to rendezvous with his fellow Corpse Grinders. It was a twenty-minute drive, with Ildiko at the wheel of her pirated Volvo. Morph was in the back, as the front passenger seat was taken up by a carefully balanced, quivering, transparent plastic bag filled with water and tropical fish. The exotic creatures swam backwards and forwards in their fragile polythene home, the water vibrating in the thrum of the engine.

Morpheus was drumming against the back of the seat with real drumsticks, getting himself psyched up.

'Meetchooo in Gomorraaaahhhh!' he sang tunelessly, beating the hell out of the leather head-rest.

'Maybe that's not so good for the fish,' called Ildiko over her shoulder. Her father had been waiting for these little beauties to arrive for months, and wouldn't be too happy if

his decision to let his daughter pick them up for him from the city resulted in their being dead on arrival.

'Survi-i-ival of the fiiitte-e-e-est!' sang Morpheus, quoting the title track of Corpse Grinder's first album. He drummed less aggressively, though.

To be honest, he was feeling like hell, and even the exertion of hitting his drumsticks on the back of a car seat made the blood in his head pound. He squeezed the sticks hard in his fists, breathed deep, pressed his knuckles into his leather-clad knees. The biker trousers, usually like a second skin to him, were cold and clammy. His bare arms were pale and goose-pimpled, yet his anorak was on the front seat, a nest for the wobbling fish bubble, and the bother of extracting it seemed too great. Always in the past he had driven to gigs wearing only his stage T-shirt; sheer adrenalin had kept him warm, even if the car had no heating and the temperature outside was below freezing. Today he was shivering.

'Are you sure you're all right?' called Ildiko, when a sharp bend in the road provoked a heavy sigh from him.

'Aspirin poisoning,' he groaned. His stomach and intestines had turned to hard rubber inside his abdomen, a solid mass of anatomical sculpture with no fluid function. A dark mass of pain pulsed behind his left eye and brow. He pressed his forefingers against the bridge of his nose, harder and harder, until it seemed they were in danger of bursting through the bone of his skull (a very 'heavy metal album cover' scenario, he had to admit).

'Stop the car.' His own voice was alien to him, a weedy, nasal sound, indistinct above the noise of the engine and the rushing in his head.

'It's only another couple of minutes,' said Ildiko, 'to my parents' place.' She checked the rear view mirror. There was a car jam-packed with post-adolescent Hungarians right behind

them, a Peugeot crammed to the roof with excited young men ready to raaahk.

'I'm going to be ...'

Morph lurched sideways, wound the window down at desperate speed, and heaved a hot gush of vomit into the air. It spurted out of his mouth and nose like beer from an agitated can, and splattered the side of Ildiko's car, wind-blown, in a long yellow stream. Smoothly, Ildiko slowed down and pulled off the road, allowing the traffic behind to roar past.

Morpheus fumbled the door open and fell out onto his hands and knees in wet frosty grass. He vomited more: convulsive gouts of it that made his head almost explode with agony. Ildiko's arm around his back triggered a fit of shivering.

'H-how are we doing for time?' he panted.

Morpheus woke up in a dark room surrounded by ceramic milkmaids and carved statuettes of reindeer. He was in bed – not Ildiko's aromatic little nest, but a strange king-size rococo layer cake of quilts and embroidered coverlets and ironed cotton sheets and fur-lined pillows. He might have been an ancient warrior on a funeral bier, floating onto a dark lake just before being set on fire.

A crack in the bedroom door admitted a pale antique glow from the hallway. Ildiko's parents had always been wealthy, even before Hungary's threadbare Iron Curtain was impatiently swept aside. Their house was a Viennese-style monstrosity, a nineteenth-century hunting lodge hidden inside a three bedroom bungalow, a Black Forest gateau cunningly concealed in a crispbread wrapper.

It was deathly quiet. Usually when Morph visited, Pavarotti or Carreras were warbling from the superannuated sound system. Ildiko's father was the sort of man who

believed that CDs could never compete with the lustrous, organic tones of old fashioned vinyl, especially when channelled through Russian-made speakers the size of shipping crates. Being rather deaf, Ildiko's father liked to play his imported tenors quite loud, but right now, there wasn't a whisper of an aria to be heard.

Morph sat up in bed. He was dressed only in his T-shirt and underpants, lightheaded and weak as a kitten.

'Ildiko!' he called softly.

She appeared in the doorway almost at once, holding a coffee mug shaped like a squirrel.

'A doctor came,' she explained. 'You've had a shot of painkiller, and something for the vomiting. Migraine, she said.'

'The concert . . .'

'It's long over. Zoltan from Ferfiak filled in for you.'

'Zoltan? He belongs in a post office, stamping the Christ out of letters . . .'

'Maybe so. But he filled in for you. They're on their way to Bratislava now.'

'Bratislava? What?' He swung his legs out of the bed and tried to stand, but felt as if two feet were unfeasibly few for this challenge.

'It's next day already,' Ildiko said, opening the bedroom curtains a bit. Undeniable daylight shone in. The dyed sheepskin rugs on the floor lit up caramel and gold. Morpheus noted that he could cope with these things now, that the sunshine was well within the range of his endurance. He was thirsty and a little peckish; his innards were empty as a bass drum.

'I've got to get to Bratislava,' he said. There was a crust of dried blood on his thigh, where the needle had gone in. He didn't remember the doctor at all, though he vaguely recalled his own arrival at Ildiko's parents' place: the ecstatic barking

of the dog, the embarrassment of being half-carried across the threshold, his limp arms slung round the shoulders of a midget middle-aged couple, the surreal passage past book-shelves crowded with Goethe and knick-knacks, stuffed antelope heads, crocheted farmyard scenes in teak frames, the door of the 'guest' bedroom with the smiling graduation photo on it, the spare plastic goldfish-bowl they'd given him to vomit in, the divine relief of being stationary and warm and in the dark.

'See if you can make it to the toilet first,' suggested Ildiko. Standing there cradling her squirrel mug, she looked calm and happy. She always enjoyed seeing her old room again, to remind herself why she now led a life of rumpled minimalism.

'I puked on your parents' hallway carpet,' said Morpheus, remembering suddenly.

'Don't worry, it fits right in,' said Ildiko. 'Besides, they're over the moon about their new cichlids.'

Morph pictured Mr and Mrs Fleps sitting in their front room, Pavarotti forgotten as they stared in a trance-like state of devotion at their latest imported fish. He chortled and allowed himself to slump back onto the quilt.

'You look cute on this big bed,' said Ildiko, tugging the covers out from under him, tucking him back in.

'I feel like ... like death warmed up,' he groaned, but this evidently wasn't a Hungarian turn of phrase, because she replied,

'I don't think that's something my parents have in the house. How about a bowl of chicken soup?'

'Just ... coffee, thanks.'

'How about a cup of tea, in a squirrel mug? Expensive English tea, bought by my daredevil dad on the black market in 1977. Maturing in the tin ever since, just waiting for you to come along.'

He closed his eyes wearily. 'My band has left me,' he said, in a voice from the Hadean depths.

By evening, Morpheus was up and about, if a little shaky. In the same room with the benignly attentive Mr and Mrs Fleps, the over-friendly German shepherd and the successfully integrated tropical fish, he spoke on the telephone with Cerberus.

'Slayer have *had* it,' enthused Cerb in his strong Ayrshire accent. 'They're old men. We're gonna murder them all across Europe.'

'What about me?' said Morph.

'We'll save the death blow for you. Catch up with us when you can. Meet you in Gomorrah!' Cerb was raving, high on adrenaline. He was about to go onstage in Bratislava, and sounded as though he was surfing on a huge tidal wave of adulation – or as if he'd succumbed to a cocaine pusher.

'How are they coping?' asked Ildiko when Morph hung up.

'I don't know,' he said. 'OK, I think.'

Morph was hungry by now, but reluctant to endure a three-course meal under the watchful gaze of Ildiko's parents, the dog, two of El Greco's saints, and the stuffed head of a fox.

'I'll take you out for a snack,' whispered Ildiko, reassuring her parents that 'Miklós' needed some fresh air.

They left the house, blinded by the porch lights and stumbling hesitantly until they found their footing on the moonlit main street. Morph's legs functioned like newly purchased equipment, not yet broken in. He looked up at the sky, clearer here than in the city. The patterns of the stars were unrecognisable, nothing like the ones above his own parents' house in Ayrshire.

At the end of the street was a grocery store, closed, and a tavern called the Blaha. They went in and seated themselves at a table, thereby doubling the number of serious diners instantly, although there were half a dozen folk drinking beer and wine. A trio of local musicians – guitar, accordion and drums – were playing restrained renditions of pop standards. Observing Morph and Ildiko's arrival, they judged that the demographics of the Taverna Blaha had changed sufficiently to justify a switch from Abba to U2. A cat-eyed girl Ildiko had gone to school with wandered over to take the order.

'Somloi Galuska,' said Ildiko, without looking at the menu.

'Bacskai Rostelyos,' said Morph, after some deliberation.

'Are you sure?' Ildiko whispered to him. 'So soon after chucking up?'

'Mind over matter,' he smirked.

The band played U2 until the food arrived, then slimmed down to a duo for 'Nothing Compares 2 U'. Morpheus watched Ildiko spoon her vanilla cream cake into her perfect mouth; Ildiko watched Morpheus devour his roast beef in tomato sauce. The clientele of the Taverna Blaha kept a casual eye on Ildiko Fleps and her long-haired boyfriend from Scotland, England.

'Does it bother your parents,' he said in between mouthfuls, 'that we're not married?'

'Of course it bothers them, you idiot,' she said, and licked the icing sugar off her fingers.

'Then let's get married,' he said.

A cheer went up from among the middle-aged folk at the bar. There was a scattering of applause. Morpheus figured they must be showing their appreciation for the musicians.

'Idiot, idiot, idiot,' smiled Ildiko, shaking her head. 'Come on, let's dance.' And she pulled him to his feet.

'I'm still woozy from the drugs,' he hissed in her ear as

she pulled him close to her. The accordionist played a tremulous fanfare.

'I'll hold you up till the roast beef takes effect,' she whispered back.

The band, complemented to the full trio once more, launched into a slow waltz version of 'Bonnie Banks of Loch Lomond'.

'I can't dance to this sort of thing,' Morph murmured anxiously into her hair.

'Just hold me tight,' she said, directly into the ear that was the less deafened of the two. 'Close your eyes, and pretend we're in bed together.'

They shuffled around on the polished floor of the Taverna Blaha for a while. An elderly man tapped an aluminium ashtray gently on the bar, one-two-three, one-two-three, to help the drummer keep time. The accordionist carried the tune, allowing the bald, moustachioed guitarist to attempt a few power chords of Dire Straits intensity.

Meanwhile in a Slovakian city far, far away, a death metal band was blistering its way through its demonic repertoire. Hordes of demented fans were synchronising their movements with every leap and lunge on stage. A drummer who might be mistaken for Morpheus was flailing away behind his fearsome armoury, putting the boot into the bass drum, bashing the Christ out of the cymbals. Close to the speakers, the noise would be titanic. Outside the venue, it would be a muffled din. Half a mile down the road, no trace.

In the Taverna Blaha, the noise levels were rising slightly. The waitress was clearing plates from the tables. Sleet clattered against the windows. The band played on, and Morph and Ildiko were still dancing. Morph kept his eyes focused on the oscillations of Ildiko's feet, willing himself not to kick his fiancée's toes. He was doing pretty well for a beginner.

The strain of playing 'Loch Lomond' in waltz tempo was beginning to show on the musicians, though. The accordionist leaned over to the guitarist and whispered something in his ear. Two sets of grey moustache nodded in unison, and the music metamorphosed smoothly into an old pop hit by Fonograf Ensemble. Ildiko leaned into Morph's chest and muffled her giggles in his shirt. He squeezed her tight, flexing the muscles of his powerful forearms against her warm back. He stopped looking down at his feet, rested his cheek on her shoulder instead, and kept moving.

'Yes,' she said. 'That's it, you've got it.'

TABITHA WARREN

Dear Sir,

Further to your obituary of Tabitha Warren on the 3rd of November, I believe I was the last journalist to interview her before her death. On the basis of our meeting, I wrote a feature article for the Independent *which, thanks to some heavy pleading by Jack Warren, was never published. If it* had *been published, the inaccurate picture of Tabitha's last years, as reproduced in your obituary, would never have gained currency.*

The 'authorised version' of events is that Tabitha's last book was Cat's Paw, *and that she saw no need to add to her body of work, having achieved everything she'd ever hoped for — including, it must be said, extravagant wealth. You yourself repeated the oft-quoted story of how she once burned a twenty-pound note over a restaurant candle, sighing that in the time it took the money to burn, twice that amount would have accrued in royalties.*

In all honesty I wasn't a fan of hers when I was assigned to the interview. My taste in fiction was more 'literary' and, despite Tabitha Warren's supposed cross-over appeal, I personally found her oeuvre *lightweight. Her endless series of novels featuring angst-ridden animals as narrators struck me as entertaining but gimmicky –* Watership Down *with Kafka pretensions, as I would put it in the article. But my editor thought she was the bee's knees and, besides, there was a rumour that another book was about to emerge from what was affectionately known in the trade as 'the warren'. ('Affectionately', not because Tabitha and her husband were well-liked, but because of the amount of revenue and media hype a new addition to the Tabitha Warren franchise was sure to generate.)*

Conscientious as always, I forced myself to re-read the most universally well-received of all her novels – her debut, A Dog's Life. *I admired the way the disintegration of Neil and Catherine's relationship is observed through the innocent eyes of their Jack Russell, but even in the most heart-tugging passages, I was nagged by a sense that the alienness of the dog's perspective is a cop-out, a failure of the author to take responsibility for her own cluelessness about human motivation. This failure cripples all her books; for all her cleverness, we know perfectly well that they are not written by cats, dogs, dolphins, rats, and all the other zoological protagonists she worked her way through, but by a woman who never quite got the hang of being human. It was this basic contradiction that I was interested in addressing when I went to interview her.*

Security was tight, even by the standards of paranoid best-selling authors. I was driven to her mansion in a limousine with darkened windows, and was chattered at constantly by Tabitha's agent, just in case I was managing somehow to plot the route. I was made to sign a document promising I would not ask questions calling 'undue' attention to Mrs Warren's advanced age, her physical appearance or her relationship with her husband. I was to use a notepad, not a tape recorder – although any fabrications would be pursued vigorously

through the courts if need be. Photographs were verboten, *as was any discussion of the Warrens' legal battles with their disgruntled children.*

'Tabitha and Jack are sick to death of distorted journalism,' the agent told me, narrowing her eyes meaningfully as we drove through Devonshire to our secret destination. 'If they see yet another article along the lines of, 'crazy old Tabitha Warren living in her lonely mansion with only her pets to love', they'll hit the roof.'

I signed the document, but when I finally arrived at the Warrens' house, I couldn't help thinking that if the Warrens were going to hit the roof, at least their roof was A-listed by English Heritage, decorated with Elizabethan turrets, and an awfully long way off the ground.

Still, my initial impression of Tabitha was more favourable than I expected. She seemed embarrassed, even upset, by the fuss that was being made around her. She had come out to meet me as soon as the car pulled up, greeted me with a smile, and suggested, 'Shall we do it here, in the sun?' But her agent and her husband immediately hustled us inside. Then the agent took ages to leave, scolding me for all sorts of things she was convinced I was scheming to write. Then her husband took over, claiming that his arrangement with the Independent *was that he and Tabitha be interviewed together. He stood next to the chair where she was sitting, his huge mottled hand hooked over her tiny shoulder, a lugubrious hulk in a truly horrid double-breasted suit.*

When I insisted on speaking to Tabitha alone, he backed down but still didn't grant us full privacy. Minutes after he'd left the room, I could hear him in the adjacent study, pretending to be sorting fan mail.

'What a welcome,' I said ruefully, deciding on impulse to test out Tabitha's erudition. 'I feel like Charlotte Corday.'

'Oh, stab away my dear,' she said, without missing a beat. 'As long as your knife is clean.'

She grinned. Her face was a mask of wrinkles underneath her expensive bob of jet-black hair, but she looked elegant and striking. The author shot that HarperCollins kept using on the backs of her books might have been taken twenty years before, but she was still giving it a run for its money. Her body was in good shape, too; slim, and clad in black leggings under a loose peasant dress — designer peasant, made by ritzy French couturiers.

'Anyway,' she continued, leaning forward to whisper, 'it's not you they're worried about, it's me. They're all afraid I'll disgrace myself.' And she widened her big green eyes theatrically.

The first ten, fifteen minutes of the interview went pretty much the way interviews with Tabitha Warren were wont to go. She rabbited on (if you'll excuse the expression) about how she felt that she could really put herself inside the minds of animals, and how she thought there must be a bit of that in all of us, or her work wouldn't have attracted such a big readership. While she spoke, a variety of subdued, pampered-looking pets wandered in and out of the room — a Persian cat, a Siamese, a mammoth sheepdog, and, yes, a Jack Russell. They sat at her feet and allowed themselves to be patted for a while, then dawdled out again. Their claws ticked on the great expanse of polished mahogany floor. Through the French windows I could see the limousine parked outside, its driver reading a newspaper, waiting for me to finish. Tabitha's agent was out there somewhere, too, exploring the immaculate gardens in the company of her mobile phone.

I told Tabitha I'd heard rumours that she'd written a new book. Her face lit up for a moment, but then a loudish thump sounded from the study, and she went glum.

'No,' she said. 'Cat's Paw was the last. Thirteen novels is quite a pile. I ask myself, does the world really need another book by me?'

'Many people would think so.'

'There is only so much one can do, don't you think?'

'Within a narrow field, yes.'

Her eyes twinkled in pain, but it didn't seem to have its origin in my remark. She fidgeted in her armchair, drawing her knees up to her chin, a curiously childish posture for a woman of seventy-odd.

Suddenly there was a telephone trill from inside the study. Jack Warren answered it, and, after a distinctly audible 'Yes?', lowered his voice to a murmur. It was a strange kind of murmur, though: not a considerate murmur, or an adulterous murmur. An agitated murmur, the sound of a man called unexpectedly to account for some unforgivable sin. Tabitha and I both noticed it; our interpretation was identical and we knew that it was.

Instantly, she leaned forward in her chair, her chin slipping between her knees.

'It's one of the children, you can bet on it,' she said. 'He should've let the machine handle it.'

I didn't know how to take this. If I'd been a tabloid hack, I suppose I would have seized my chance, asked her about the family strife, the daughters' accusations that Jack kept Tabitha a prisoner in her own house, that he'd had a harem of mistresses over the years, that she had no say in the running of her business affairs. But all I could think to ask was,

'Have you ever thought of writing something totally different?'

She slid down off her chair, squatted on the floor in front of me. The sheepdog sidled up to her, squatting down too.

'Oh, I have, I have,' she said.

She was an unsettling sight, sending a chill down my spine even now as I recall it: an old, old woman with thin limbs wreathed in black cotton, rocking on her haunches, never for an instant taking her eyes off me.

'Is it fear of disappointing your fans that stops you trying it?' I suggested.

The question bounced off her like a ball of wool. I might just as well have asked her about the temperature on Mars or the latest football score from Sicily.

'You don't understand,' she whispered, her big eyes animated and furtive. 'I've already written it. All this palaver I come out with in interviews, of "There's nothing more to say" – it's all lies. I have to lie, you see.'

'Who makes you lie?'

She tipped her head in the direction of the study. Her black fringe fell in front of her eyes.

'But why?' I said, feeling out of my depth. 'Is this new book about him?'

She shook her head vigorously, like a child. Her little black mane swept back and forth.

'So why doesn't he want it published?'

'I don't know,' she whined softly. 'Who can guess what goes through his head?'

Before I could think of anything else to say, she was crawling across the floor, heading for an antique bureau, talking all the way there.

'My earlier novels are no good, no good at all. False, fake, cowardly. The mind in them isn't an animal mind. It's a human mind dressed up in animal clothes. A human voice with a slight animal accent.'

I was surprised by this last phrase. It was sparkier and more impressive than anything I'd read in her work. In fact, it eroded my condescension towards her and I was moved to treat her as a big grown-up writer – at the same time as I was watching her crawl on all fours.

'Uh . . . well, that's an unavoidable problem, surely,' I tried to reassure her, 'with anthropomorphism?'

She'd found what she was looking for, hidden under the bureau. It was a sheet of paper, soiled with house dust and dog hair.

'Here,' she said, sliding along the polished wood towards me. 'This is my new book. I keep bits of it stashed everywhere, so he won't find it. Don't read it now, there may not be time. But take it; keep it safe.'

Blushing and awkward, I folded the handwritten text into a smaller square and slipped it into my jacket.

'It's called The Window Is Not Open,*' she said. 'It's a tale told by a cat.'*

'Oh yes?' I said as brightly as I could, but something in my voice must have betrayed my disappointment.

'No, no, not like Cat's Paw,*' she whispered intensely. 'This one really is told by a cat. Unadulterated. No human interference. Pure cat. A book that cats themselves would read, if cats could read.'*

'Have you tried reading it aloud to yours?'

She glared at me chidingly, clambering, backwards, into her arm-chair again.

'You're making fun of me, dear, but I don't care. What I've given you will convince you. Of course I've had to make a compromise, writing it in English. But that's the only compromise I've made.'

I had to struggle to keep a straight face, even though, later when I got to read her illicit scribblings, I realised she was quite right. This is the extract that nestled in my jacket pocket: (Please note that I have no idea if this was the beginning of the book, the end, or from the middle)

Time before, here a mouse was. Time before, here a mouse was. Time before, here a mouse was. Time before, here a mouse was. Time before, here a mouse was. Time before, here a mouse was. Grass rustle. Mouse? Mouse? Not mouse.

Time before, here a mouse was. Time before, here a mouse was. Time before, here a mouse was. Time before, here a mouse was. Time before, here a mouse was. Time before, here a mouse was. Time before, here a mouse was. Time before, here a mouse was. Time before, here a mouse was. Time before, here a mouse was. Time before, here a mouse was. Time before, here a mouse was. Time before, here a mouse was. Grass rustle. Mouse? Mouse? Not mouse.

Time before, here a mouse was. Time before, here a mouse was. Time before, here a mouse was. Time before, here a mouse was. Time before, here a mouse was. Time before, here a mouse

was. Time before, here a mouse was. Grass rustle. Mouse? Mouse. Come, mouse. Come. Yessss!

Mouse is mine now. In my mouth, warm pulse. On my tongue, heart beat. Come mouse. Come to my house. My house full of mouses, a place for play. This is the way: the grass, the hard ground, the window. Inside my house, my master. Are you big enough for him? Don't break yet, be alive. Alive for him. My master's giant hand will touch all of me in master love. His hand, stroking me, like too many tongues.

But the window is not open. The window is not open. Mouse in mouth, warm pulse, heart beat, but the window is not open. The window is not open.

Sitting there in Tabitha Warren's swanky front room, I was suddenly aware of an acrid smell. Tabitha was squatting on her armchair,

a faraway look in her eyes as her husband hurried in from the study.

Jack Warren glanced first at Tabitha, then at me, then at the door to the outside, an unmistakable signal that the interview was over. He took up his former position at Tabitha's side, laying his hand on her shoulder in a gesture (I now thought) of protectiveness and sorrow. Whatever he had just endured on the telephone had knocked the sheen of composure off his face, adding red rims to his eyelids, disordering his thin grey hair. The smell was pungent now, attracting the sheepdog, who padded up to Tabitha's chair and sniffed around it.

'My wife is very tired,' he said, to get me moving.

Tabitha twisted her head and looked up at him, following the length of his arm all the way up to his pained face.

'Oh but I'm not a bit tired, Jack,' she protested mildly.

'Nevertheless, darling,' he sighed, stroking her hair. 'Nevertheless . . .'

I got up and, for courtesy's sake, crossed over to the pair of them and, rather formally, shook their hands. Jack Warren's was warm and dry, if somewhat weak; Tabitha's was clammy, an eager squeeze with a hint of nails that needed cutting. Her parting words to me were:

'Remember, dear: all I've achieved so far has been just . . . toying. The best is yet to come.'

I feel that perhaps these should be immortalised as Tabitha Warren's last words, rather than the ones you quoted in your obituary – supposedly overheard by one of the nurses who cared for her in the final phases of her dementia. These bitter remarks that she reputedly made about her husband – a man who was no longer around to defend himself – don't sound much like Tabitha Warren's voice to me, and I would question the journalistic ethics of quoting them. After all, more reliable sources than this (suspiciously nameless) nurse insist that in all the lonely months and years after her beloved Jack's death, Tabitha never spoke again.

Yours, etc

VANILLA-BRIGHT
LIKE EMINEM

Don, son of people no longer living, husband of Alice, father of Drew and Aleesha, is very, very close to experiencing the happiest moment of his life.

It's 10.03 according to his watch, and he is travelling down through the Scottish highlands to Inverness, tired and ever-so-slightly anxious in case he falls asleep between now and when the train reaches the station, and misses his cue to say to Alice, Drew and Aleesha: 'OK, this is Inverness, let's move it.' His wife and children are dozing, worn out by sightseeing; the responsibility rests on his shoulders. He doesn't know that the train terminates in Inverness and that everyone will be told by loudspeakers to get out; he imagines it rolling smoothly on, ferrying them farther south, stealthily leaving their pre-booked bed & breakfast behind. This is his first visit to Scotland; the film in his camera has only two shots left; there's no Diet Coke on the refreshment trolley; his wife's

head sags forward, giving her a double chin; big raindrops skid silently against the thick glass of the train windows.

Don and his family have occupied the table seating on both sides of the central aisle: eight seats in all, for four people. He reassures himself that this is OK: the train isn't very full. Plus, he and his family are big people: Americans, head-and-shoulders above most of the other passengers. Drew, just turned fifteen, is five-eleven; Don is six-two. Both of them have hands like boxers. Three hours ago, on the way down to breakfast in an overheated hotel near Dunrobin Castle, Drew had a little blow-out and said 'Fuck *you*, Dad', but they've made up since then, and Don is two minutes away from the big moment.

Alice and Aleesha are across the aisle, slumped opposite each other, their sports bags propped in the window seats, too bulky for the overhead baggage rack. Aleesha, still a child at thirteen despite her budding breasts and chapped white nail polish, has snoozed off in the middle of reading *Harry Potter and the Half-Blood Prince*. Her thin arm dangles in the aisle, bracelets of chewed multi-coloured cotton hooped around her knobbly wrist. Her mother is dreaming uneasily, digging her head into the back of the seat as if registering her frustration with its pitiless design. Alice is forty, and hates being forty. Every month, three days before her period, she starts complaining about her body and its worsening imperfections, and Don has to tell her whatever she wants to hear, which takes some guessing.

The happiest moment of his life so far, besides the one he's about to experience, was when he saw Alice waiting for him outside what was then still called Kentucky Fried Chicken, and she smiled at him, and they both knew they were going to drive straight to Ben and Lisa's empty beach house and make love to each other for the first time. Those

three days at Ben and Lisa's place were magnificent, and he felt such joy in bed with Alice, getting to know her in that way, but her smile when he approached her – that smile of welcome and anticipation and conviction that she was doing the right thing – that was a more memorable thrill than anything they did afterwards. Standing in that doorway under an icon of Colonel Sanders, she was wearing a little black dress with a tan raincoat loosely buckled over it: very French, or so he thought then, never having been to France but having seen movies set there. (He and Alice finally visited Paris in '97, but were kind of distracted by arguments with the kids about the Louvre versus Eurodisney.) Today his wife is wearing a khaki-coloured T-shirt and a loose flannel shirt over that: drab, utilitarian travelling gear.

Don looks down under the table. He's wearing trainers on his huge feet, military pants. In Scotland, 'pants' means underwear. His military pants have lots of pockets and zips and drawstrings and toggles, more than anyone could find a use for. It's a fashion thing, and he wonders if he's too old for it. Yesterday, Aleesha was sitting next to him on a different train from this one, and she unzipped a pocket in the calf of his pants, just to see what was in it. It was a toddlerish action, an innocent gesture of playfulness and boredom, but he felt the charge of her maturing sexuality and was disturbed by it. 'That's kinda dumb, Dad,' she'd said, dabbling her fingers in the unzipped slit of fabric, a pocket too narrow for anything bigger than a pen, assuming you'd want a pen stowed against your calf. Idly, Aleesha had zipped him up again.

He looks across the table at his son. An inflatable neck-cushion is acting as a pillow for Drew's cheek; his brow rests on his muscular forearms; his hands are loosely balled into fists. From this angle, he's not the world's most good-looking kid. His nose is in the process of mushrooming into the same

bulbous schnozzle that all the males in Don's family have had for generations; his lips are swollen, bee-stung, more feminine than Aleesha's – an observation that would enrage him if he knew. And, all over his skull, where there used to be a shaggy brown mop of Heavy Metal hair, is now . . . The Haircut. The haircut they argued over endlessly.

'You can't bleach your hair like Eminem. You'll look like an idiot. *He* looks like an idiot.'

Drew had sighed, his shoulders hunched against the weight of the pre-senile ignorance being heaped on them.

'Eminem is cool. Besides, it's my hair, and my money.'

Frightening, how a sentence of only ten words could provide fuel for so many hours of fierce dispute over a period of days. Whose money *was* Drew's money? What did he have to do to make it his own? Was it his if he chose to spend it on boy scout crap or some old Bruce Springsteen record, but not if he spent it on Eminem? And whose hair was Drew's hair, exactly? (Don felt like a maniac arguing about this, but on the other hand wasn't it true that he and Alice had created that hair, and the head on which it grew, one night – or maybe one day – fifteen years ago? Every follicle on Drew's scalp was made according to their secret genetic recipe, and nurtured from egg to brunette boy.) Who did Drew think he was fooling, pledging fellowship with ghetto youth and the hip-hop scene, chanting along with lyrics about smacking bitches and fuckin' wid de wrong niggaz, when he was a white kid living with his folks in the suburbs of West Springfield, with a holiday in Scotland on the horizon? To which Drew's response was that maybe he wouldn't be living with his folks much longer, not the way their attitude was making him puke, and they could shove their trip to Scotland, he'd rather hang out with his friends here, and anyway, Eminem was white, so what's your problem?

Which provoked Don to tell his son exactly what his problem was. Eminem, he said, was a walking invitation for kids to give up on everything and wallow in negativity. Thanks to rap stars like him, kids were being sold pessimism the way they were once sold chewing gum. Kids who were too young to know a damn thing about the big wide world were coming to the conclusion that Planet Earth was rotten to the core and there was nothing to be done about it except buy CDs and T-shirts.

Alice, trying to stop the conflict getting too global, suggested that Eminem had the right shape of face for bleached, close-cropped hair, but that it wouldn't suit Drew's features at all.

'It's only fuckin' hair!' Drew had yelled. 'What *is* it with you people?' He was cursing a lot lately, whenever he got mad, mostly at his father, but even sometimes at his mother. Every time he yelled Fuck, Aleesha would flinch, as if someone had just thrown a glass against the wall.

Now, Drew lies sleeping on his inflatable cushion, his arms freshly sunburnt, his hair close-cropped and creamy-white. His shoulders are well-muscled, almost a man's shoulders, and Don realises all of a sudden that his son is better-built than Eminem can ever be – taller, stronger, fitter, handsomer.

Aleesha wakes from her doze, looks at the window in case it's Inverness already, then looks to her father for confirmation that it's not. He shakes his head and she smiles. Why the smile? He doesn't know, but he smiles back.

Aleesha leans sideways into the aisle, stretching her arm across the empty space towards her brother. In her hand is the comb she was using as a bookmark just before she fell asleep. Carefully, oh-so-slowly, she runs the teeth of her comb through her brother's hair. Time slows right down. The comb lifts the

nap of Drew's crop, revealing rich brown roots under the bleached exterior. The way it lifts and resettles as the comb passes through it is mesmerising, like watching wheat being rustled by the breeze.

Drew doesn't stir; he's either deeply asleep or determined to ignore his sister. She combs on, tenderly, aware of her dad watching her, aware of the spell she's casting over him. Drew's hair lifts and re-settles, lifts and re-settles, the bristles soft as a brand-new paintbrush, luxury bristle, mink fur. It's a good haircut after all, damn it. In fact, it's the best haircut Drew has ever had, the best haircut on this train, the best haircut in all of Scotland north of Inverness, maybe the best haircut in the world.

Out of the corner of his eye, Don sees Alice repositioning herself, laying her head down on her bag, shifting her weight from her butt to her side. The swell of her butt is sexy, and he gets a glimpse of her naked flesh where the T-shirt has come untucked from her jeans. He still wants her. He's looking forward to the next time they're alone together in a bed, at home or not at home, anywhere where he can run his palms over her warm skin and stroke her hair off her face.

His son snoozes on the table in front of him, a big man of a son, hair feathery and vanilla-bright, almost *too* bright in the sunlight, and above it hovers the beautiful hand and arm of his daughter, coloured cotton bracelets dangling from her wrist, which flexes rhythmically as she grooms the white pelt of her one and only brother, grooms him pointlessly, for he's as combed as combed can be, except that there *is* a point, because this is the happiest moment of Don's life.

In thirty seconds from now, a refreshments trolley will come down the aisle, and Aleesha will be asked by a stunted guy in a uniform to move her arm please, and she'll put it back and Don's happiness will ebb a little, just enough to

make it no longer the happiest moment of his life, but that's OK, because it was a long moment, longer than Alice's smile in the doorway of what has since been renamed KFC. In fifty seconds from now, Aleesha will ask her mother if she can have a chocolate bar, and Drew, still slumped motionless on the table, will say, in a deep voice and distinctly, 'Is there any Pepsi?' In half an hour, they will be in Inverness; in three days they will be home; in two years, Aleesha will announce to her parents that she's always hated the name Aleesha, it sounds like one of those dumb-ass names that black people invent, and she's going to call herself Ellen from now on. And in five years, despite her parents' confident predictions, Ellen won't have grown out of being Ellen, she'll still be Ellen and she'll have had an abortion and her smile will be different, lopsided and a little discoloured by smoking, but she'll be engaged to a man who adores her, and pregnant with a baby she intends to keep.

And by then, Drew will be living in South America somewhere, and Don and Alice will never see him anymore, and their friends will say that they must be very proud of what he's trying to achieve there, and they'll say yes, they're proud, and they'll show these people a photograph of Drew on a construction site in what looks like a shanty town, and he'll be wearing glasses perched on his gigantic schnozzle, his dark brown hair slicked with water and sweat. And Alice will go and make coffee, walking stiffly because of her tennis shoulder which isn't tennis shoulder at all but the first signs of the illness that will kill her when she's fifty-nine, and after that Don will tell everyone he'll never be able to love another woman, but three years later he'll marry one of the people he said this to, and she'll be warm and funny and a great cook and not as good in bed as Alice but he'll never tell her that, he'll die before he tells her that, because she'll make

him happy, happier than he ever expected to be in his old age, happier than any of the other miserable old coots that live in his neighbourhood, happier than he's ever been in fact, except for maybe a couple of isolated moments, like the smile of a young woman waiting to be his lover, her face glowing in the light of a fast-food franchise, and like the hand of his daughter floating above the head of his son, on this morning in a Scottish train, the haircut making everything worthwhile, shining so bright it leaves a pattern on your retina when you close your eyes, vanilla-bright like Eminem.

THE FAHRENHEIT TWINS

In Memory of Panda and Shiro

At the icy zenith of the world, far away from any other children, Tainto'lilith and Marko'cain knew no better than that life was bliss. Therefore, it *was* bliss.

Certainly they had plenty of space to play around in – virtually unlimited space. All around their house, acres of tundra extended in all directions, unpunctuated by fences, roads or other dwellings. A team of huskies could easily pull a sled with the little bodies of Tainto'lilith and Marko'cain on it, for miles, without even losing the frisk in their step. Time was also no problem: in almost perpetual Arctic twilight, there weren't any rules about being back by sunset. The only thing the children's mother absolutely insisted on was that they never leave the house without a compass, since the tundra looked much the same in all directions, especially

when the snows were fresh. During the darker months, even the uncannily keen vision of the Fahrenheit twins was strained by the gloom, and navigation by the light of the moon on a sea of grey snow was impossible.

Still, however dark and treacherous, all that they surveyed was their domain. Nominally, the island of Ostrov Providenya was part of an archipelago that belonged to the Russians, but in reality no law extended far enough to include this barren wasteland encircled by a shifting morass of ice. The Fahrenheits were monarchs here, and their two children prince and princess.

'What lies beyond?' the twins once asked their father.

'Nothing special,' Boris Fahrenheit replied without looking up from his journals.

'What lies beyond?' they then asked their mother, knowing she tended to see things rather differently.

'Oh, darlings, too much to explain,' she teased. 'You'll see it all, when you're tired of this little paradise.' And she ruffled their unwashed hair, in that distantly affectionate way she had.

Physically, there was little in common between parents and offspring. Boris Fahrenheit was a tall thin German, grey of face and silver of hair, walking always slightly stooped as if the weight of his oversized knitted pullovers was too much for his skeletal frame to bear. Una was also tall, a blue-eyed, rosy-cheeked Aryan beauty with dyed black hair cut short in a between-the-wars style. She walked erect, keeping all the flesh firm. She was fifty-nine years old, and had produced her children well past the age where such things were considered feasible.

Tainto'lilith and Marko'cain were small, even for their age, which was somewhere between nine and eleven. No one had recorded the birth, and it was now too long ago for Boris

and Una to recall the exact date. The children were clearly not adolescent yet, anyway. They tumbled around below the furniture, giggling, rounded with puppy fat. They smelled sweet. They wore without complaint the embroidered seal-skin jumpsuits sewn together for them by their mother. They conversed with the huskies as equals.

Their hair was naturally black, hanging long over their ivory-white faces. Each pair of cheeks was sprinkled with cinnamon freckles, as well as a scattering of tiny puckered scars from a mysterious disease that had thankfully run its course without needing medical attention. Their brown eyes were large, with something of the seal about them: all dark iris and no whites, or so it seemed. They resembled neither their father nor mother, despite the fact that the Fahrenheits were, at the time of the twins' conception, already long exiled from past friends. But Boris and Una had been shaped and coloured by the Old World, and their children by a sub-Polar archipelago, whose glacial contours could not even be mapped.

More than anything else, the twins' characters were formed by benign neglect. To their father, they were an indulgence of their mother's which he tolerated so long as it didn't interfere with his research. To their mother, they were like robust little pets, pampered and cooed over when she was in a frivolous mood, forgotten about utterly when she had better things to do. Typically, she might spend hours bathing them and massaging whale oil into their skin, scolding them for spoiling their beautiful young flesh with so many calluses and scars; then for the next week she might scarcely notice their existence, nodding absentmindedly as they tore away into the icy night.

In any case, Boris and Una Fahrenheit were themselves

often away from home, advancing the progress of knowledge. Specifically, they were away visiting the Guhiynui people, on whom they were the world's foremost authorities. The Guhiynui being mistrustful of strangers, however, progress was slow, at least on fundamental issues. Una's book on Guhiynui handicrafts had already been published and she was compiling another on their cuisine, but there was no end in sight on Boris's long-awaited history, and despite the Fahrenheits' best efforts the dark secrets of the Guhiynui's sexual taboos had not yet been illuminated.

Of course, it was the Fahrenheits who must travel to the Guhiynui, not the other way around. And, because Boris and Una always travelled together, it transpired that Tainto'lilith and Marko'cain were often left alone in the house, with only the dogs for company, for days or weeks on end. This made them uncommonly self-sufficient, in a way that would have astounded visitors – if there had ever been any visitors.

The existence of Tainto'lilith and Marko'cain was in fact a secret from anyone in the green parts of the world. Few people had even heard of the island where the Fahrenheits lived, let alone the specifics of its invisible, unreachable population. Una had given birth at home, midwifing herself. Stoical in the face of the duplicated results, Boris had constructed a second cot identical to the first, the memory of how it was done still fresh in his mind.

The indistinguishable cots were apt. In all respects except genitals, Tainto'lilith and Marko'cain were identical twins. Their expressions were the same. There was even the same amount of light inside their eyes, a difficult thing to reproduce exactly.

One day their mother told them a story – a true story, she insisted – about how a future would come when their bodies would change beyond recognition. Tainto'lilith would grow teats, and Marko'cain would sprout a beard.

'Oh ho!' they chortled.

But their mother was serious, and this sewed a needle of anxiety through the tough skin of their hearts. From that moment on, the challenge of arresting the advance of time became a priority for Tainto'lilith and Marko'cain. The years must not be allowed to pass: they must be kept in check, securely corralled in the present. But how?

The answer must lie, the twins felt sure, in ritual – ritual being a concept that was much discussed in the Fahrenheit household, in reference to the Guhiynui. But Boris and Una were mere observers, too European to understand ritual in its visceral origins. Their black-maned, seal-eyed children were already devising a way to control the workings of the universe with such ready-to-hand materials as Arctic fox and knife.

Tainto'lilith and Marko'cain had never met the Guhiynui, but their minds seemed to work similarly – as Una always remarked whenever she saw her children setting off for some solemn ceremony, sled laden with improvised talismans, fetishes and ju-jus.

'Ah, if it was *you* two trying to unlock the Guhiynui's secrets,' she flattered them, 'instead of old Boris, you would get results in a hurry, wouldn't you, my little angels?'

In fact, the twins were capable of great patience when it came to ritual. Certainly, like all children they were impetuous and never walked if they could run, but magic was a different thing from play. It was grand and elemental and couldn't be rushed. You could wolf your dinner or jump recklessly into the embers of a bonfire, but picking at the threads of the fabric of time required more caution.

To crack the 'teats and beard' problem, for example, Tainto'lilith and Marko'cain planned a ritual which could only be performed once a year, at that potently magical moment when the summer sun rose above the horizon at

last. Shortly beforehand, they would trap a fox, and make a cage for it – well, they'd have to make the cage first, perhaps. Then they would take the fox to the horizon and fasten it in position, its head facing where the sun was going to rise. Taller than their captive, the children were sure to spot the first glow of light coming, and, just as the fox was about to see it, Marko'cain would pinion the animal's head with his knees while Tainto'lilith stabbed out its eyes.

Afterwards, they would kill it, although this wouldn't be an essential part of the ritual – merely a gesture of mercy. And every year, they would repeat the ritual with a fresh fox, an eternally reincarnated fox that would always close its eyes rather than witness the changing of the season.

'Do you think it will work?' said Tainto'lilith.

'I'm sure of it,' Marko'cain assured her. 'I feel it in my testaments.'

Having said that, there could be no doubt.

The great house where the Fahrenheits lived stood out from the landscape like an abandoned space ship on the moon. It was a domed monstrosity of concrete, steel and double-glazed glass, attached umbilically to a generator and humming gently all the time. Inside, it was decorated and furnished in the schmaltziest Bavarian style, with intricately carved cuckoo clocks, chocolate-brown tables and chairs, embroidered tapestries, glass cabinets filled with miniature poppets of all nations. A massive oil painting of golden reindeer in a forest of broccoli hung above the fireplace, which was never lit because the central heating took care of all that. There was no vegetation outside anyway, so nothing to burn except (if need ever be) the furniture and the Fahrenheits' books and papers.

The kitchen was a Baroque wonderland of polished wood and brass; dozens of weirdly-shaped implements and

utensils hung in neat rows on the walls. Few of them were ever used. All the Fahrenheits' food came from a freezer the size of a Volkswagen, and Una boiled or baked it either in the grey pot with the cracked wooden handle or the singed pink ceramic oven dish, according to what it was. She was a pathologically forgetful cook and any meal not prepared by the children was likely to be a challenging affair, though occasionally she did get into moods when she would create elaborate pastries or even soups.

'You need vitamins, minerals, and all those mysterious little trace elements,' she would enthuse, serving each of her children some extraordinary treat on the special plates with the silver rims. 'You can't live on rubbish all the time, you know.'

The twins' bedroom was painted mauve, as a bisexual compromise between pink and blue. Very little of the walls showed through, though, because of the density of prints and bookcases and shelves piled thick with knick-knacks. All these things had belonged to Una when she was a child; she had insisted on taking them with her to the island for her own personal, sentimental reasons, long before she had conceived of Tainto'lilith and Marko'cain. Over time, more and more of it was passed down to the children. Her eyes would mist over, and she would rush to fetch something from a locked cabinet or even a suitcase.

'Here, I want you to have this,' she would say, brandishing some ancient ornament or faun-coloured book. 'If you promise to take care of it.'

From careful study of these things – the little wooden horses with real manes and tails, the crystal baubles with cherubs inside, the music boxes that played Alpine melodies, the stuffed mouse with the Tyroler hat, green velvet jacket and lederhosen – Tainto'lilith and Marko'cain pieced together an impression of who on earth their mother might be.

Conversation was considerably harder to come by. Una addressed perhaps a hundred sentences a year to her children, or even less if repetitions weren't counted.

In view of this scarcity, the twins were compiling a 'Book of Knowledge', in which they faithfully recorded all the things their mother said to them. Not the half-hearted scoldings or the offhand domestic instructions, but anything more pregnant. The book — a hundred or so blank pages bound in stiff, intricately patterned covers — was a sacred object and mistakes were not allowed. Every word, every letter proposed for inclusion in it was discussed by the twins beforehand, practised on scrap paper, then inscribed onto the creamy white pages with great care. Appropriately enough, the first thing written into the book was what their mother had told them about the book itself when she'd presented it to them.

'This book was once a tree.'

It was an intriguing thought. The Fahrenheits' house was infested with paper — hardbound texts, maps, German romances, very old newspapers, glossy magazines flown in from Canada, plus of course Boris and Una's own mountains of notes and journals. All these, if mother was to be believed, had once been trees. The notion was doubly potent because the children had never seen a tree, except in books.

Their own attempt to grow such a miraculous thing for themselves, by pulping a book into paste and burying it in a compost of excrement and yeast, had not been successful.

Disappointed, they'd worked up the courage to knock at their mother's study, to ask her the exact recipe for trees.

'Not now, darlings,' she warned them, leaning further into the pearly light of her desk lamp.

One day, Boris and Una Fahrenheit returned from yet another visit to the Guhiynui, landing their grimy blue-and-silver

helicopter just outside the house as usual. They disembarked, one from each side of the cabin, stooping under the whirling blades. Tainto'lilith and Marko'cain watched them from the dining room window, through the trickling shimmer of condensation. Four cuckoo clocks, in various rooms of the house, started cooing simultaneously. In the snows outside, a chaos of huskies swirled around the grown-ups, barking and snuffling.

It was obvious, even before Boris and Una reached the front door, that they were in an unusually subdued mood. They were neither arguing like bitter enemies nor (as was equally common) discussing their findings like affectionate colleagues on the brink of a breakthrough. Instead, Una walked into the house silent and pale, pausing only to let her coat fall to the floor before disappearing into the bedroom.

Boris, a few steps behind, followed her to the bedroom door, then thought better of it. He left the house again, and busied himself putting the helicopter away. Tainto'lilith and Marko'cain watched him through the glass, wiping the condensation away with their pyjama'd elbows, *pwoot woot woot.*

Eventually their father was ready to give them an explanation.

'Your mother has eaten something that disagreed with her,' he said. 'Don't be surprised if this ends badly.'

This was the sum of his thoughts on the matter, but it was enough to galvanise the twins into action.

For the next three days, Tainto'lilith and Marko'cain put aside all childish things in order to nurse their mother in her bed. Holding back offers of nurture only during those arbitrary hours of 'night' when their parents were actually sleeping together, they devoted every remaining minute to a routine of snacks, cold compresses, warm towels, fizzy pills and hot water bottles.

'Oh, you are such little darlings,' Una beamed at them, her face glowing like a gas flame. 'My own mother couldn't have nursed me better than you two are doing.'

Pride in this distinction didn't blind the twins to the fearsome obstinacy of their mother's illness. As the days passed, they grew stoical in their acceptance of the prophesied 'bad end', which in their minds was their mother having to be transported hundreds of miles to the nearest hospital.

Instead, she died.

Bringing the breakfast as usual, the twins found their father loitering outside her bedroom, fully dressed.

'She's dead,' he said, then smiled a ghastly smile as if trying to reassure them that he would not let a thing like this cast a shadow over their welfare.

'But we have her breakfast,' said Tainto'lilith.

'It's all right, you weren't to know,' said Boris.

Seeing that the twins were not taking his word for it, he stepped aside to let them into the bedroom where, at some uncertain time during the night, his wife had finally left him. The event seemed to have rendered him oddly lenient, almost tender.

Tainto'lilith put down the tray of tea and oatmeal just outside the door, and followed her brother in. Una Fahrenheit was lying horizontal in the bed, sheets pulled up to her chin. Her flesh was the colour of peeled apple. Her mouth hung slackly open, her eyes were only half shut. There was nothing happening inside her skull; it was deserted.

Boris stood in the doorway, arms loosely folded, waiting for Una's children to confirm the correctness of his judgement.

Tainto'lilith and Marko'cain dawdled around the bed, sobbing and snivelling softly. Then, briefly, they wailed. In

time, they stopped moving and made a little space for themselves on the edge of the mattress next to their mother's body. They sat there, shoulder to shoulder, breathing in turns. Outside the bedroom, the tongues of dogs slurped at oatmeal and cold tea.

'What happens to her now?' Marko'cain asked the shadowy figure in the doorway.

'Burial,' said their father. 'Or cremation.'

'Oh,' said Marko'cain. He was thinking angels might still come down from the snowy sky and scoop his mother's body up to Heaven. Hidden somewhere far beyond the featureless gloom of the Polar atmosphere, there might be an exotic paradise of teak and lace, laid out ready for Una Fahrenheit. Perhaps only the reinforced concrete of the ceiling was keeping the angels from getting in.

'I'll leave the final decision to you,' said Boris, with a heavy sigh. 'Don't think too long about it, though.'

Left alone with their thoughts, Tainto'lilith and Marko'cain wept a little longer, then began to plan for the future.

They were angry, of course, that the opportunity of saving their mother had not been offered them. Had they seriously imagined she might die, they would certainly have done something to stop it. The universe was not above agreeing to bargains of various kinds, providing enough advance warning was given.

But she was dead now, and that was that.

'We are orphans now, like in the storybook of *Little Helmut and Marlene*,' suggested Tainto'lilith.

'Well . . . not really,' frowned Marko'cain. 'We have a father.'

'For how much longer?'

'He looks quite well.'

'That's not what I meant.'

'You think he will leave us now that mother is gone?'

'It's possible,' said Tainto'lilith.

'Ours is the only house on the island,' objected Marko'cain.

'He may go and live with the Guhiynui. He knows them a lot better than us, and some of them are bound to be women.'

Marko'cain considered this for a minute, then said,

'We are talking about the wrong things.'

Behind them on the bed, the body of their mother was waiting.

'True,' said Tainto'lilith.

The important question was, what ritual would be the right one for their mother – not simply in the matter of removing her body, but also in commemorating all she had been in spirit. She was, after all, no mere piece of refuse to be disposed of.

'We buried Snuffel,' recalled Marko'cain. Snuffel was the children's pet name for Schnauffel, one of the huskies who had died a couple of years before. They had buried him near the generator, in the lush soft earth surrounding the hot water pipes. An elaborate ceremony had accompanied the burial, involving recitations, toys and raw meat.

'Snuffel was a dog,' said Tainto'lilith. 'Our mother isn't a dog.'

'I'm not saying we should do it exactly the same. But we could bury her along with her favourite things.'

'She would hate to have her things buried. Whenever she gave us something, she was always upset if we got it dirty.'

'But won't she be in a box?'

'I don't know. Father didn't say anything about a box.

And you remember when we asked about making the fox cage, he said he had no wood to waste on such foolishness.'

Marko'cain sat slumped in thought. Outside the door, the dogs' tongues stopped lapping and their soft clicking footfalls faded away. These things and more were made audible by the silence of their mother on the bed behind them.

'I think,' said Marko'cain at last, 'Mother should be buried in very deep snow. Then, if after a time we decide we have done the wrong thing, we can fetch her out and she will still be good.'

For some reason this made Tainto'lilith cry again. Her brother put his arm around her convulsing shoulders. The bed shook gently, its three burdens bobbing up and down.

'She wouldn't *like* to be buried in snow,' sobbed Tainto'lilith.

Marko'cain bit his lower lip and frowned.

'Dead people don't feel anything, do they?'

'Don't they?'

'It's in the Book of Knowledge, I'm sure.'

They went and fetched the Book of Knowledge, and found the relevant page. Sure enough, there it was: *Dead people don't feel anything.*

The physical act of fetching the Book of Knowledge, quite apart from what was in it, helped the twins feel a little better somehow. It got them out of their mother's bedroom for a minute, allowing their accumulated grief to escape like harmful fumes into the hallway. When they returned, the bedroom seemed airier and more benign. Una Fahrenheit was lying exactly where they had left her, unchanged to the smallest wisp of hair and glint of tooth. So clear was it from this that her spirit had departed, that the children lost much of their terror of the body she'd left behind. It was a husk, no longer truly their mother – more like their mother's most

treasured possession, which had been given to them as a parting gift.

All they had to do was decide how best to pass that gift on to the universe. There was, after all, a possibility that their mother was taking a lot more interest in her children now that she was dead and her splendid body was in their care. Always so well-preserved in life, she might be watching them anxiously from somewhere up above, to make sure she wasn't mistreated or neglected in death.

'I still don't like to think of her frozen,' said Tainto'lilith, 'even if she can't feel it. She is our mother, not a piece of lamb in the freezer.'

Marko'cain nodded, accepting this, but then an instant later he frowned, stung in the forehead by a new idea.

'Perhaps we should eat her,' he said.

'Oh! What a horrible bad thought!' cried his sister.

'Yes, so there must be power in it,' he reasoned.

Tainto'lilith bit her lower lip, thinking. All ideas must be considered carefully. The universe knew what was best for everyone, even if the way to its heart might sometimes be hard to understand.

Gamely, she tried to imagine the universe smiling down on such a hideous ritual, tried to imagine being brave enough to sacrifice her own feelings to it. Certainly there was a potent appeal in the idea of making their mother disappear inside them, rather than abandoning her body to parasites or the elements.

'She is too big,' said Tainto'lilith at last. 'If I could eat her like an apple – or half an apple – I would do it.'

'We could eat a little of her for the rest of our lives,' suggested her brother. 'Eat nothing else, ever. That would a very strong thing to say to the universe.'

'This is silly talk,' sighed Tainto'lilith. 'I am feeling sick. Think of the hair.'

'We could do something else with the hair.'

'This is silly talk.'

'Yes, you are right.'

Crestfallen, they sat on the edge of the bed, the Book of Knowledge lying closed on the floor at their feet.

'Well . . . what is left?' said Tainto'lilith after a while.

'The best thing,' said Marko'cain.

'What do you mean?' said Tainto'lilith.

'All that we have thought of so far is no good,' said Marko'cain. 'So, the best thing is still left.'

That was cheering. They pondered with renewed vigour.

'Father seemed most in favour of cremation,' remarked Marko'cain. 'That is, burning her.'

'How do you know?'

'It was the way he spoke the word.'

'He said he would let us decide, though.'

'But not to take too long.'

'What time is it?'

'I don't know. The cuckoos will tell us soon.'

'I don't like the thought of burning mother,' fretted Tainto'lilith. 'It is worse than eating her. It's like starting to cook her and then forgetting, and coming back to find her all black and ruined.'

'The Guhiynui burn their dead people, I'm sure I heard father say.'

'Every tribe has its own rituals,' Tainto'lilith said, struggling with hand gestures to make him understand. 'The universe knows we are not Guhiynui. The universe isn't stupid. We have to do something that is right for the tribe that *we* are.'

'You think we are a tribe?'

'Of course we are a tribe.'

'Just the two of us?'

'There are more of our kind where our mother and father came from. That's our tribe.'

'Father says they are all imbeciles and back-stabbers there. And mother said once that they let the streets get dirty, and another time that the trains are always late and full of rude people who will not stand up for a lady.'

'Still they are our tribe.'

Marko'cain had become agitated, picking at little scabs on his knuckles and shuffling his feet.

'I can't remember why we are talking about these things,' he said despondently.

'Neither can I,' admitted Tainto'lilith.

'If only mother could tell us what she wants done.'

'Perhaps she will send us a sign.'

'Perhaps father will come back soon, and tell us we've run out of time.'

As if to confirm this, several cuckoo clocks went off at once, filling the house with the sound of mechanical bird-song.

After much discussion, the twins finally worked up the courage to tell their father they wanted to take their mother away with them into the wilderness. Once they were far enough out there, they would wait for a signal from the universe as to the best thing to do with the body.

Surprisingly, Boris Fahrenheit agreed.

'You *are* little primitives, aren't you?' he commented, with new respect. 'I had thought of commissioning some sort of Christian minister to fly out here and do the job, but I'm sure you would do better. You are blood, after all.'

Uncharacteristically, he began running about like a maniac, gathering together the necessaries for their journey.

'With the extra weight, the dogs will be slower, and will

get hungry and thirsty sooner: you must allow for that,' he cautioned, filling a large canister with boiling water.

'You must take a hamper of food for yourselves,' he went on. 'And food for the dogs. And fuel for a fire, if . . . if you need to make a fire. And I will fetch the compass for you. That is essential.'

Within half an hour he had organised them, hamper and all, and escorted them out of the house. In all those thirty minutes, from the moment the twins had announced their intention right up to the moment they stepped onto the snows, he scarcely stopped talking, reminding them of all the things they must do to keep safe. It was a totally unprecedented and, in the circumstances, bizarrely maternal display of fuss. Had there not been an important mission to accomplish, the twins might have considered inaugurating a whole new Book of Knowledge, merely to contain all the advice and instruction their father was shovelling onto them now.

They stood together in the chill wind and the horizon-less gloom, the three remaining members of the Fahrenheit family. The huskies were harnessed and ready, their breath clouding silver in the tungsten porch-light. The corpse of Una Fahrenheit, wrapped in furs and bound with leather straps, was secured on a long sled, shackled behind the twins' buggy like a tenacious seal.

'And remember!' Boris shouted after them as they slid away towards the wasteland, 'If you need to send up a flare, avert your eyes as you fire!'

Faces blushing hot with mortification and fear, Tainto'lilith and Marko'cain urged the dogs to go faster, to escape from the avalanche of unwanted love.

For what seemed like eternity but was probably only an hour or two, the twins raced full-pelt across the sugary tundra.

'Faster!' shouted Marko'cain.

'Quicker!' shouted Tainto'lilith.

Of course the dogs were wild with enthusiasm at first, but then their pace slackened, not so much from exhaustion as from anxiety – the need to be reassured that there were fellow mammals behind the reins and not some sort of unfeeling machine. Flicks of the whip against their flanks goaded them back up to speed.

Even as they ran, the dogs tried to turn their heads, straining to catch a glimpse of the children they loved so dearly, who had never driven them so hard for so long before. But Tainto'lilith and Marko'cain ignored the appeal, identically determined, hunched down low in their buggy, blinking stoically against the upflung snow.

It was as if they feared that if they stopped or even looked around, their father would still be running after them, clutching a thermos flask or an extra pair of gloves.

'It's mother's death that has done this to him,' said Marko'cain when they finally stopped to let the huskies rest. 'He will feel better when he has had a sleep, don't you think?'

'I don't know,' said Tainto'lilith, blinking in the steam from the panting dogs. 'Perhaps he will be like this forever.'

Glum, they turned to look at their mother on the bier behind them. Her face, which they had not been able to bring themselves to wrap up like the rest of her body, was snow-grey in the twilight.

'She looks worried about something,' fretted Tainto'lilith.

'It's because you are looking at her upside-down,' suggested Marko'cain.

Tainto'lilith contorted her head to test this theory. Her black mop of hair swung free from under her furry hood, and

she palmed it tight against her cheek while examining her mother's physiognomy.

'No, she still looks worried,' she concluded.

'The cold has made her complexion paler,' said Marko'cain, secretly afraid of where this line of enquiry might be leading them.

'No, it's in her expression,' said Tainto'lilith. 'In her brow.'

'She has a few wrinkles there, that's all,' explained her brother, as if the subtle workings of ageing held no secrets for him. 'In life, she kept them moving around so we wouldn't spot them. Now, they're still.'

'It's more than that,' insisted Tainto'lilith. 'I hope she wasn't worried about something as she was dying.'

'What would she have been worried about?'

'Us, for one thing.'

'We are two things.'

'Precisely.'

'She knew we would take care of each other.'

'You think so?'

'She must have, or she would have done more for us herself while she was alive.'

For several more minutes they sat there, their seal-coated forearms resting on the back rung of their buggy, their faces pensive, staring down at the glacial upside-down face of their mother. Then they got up to stretch their legs, and to pour some of the hot water from the canister onto the snow, so that a tepid pool formed from which the dogs could drink.

All round them, in all four directions (– but why only four? – in all three hundred and sixty thousand directions! –) the landscape looked exactly the same. Only the sky differed, varying from greyish indigo to pale purple.

'Where are we going, exactly?' enquired Marko'cain.

'We've been going south, I think,' said his sister, stroking

her favourite husky, allowing the bewildered animal to lick her furry fingers. 'Is the direction important?'

'The universe hasn't taken any notice of us so far,' said Marko'cain. 'Maybe if we go to where the land ends, it will understand that we need help.'

Tainto'lilith had knelt down in the snow, butting her cheek and nose playfully against the snout of the husky. The dog leaned close into her face, almost wetting himself with relief.

'Our island is only small,' Tainto'lilith said, as the other dogs began to pant for their turn. 'We are bound to get to one of its edges soon.'

Marko'cain fetched out the compass, and consulted it, turning round and round as if playing a game, his black boots trampling a hollow in the snow.

'Ho!' he said. 'This is a strange thing: the compass is pointing to a different north whichever way I turn.'

Tainto'lilith gazed up into the stratosphere.

'Perhaps we have reached the Pole,' she murmured.

'The Pole is the other way,' said Marko'cain, frowning. 'I think this compass is broken.'

His sister sidled close, examining the pristine-looking instrument nestling in the grubby palm of his glove.

'The glass is perfect, and the arrow is wobbling just like normal,' she pointed out.

'It's broken inside,' declared Marko'cain, 'where we can't see.'

He shuffled around in a circle again, to demonstrate how north had lost its meaning. Tainto'lilith shuffled with him, and the huskies, smelling a new kind of play, paced around them in a wider circle.

'You are right,' she said. 'But it doesn't matter. The dogs know the way home.'

And they stowed the compass somewhere safe, for their father to mend when they returned.

It took longer to reach the shore of Ostrov Providenya than the twins expected. A whole day's worth of hours, perhaps more. Perhaps two entire days. There was a feeling the twins always got when they had neglected to sleep, a feeling as if their eyeballs had been carelessly left lying about somewhere, and had dried out. Then again, maybe this time it was the weeping that had caused it. Maybe they had only been travelling for a day after all.

And yet they really hadn't thought their island big enough to permit such a long journey as they had made. At their first glimpse of the sea, when it was still a long way off, the twins wondered whether perhaps they'd passed the end of the land a long time ago, and had ever since been traversing an appended halo of frozen sea-water.

However, when at last they were drawing near to the strand, all doubt was swept away. They could see the waves breaking against an undeniably substantial shore of stone, an igneous corona around the rim of the softer earth.

The twins whooped in unison, waving fists in the air as if their advance towards the sea were a battle charge.

Even from a distance, it was obvious that this strip of Ostrov Providenya's shore was only very narrow, and yet it seemed to have some influence inland: the ground on which the twins were travelling grew deceptive beneath them. Oh, the snowy tundra *looked* the same as all the terrain they'd been sliding over from the beginning, but it wasn't the same. Violent bumps and scrapes under the skis of the buggy warned them that the crust of snow was hazardously thin. They glanced behind them: two long lines of dark earth trailed in their wake, and the frozen body of their mother was jolting against its straps.

Hastily, Marko'cain and Tainto'lilith reined the dogs in. If the sea-shore was the place where the universe intended to give them its verdict, they would have to travel the rest of the way there on foot.

With the sleds at a standstill, quiet descended – or what would have been quiet a few miles back: instead, the air was a-buzz with the sound of waves. This was an awesome novelty for the Fahrenheit twins; not the vastness of the ocean, because they had grown up with vastness, but the sound of it. All their lives, circumambient silence had suggested to them that their little family and its machines must be the only animated things in the world: everything else just lay there, still. Even the occasional storm seemed nothing more than a stirring of white dust, a redistribution of lifeless snow by the careless opening of some big door in the universe. As soon as that open door was noticed by whoever was responsible for these things, it would be shut, and silence and inertia would be restored. Here by the sea, however, the illusion was shattered. The great waters were in constant motion, bawling and hissing to each other. Their hubbub was fearsome and relentless, and next to it the voices of the Fahrenheit twins were feeble, barely audible, swallowed up by a larger life.

All this the twins observed and understood in a moment, but even in their newfound humility they found reason to hope. Perhaps the grand restlessness of the sea, its deafening roar of collective purpose, only served to prove how much power it had to help them.

Tainto'lilith and Marko'cain had stopped thirty yards or so from the shore. Dismounting from their buggy, they stumbled around, stiff-limbed, calming the huskies. The ground beneath their feet crackled and sighed. Here and there, sparse vegetation poked through the thin snow, like limp green beans emerging from an inedible expanse of mother's powdered

potato. In the near distance, tortured rock formations – volcanic froth frozen in time – fringed a stony shore. Startled by the arrival of the Fahrenheit twins' little cortège, a colony of white birds billowed into the air, a swirling cloud of wings.

'This is the place,' affirmed Tainto'lilith.

The dogs were very hungry by now, and so the Fahrenheit twins fetched out the tins of food from either side of their mother's body.

'There is a tin opener, I hope?' said Marko'cain, holding one of the tins aloft from the slavering jaws of Snuffel Junior.

'Of course there is,' Tainto'lilith reassured him, bringing the glittering tool to light. 'Father has thought of everything.'

Disappointingly, however, the contents of the unlabelled cans, when the lids were cut off, did not appear to be dog food – at least no dog food the twins had encountered before.

'What is this stuff?' frowned Tainto'lilith, peering into the tomato-red goo.

'I'm not sure,' admitted her brother. 'Let's see what the dogs think.'

They tipped two cans-full of the substance onto the ground, where it spread into a globulous pool of gore, enriched with pale seeds. The huskies approached eagerly, sniffed, then looked up at the twins in puzzlement.

'This is bad news for us,' said Marko'cain.

'Worse news for the dogs,' said his sister. '*We* have food, at least.'

'Yes, but we need the dogs to get home. They are hungry and cold. Soon they will get weak and bad-tempered.'

'Let's make a fire, then, and cheer them up.'

Tainto'lilith and Marko'cain walked to the shore, feeling the strange new pressure of stones against the soles of their boots. Accompanied by the cloud of cooing birds, the twins

searched the rocky strand for something to burn. There was
nothing. However, they did find a big bowl-like metal object,
ochre with rust – a fragment of a ship, perhaps. They carried
it back to where the sleds and huskies were, with the idea of
filling it up with fuel like one of those flaming braziers in
Hansi and the Treasure of the Mongols.

'Remember to stand well back,' counselled Marko'cain as
Tainto'lilith prepared to drop a lighted match into the oily
pool.

The match fell into the liquid and was instantly extinguished. A second match did likewise. One after another, the
little sticks of flaming wood were sacrificed to the same
greasy fate. Eventually a faint aroma of singed fried food,
familiar to the twins from their mother's meals, began to venture through the air.

'This is cooking oil,' said Tainto'lilith.

A finger-dip's taste confirmed she was right.

'We should have packed our own supplies,' said
Marko'cain, putting his glove back on. 'Father was not thinking very clearly.'

'He certainly was in a state.'

Perplexed, the twins perched themselves on the edge of
their mother's sled and considered their lot. The huskies
whined and snuffled nearby, investigating every clump of
vegetation and bird dropping in case it was edible. They were
well-behaved so far, but it wouldn't last. Soon they would
realise that the twins, and the body of Una Fahrenheit, were
the only meat for miles around.

In the skies above, contradictory messages were being
sent. A subtle orange glow on the horizon promised the
dawn, at long last, of the Arctic summer. Then again, there
were massive clouds in the sky and the occasional flicker of
light, threatening a thunderstorm.

'We are going to need some shelter,' predicted Marko'cain.

'If we get too comfortable, the universe may think we don't need any help.'

'I'm sure we will not be able to get too comfortable.'

They harnessed the dogs again, and travelled along the shoreline at a funereal pace. The heavens were crackling with electricity, which made the animals uneasy and distractible, tugging against the reins. The waves crashed louder and louder, sending spray so far inland that it spattered the cheeks of the Fahrenheit twins.

After another mile or so, something extraordinary could be seen, sprouting up from a hillock.

'Is it a tree?' wondered Tainto'lilith, urging the huskies on. But it wasn't a tree. It was the giant blades of a helicopter, all on their own without a vehicle to be attached to. Someone had carried the great metal cross here, buried one of the blades deep in the ground, and thus created a monumental steel crucifix.

'We should be careful,' said Tainto'lilith. 'If lightning comes, it will probably strike that cross.'

Marko'cain nodded, deep in thought.

'Perhaps this is the message from the universe,' he said, as they drew nearer.

'About mother?'

'Yes. Perhaps we should stand her up against that cross, and invite the lightning to strike her.'

As if in support of this idea, a bright tendril of electricity whipped across the sky, lighting up everything for a moment with tungsten clarity.

'Do you really think so?' said Tainto'lilith dubiously. 'Don't you think it might . . . it might make her . . . come back to life?'

'Back to life?' breathed Marko'cain. 'No! Do you think so?'

'I can imagine it happening.'

Marko'cain stared at the cross, then into his embroidered lap, imagining it for himself.

'That frightens me,' he admitted at last.

'Me too,' said Tainto'lilith.

'Let's wait for a different message.'

A few hundred yards further on, they found the helicopter from which the blades had come. It was bigger than Boris and Una Fahrenheit's machine, and in better decorative order, except of course for the missing blades and (on closer examination) its belly, which was all crumpled and ruined. Plainly, it had crashed, and failed to get up again.

The Fahrenheit twins went to investigate the wreck. They peered through the perspex windows, then flipped open one of the doors. There were seats for six passengers, but no-one inside, despite complex skeins of blood patterning the upholstery. No doubt at least one of the people who had lost that blood was buried beneath the great metal crucifix nearby. Those who had done the burying had moved on, seeing no point in staying with the husk of their flying machine. Tainto'lilith and Marko'cain would have done the same. After all, (as they quickly ascertained) there was no food in the helicopter anymore, and all the flammable stuff had been taken out of it. The twins walked back towards the growling dogs, empty-handed.

'We could sleep inside it, maybe,' said Marko'cain, looking back.

But next instant, a flash of lightning struck the steely hull, exploding the windows like the skin of a giant balloon, branding a helicopter skeleton shape on the twins' retinas. In terror they covered their eyes, but the flare of luminescence

faded almost immediately, leaving only a blueish flicker fidgeting over the blasted paintwork.

They hurried back to their sleds, where the dogs were barking and howling frantically.

'Be calm! Don't fear!' they counselled the animals, too fearful themselves to extend their hands. Even Snuffel Junior looked as though he might bite instead of submitting to a placatory stroke.

'Good dogs!' cried the twins without conviction, taking a step towards the phalanx of snapping canine teeth and saliva, then taking a step backwards.

However, just as the children were on the brink of conceding they'd lost control, the tension was resolved from an unexpected quarter. One of the dogs, a little removed from the others, detected a hint of movement where no movement should be, and, with a yelp of glee, bounded away to investigate. All the other dogs stopped their barking and turned their heads, nostrils agape.

Over at the helicopter hulk, whose metal skin was still hazy with smoke, a small hole in the torn fuselage was apparently giving birth to a flurry of animal life: a family of voles, shrieking in distress. No sooner had the first one found its feet on the snow than it was snaffled up in the husky's jaws. An instant later, all the other dogs had pounced in unison, and the twins' view of the squirming litter of disoriented rodents was blotted out by a scrum of haunches and wagging tails. Furious growling quickly subsided when it became clear that there was enough for all.

'We are lucky,' said Marko'cain as the dogs gnawed at their miraculous feast. 'Such things can't happen very often.'

'We should eat something ourselves,' sighed Tainto'lilith, weak and shivery now that the crisis was past.

Marko'cain walked over to the sled and fetched the big bag of provisions out of it. He unbuckled it and peered inside.

'Ho! This is a puzzle,' he exclaimed. 'The hamper our father packed for us is empty.'

'Empty!' cried his sister. 'But it was full when we set off! Did the dogs eat it when we weren't looking? Did it fall out, maybe, as we were moving along?'

'No . . .' Marco'cain was pensive, grappling with ambiguities. 'I shouldn't have said it was empty. It has some . . .' – he rummaged – 'some big crumpled-up papers in it, and a heavy book called . . . *Principia Anthropologica*.'

The Fahrenheit twins stood for a while with the hamper at their feet, warming their hands inside their armpits, listening to the waves on one side of them and the crunch of bone against gnashing teeth on the other.

'Do you think perhaps our father is trying to kill us?' said Tainto'lilith.

'Why would he wish to kill us?' said Marko'cain.

Both of them did their best to imagine, willing themselves to transcend the limitations of childish thought.

'He might think we are trouble to look after, now that mother can't do it anymore,' suggested Tainto'lilith.

'But we've been looking after ourselves, haven't we?' protested Marko'cain. 'He doesn't often notice we are there.'

'Maybe that's the problem!' declared Tainto'lilith. 'He doesn't notice us very often, so perhaps in his mind we are still babies, needing milk and love.'

'Well . . .' frowned Marko'cain. 'We will need *something* to eat soon, or we will die.'

Warily, the Fahrenheit twins sampled the tomato-red gloop in the tins. It was, unsurprisingly, tomato. They spooned it

into their mouths, glob after glob, crimson juice running down their chins.

'This will keep us going,' said Tainto'lilith as cheerfully as she could.

'We need a message from the universe,' retorted Marko'cain. 'And we need it quick.'

When they had eaten as much of the chilly, snot-textured fruit as they could stand, they sat at the edge of their mother's sledge again, facing the sea. A pearly glow was growing on the horizon. Summer was about to come up.

In normal circumstances, this would have been a cause for ecstatic celebration, but just now the Fahrenheit twins had other things to think about. With great earnestness, striving not to be distracted by their sleepy heads, sick stomachs and the uneasy sense of their unfinished mission, Tainto'lilith and Marko'cain discussed their chances of survival – not just in the short term, but in the event that they were no longer welcome at home.

The discussion began well enough, with an accurate inventory of their meagre supplies and a head-count of the dogs, but when they moved on to speculate about more slippery intangibles – like their father's true desires or the reliability of supernatural aid – their tempers began to fray. Over and over, they were forced back to the same conclusion: that they had no-one to rely upon but each other.

'We must each consider our strengths and weakneths,' said Marko'cain.

'But we are both the same!'

'Not inside our underpants.'

Tainto'lilith sighed in exasperation. Testaments and pee-holes were equally useless in the face of an unfriendly universe, as far as she was concerned.

'We are the same,' she said, digging the heels of her boots

through the crust of snow, gouging into the hard dark earth. 'Same, same, same.'

Unnerved by the intensity of his sister's conviction, Marko'cain swallowed hard, trying to keep his disagreement to himself. He gazed out across the swirling surf, as if soliciting the sea's ideas, but really he was comforting himself, sending confidential reassurances to his slighted genitals. Tainto'lilith smelled his estrangement instantly, of course.

'Why *shouldn't* we be the same, anyway?' she demanded.

Marko'cain kept his eyes on the sea, dignified in his appreciation of the wider picture.

'If there really is no difference between us, it would mean that neither of us can know anything that the other doesn't,' he pointed out.

'Is that dangerous?' his sister wondered.

'It could be.'

There was a pause.

'I can't imagine how.'

'Neither can I,' said Marko'cain solemnly. 'That gives danger the advantage.'

'Now you're just being silly,' Tainto'lilith scolded him. 'Like when you used to make me frightened in bed as we were about to fall asleep, by saying that a bear might come through the window and eat us.'

'Bears came to our house all the time,' retorted Marko'cain defensively. 'You saw their footprints in the mornings.'

'Footprints don't kill,' sniffed Tainto'lilith, hugging herself. 'All those years, all those bears, and what did our mother die of?'

The question, released as an innocent puff of rhetorical vapour, hung in the air, cloudier than expected.

'We don't know what she died of,' said Marko'cain at last.

'No,' admitted Tainto'lilith.

'It could kill us too.'

'I don't think so.'

'Why are you so sure?'

'I feel very well. You not?'

'I'm hungry and tired and cold.'

'Me too, but those things can be fixed.'

'I hope so.' Marko'cain seemed unconvinced, even as the first ray of sunshine began to creep across the ocean towards them. Something – a suspicion – was nagging at him. 'Perhaps father killed mother. He said she ate something that disagreed with her. Perhaps we have now eaten the same thing. A deadly poison.'

'What nonsense you are talking!' grizzled Tainto'lilith, pointing to the discarded tins at their feet. 'It's just tomato, from our own storehouse. Mother would have eaten something strange. Guhiynui food.'

'Still . . .'

Wave by wave, the sea was turning from grey to silver. The birds were going mad with joy. Elongated black shadows were unrolling like tongues from the rocks on the shore, the sleds, the empty hamper, the tins. Even the blades of grass, prickling up through the increasingly slushy snow, cast magnified javelins of shade before them.

'What would father want to kill mother for?' said Tainto'lilith.

'They argued all the time,' Marko'cain reminded her, waving his hands about to demonstrate.

'Not all the time.'

'More than half.'

Tainto'lilith's brow furrowed as she made a few calculations.

'Exactly half,' she concluded.

Marko'cain, knowing she was right, slumped a little. Then he was pricked by another memory.

'Father told us once that he wouldn't trust her as far as he could throw her. She is as bad as the Guhiynui, he said.'

'Yes, but another time mother said he couldn't possibly manage without her. Without a woman, he's helpless like a baby, she said.'

'Are you sure?'

'It's in the Book.'

They sat in silence, picturing their father shambling to and fro in the Fahrenheit house, his uncut grey hair hanging in his eyes, his pullover full of holes, his heart in pieces, his coffee cold.

'So what will happen to him now that mother is gone?' murmured Marko'cain.

'We'll help him,' said Tainto'lilith. 'If it's true that he sent us out to die, I'm sure he's sorry by now. He'll be glad to have us home, you'll see. And every year we are bigger. If he can wait a little while, we can do everything mother did.'

Having decided this, they made a fire with the *Principia Anthropologica*. Fed with five hundred and sixty-two dry pages one after the other, it burned hot and bright, but lapsed into substanceless ash as soon as the last page was added. The huskies, closely gathered around what had been such merry flames, raised their panting heads in disappointment.

'That's all, doggies,' sighed Tainto'lilith.

The storm finally having passed over, the children took shelter in the blasted shell of the helicopter, sleeping in the cabin together with the dogs. The overcrowding helped to conserve body heat: a snug interleaving of fast-breathing furry haunches and gently snoring little humans.

While they slept, the sun raised itself from the horizon. The snows glowed white, the heavens azure and pink. The temperature began to climb towards zero.

On waking, the twins extracted themselves groggily from their dense swaddling of hot flesh. The huskies slumbered on while Marko'cain and Tainto'lilith crawled out of the cabin, blinking in the sunshine.

The world had been utterly transformed by the advent of summer, and this in turn had its effect on the children's spirits. The golden-white light and long, clear views encouraged in them a placid, groundless optimism. The risk of imminent death from cold and hunger seemed, all of a sudden, remote, despite the fact that they had only a few tins of tomatoes left, possibly frozen solid. They could imagine themselves catching seabirds, picking them out of the sky with a well-aimed pebble or even pouncing on them with the stealth of a superior species. They could imagine flinging a penknife straight into a polar bear's heart.

'Oh, look!'

In the clarity of day, the twins could now see, in the far distance along the shore, thin plumes of smoke rising from a cluster of dwellings. The bulbous, vaguely pyramidal shape of these dwellings was familiar to them from their parents' notebooks. These were the whalebone-enforced domiciles of the Guhiynui.

'But what about mother?' said Tainto'lilith as her brother ran to fetch the dogs. 'What about the message from the universe?'

'This *is* the message from the universe,' Marko'cain replied, his enthusiasm inspiring the huskies to leap out of the helicopter one after the other, a fluid tumble of milky fur.

'How do you know?'

Marko'cain was already busy with the harnesses.

'I feel it in my testaments!' he yelled in triumph.

And so, the Fahrenheit twins set off for the Guhiynui village.

In strict mathematical terms, as it might be depicted on a map, the journey was three miles at most, but in practice the children had to veer several hundred yards inland to keep their purchase on the softening snow. A long thigh of land rose to shield them from the sound of the waves, and they travelled in silence and still air. This far away from the shore, the Guhiynui's settlement too was hidden from sight, though its plumes of smoke remained visible in the sky above.

With perhaps a mile-and-a-half still to go, the land assumed a bizarre topography, all peaks and hollows. Grassy mounds erupted through the snow, and rocks the size of houses were scattered all about. The dogs negotiated these obstacles warily, needing flicks of encouragement from the whip. They whined softly even as they jerked to obey, pining, in their inbred doggy solidarity, for the flat environs and the well-known smells of home. Too much novelty was spooking them.

The children sympathised, but they too were being driven. The deceptively placid face of their mother, sweating its veneer of frost off in the sunlight, was exerting a powerful stimulus behind them. They must find a place for her soon.

Then, as yet another massive boulder was looming in front of them, and with the Guhiynui settlement still a fair way off, an unexpected sound made the twins' ears prick up inside their furry hoods.

'Ho!' cried Marko'cain. 'Do you hear that?'

They reined the dogs to a halt. Ricocheting among the giant rocks was a faint but unmistakable music: the peal of mechanical birdsong.

'A cuckoo clock!' shouted Marko'cain in wonder.

'That isn't possible, is it?' said Tainto'lilith, as the cooing abruptly stopped. 'It must be a *real* cuckoo.'

'No, it is a cuckoo clock,' Marko'cain assured her. 'I even know which cuckoo clock it is. Didn't you recognise it?'

Tainto'lilith closed her eyes tightly, chasing the echoes through her brain.

'Yes,' she said, almost at once, surprising herself. 'It is the smallest one, with the two little hunters on either side, and the upside-down rabbits with the tied-up feet and the purple door.'

'Yes,' affirmed Marko'cain. 'The one that went missing from our house a long time ago.'

'Mother said it got broken.'

'And we said, Can father not mend it.'

'And she said, Don't bother your father about this, or I will be angry with you.'

'Then she said, One less clock makes no difference to the universe.'

'We wrote that down in the Book.'

'Yes. It feels like yesterday.'

'It was a long time ago.'

Cautiously, they steered the dogs in pursuit of what could no longer be heard: the invisible sonic footprints of a tiny automated thrush, which might prove to be a figment of their own delirious memories.

Once the turn was taken, however, very little searching was required. In a small snowless clearing, hidden from the wider world by towering stones, stood a single Guhiynui dwelling. In all respects it was identical to the drawings their mother had made of such dwellings in her notebooks: the whaleskin exterior, stiffened by tanning and tarring, the whale-bone framework, interwoven with rope, the absence of

windows, the thong-tied entrance slit, and the thin central chimney, poking up like a smoke-blackened wick. Only, there was no smoke coming from the chimney just now, and no sounds of life within – no evidence at all, in fact, of the communal bustle and vigorous manly activity Una Fahrenheit had often praised, shortly before a big argument with her husband.

The children dismounted from their buggy and walked straight up to the house. There was no more need for caution. The universe had them in hand, after all. The entrance flap was knotted loosely, in a shoelace-style bow. Marko'cain tugged it free, and he and his sister squeezed inside.

'Ho!'

There was no-one at home. Instinct had told them there wouldn't be, but a quick glance confirmed it, for Guhiynui houses were simple things, undivided into separate rooms. This one didn't even feel lived-in, in the sense that there was no mess or clutter whatsoever. It was a place meant for visiting.

There was no furniture to speak of, only a bed and, in the centre of the room, a potbelly stove of burnished green iron. The rest of the floor space was bare, but because the walls tapered inwards rather sharply, the whole house was still scarcely big enough for a grown-up to walk around in, and far too cold to be cosy.

And yet, from the moment the Fahrenheit twins stepped inside, they were intoxicated by the mysterious potency of the place. This was unquestionably where the universe wanted them to be. This was the message, delivered not in a voice of thunder but in the barely audible fluting of a familiar automaton.

It wasn't just the presence of the missing cuckoo clock, defiantly keeping its exotic brand of time with its delicate pendulum. No, the mystique of this place went beyond that. The

whole interior seemed to glow much brighter than the single ray of sunlight through the entrance slit could explain, and the air, for all its chill, seemed aromatic with intimacy.

Perhaps, more than anything else, it was the paintings. Everywhere on the curvaceous walls, warmly-hued cloth paintings were mounted, sewn close against the whaleskin with twine. There were images of adventure: top-heavy Guhiynui warriors sailing the seas on toy boats, or slicing each other up like sausages. There were images of hunting: seals and beluga whales spreading attenuated flippers in surrender to a hail of spears. There were images of birds, carrying tiny sleeping humans towards the sun. And, directly above the bed, there was the largest painting of all, a dynamic full-length portrait of a dark-skinned male and a slender, creamy-white female. From her stylised hairdo and the blush of rose on her cheek, it was quite obvious that this woman was meant to be Una Fahrenheit.

Admittedly the Guhiynui's style of illustration was very different from what the twins had grown up with in their mother's antique storybooks. Both bodies seemed to be floating in space, surrounded by an intricate pattern of stars or snowflakes. The feet were impossibly tiny, the legs bonelessly contorted and intertwined. No clothes had been attempted, not even underpants, leaving the figures naked but apparently impervious to the elements. The man had some kind of extra limb growing from between his legs, and Una had two mouths, one on her face and another, much larger one, on her belly. And yet, for all the primitive eccentricity of the image, its colours were lush and vibrant, and something of their mother's nature had been captured – the best side of her nature, the way she'd tended to look when she was in her happiest mood. On her face, here in this Guhiynui tribute to her, the twins recognised the expression that always came

over her when she was about to wash them and pamper their skins with whale oil.

The bed was a big nest of seal skins, all different kinds: hooded seal, ringed seal, bearded seal. It looked supremely comfortable, especially with two fluffy pillows at the far end, each covered in a pastel-coloured pillowcase embroidered with tiny edelweiss. Tainto'lilith removed one glove, and stroked the satiny braille of the coloured cotton. Then she gathered up some stray hairs, fine black ones with grey roots where the dye had failed to penetrate. Pressing her nose into the pillow, she inhaled the scent of Idyl-Geruch and Hyacinthe-Gesang, the heady perfumes of a long-lost Bavaria. Meanwhile, further down on the bed, Marko'cain allowed himself to test the softness of the seal skins under his sprawling body.

Both twins felt sick with desire to sleep in that bed, knowing very well that it was not intended for them. The perfect equation of two pillows and two children was almost impossible to resist, but resist they did. Troubled and enchanted, they struggled to their feet and looked away.

Kik-kik-kik-kik-kik, the little cuckoo clock was saying, securely mounted on the whalebone wall. *Kik-kik-kik-kik-kik . . .*

Venturing up close, the twins examined the clock's condition. Its fragile brass chain was unbroken; indeed, it had been pulled up quite recently, giving the mechanism plenty of time before needing another tug. Care had been taken, in bracketing the clock to its cetacean rib, to keep the little birdhouse straight, despite the curve of the wall. The wrought-iron pine-cone hung like a plumb-line on the end of the chain, confirming the correct orientation of the whole machine. For the clock to be working as well as this, it must, during the long intervals between Una's visits, have been

treated with the utmost respect and gentleness by the Guhiynui. Only the minuscule wooden barrel of one of the hunters' guns was broken off, but that might well have happened *en route* between the Fahrenheit house and this, Una's secret home away from home.

Without needing to confer on the decision, the twins helped each other unbuckle their mother's body from the sledge and carry her into the Guhiynui house. Reverently they inserted her into the bed, wrapping the seal skins around her, smoothing her penumbra of wet hair evenly over the pillow.

'Cuckoo!' carolled the clock, once only. It had used twelve of its cries to call them here, and must begin again.

'We must take the dogs home now,' said Marko'cain.

'And ourselves as well,' said Tainto'lilith.

'Father may not want us to come,' said Marko'cain.

'We have nowhere else to go,' said Tainto'lilith.

'Don't we? The Guhiynui village is very close by,' said Marko'cain.

'We are not Guhiynui,' said Tainto'lilith.

'They liked Mother. They gave her a bed, blankets, and everything. Even a naked painting with her face on.'

'We must go back to our Father's house,' said Tainto'lilith. 'The Book of Knowledge is there.'

Marko'cain's brow was knotted and his nostrils were flared, as though he were about to bark.

'We know everything now,' he said, with finality. 'There is nothing more to know.'

Tainto'lilith was frightened by this new hardness in him, this loss of the natural curiosity that they'd shared since tumbling out of the womb.

'Let us allow the universe to decide,' she said. 'Let us wait for another message.'

'All right,' said her brother. So they stood still, staring into the sunlit expanse of snow, and listened, and listened. The universe said nothing.

The twins lost patience and made their own minds up. They decided they would go straight home. There was, they felt, something not right about prolonging their adventures when their mission was accomplished, and the dogs seemed desperately keen to turn back. Moreover, there was a long, comfortable sledge free now, in which Tainto'lilith and Marko'cain could slumber the miles away, basking in the sun while the huskies pulled their lighter load homewards.

So that is what they did.

In one of her rare outbursts of nostalgic storytelling, Una Fahrenheit had once told her children of the express trains which carried people across the borders of deepest Europe, whisking them from country to country without anyone having to give a thought to the steering. People could play card games, read books or even sleep, and the trains would continue unerringly, drawn to the destination as if on a tight string. This was how the long journey back to civilisation felt to the Fahrenheit twins.

When at last they sensed themselves coming to rest in a warm, dark place, it might have been one of those fabled tunnels leading into a railway station, the like of which they had struggled to describe for the purposes of the Book of Knowledge. It was, in fact, the huskies' heated bunker, their concrete kennel, nestled behind the generator. The exhausted dogs were putting themselves to bed without even waiting to be untethered from their harnesses.

Tainto'lilith and Marko'cain prised themselves out of the sledge like a couple of imperfectly defrosted fish, falling onto the seagrass matting of the kennel floor. They were, they

realised, half-dead. Only their instinctive huddling together, nuzzling their faces into each other's furry hoods and locking torso to torso, had saved them from sleeping themselves into frostbitten oblivion.

'Oh, oh, oh,' they said, crawling dizzily on their hands and knees on opposite sides of their mother's bier. Snuffel Junior lifted his head from his boneless slump, momentarily concerned for the twins' welfare. Then he nuzzled back to sleep. They would live.

Boris Fahrenheit was thunderstruck at the twins' return. A rowdy influx of polar bears would have surprised him less than the quiet re-entry of his two small children, padding into the kitchen in their damp and filthy socks. He looked from one twin to the other, noting the trickly red stains on their chins and the breasts of their jumpsuits, the halo of animal hair all over them, the pink irritations in their luminous eyes.

'It's done, father,' said Tainto'lilith reassuringly, but the old man's grey complexion only went greyer.

Perhaps his discomposure was caused by a difficulty in juggling two social challenges: that of welcoming his children home and that of entertaining a visitor. For Boris Fahrenheit was not a social creature, and the matronly-looking woman who was sitting at the breakfast table, tea in hand, was surely the first visitor they had ever had.

'Oh, Bumsie!' she cried, apparently addressing Boris. 'You didn't tell me you had children!'

Boris's jaw was shuddering like an abused motor.

'I – I was keeping it a surprise,' he stammered. 'They're no trouble, really. They're basically . . . self-caring.'

'Oh, but they're adorable!' exclaimed the woman, springing up from her breakfast stool. She was a small thing, hardly taller than the twins themselves, and she had a fetchingly

dishevelled abundance of blond hair. Her skin was so tanned it was almost caramel, contrasting vividly with her white bathrobe. Her face was uncannily similar to one of the many dolls their mother had given them over the years, an impish Scandinavian poppet intended (according to the Book) to dangle from the ceilings of automobiles. She radiated nurture.

'This is Miss Kristensen,' croaked Boris Fahrenheit. 'She will be living with us from now on.'

'How do you do,' said the twins in unison, resorting to the language of the stories they had read. It seemed to be what was wanted.

'Oh, very *well!*' beamed Miss Kristensen, extending her hands in friendship, one for each twin.

Hunched behind the breakfast table, Boris Fahrenheit exposed all his teeth in a startlingly unbecoming smile.

The twins ate themselves sick on a lavish meal prepared for them by Miss Kristensen. They were too weak to sit at the table with their father, so she fed them on the floor, where they helped themselves to a cornucopia of steaming protein and starchy titbits.

'You poor, poor things,' she sang, bending down to serve them milk, not from the ample bosom that swung inside her bathrobe, but from colourful little cartons manufactured in Canada. Before they could thank her politely, she was back at the stove.

Miss Kristensen was in fact a dynamo of culinary energy, chattering in the steam of her own high-speed cooking, flipping eggs without even looking at them, happily bonding with all the utensils Una Fahrenheit had never used.

'Here you are, you secretive rogue,' she said, setting a

plate of sizzling cutlets in front of the bewildered Boris. Then, in a raucous whisper, 'I'm dying to know what else you never mentioned in your letters!'

Tainto'lilith and Marko'cain excused themselves to go off and vomit.

Hidden away in their own bedroom, feverish, hunched over a big metal bowl, they puked all the colours of the rainbow for what seemed like an age.

'We smell bad,' observed Marko'cain, during a little rest between exertions.

'It's all the tomato,' sighed Tainto'lilith.

More than anything, they were desperate for a bath. This in itself was not a problem: they were well accustomed to bathing themselves, and washing their clothes, too. But unspoken between them was a bewildering new anxiety: the possibility of Miss Kristensen volunteering to bathe them. The thought was terrifying – more taboo, somehow, than anything they had yet encountered. So, stealthily, they spirited themselves into the bathroom, locked the door, and filled the tub.

Whoops of feminine laughter and growls of paternal caution echoed through the house as the naked twins stepped into the water together.

'This is not our home anymore,' said Tainto'lilith, facing her brother across the soily, steamy broth shimmering between them. 'Things have changed.'

Marko'cain nodded in agreement.

'We have changed, too,' he said.

They glanced at each other, surreptitiously checking whether the threatened teats and beard were sprouting yet, but their outward appearances were still comfortingly identical. It was their insides that would never be the same. Something had happened to them, out there in the wilderness.

'I am angry at father,' mentioned Marko'cain, saucing himself with shampoo. 'Are you?'

'Very angry.'

'Do you think it would make us feel any better if we killed him?'

'I think we should just run away,' said Tainto'lilith. 'But with proper food, this time.'

Marko'cain ducked his head into the water, allowing his sister to paw the suds out of his scalp. When he surfaced, he said,

'Perhaps we should kill father, *then* run away.'

'What about Miss Kristensen?'

'Kill her as well,' added Marko'cain glibly.

'We don't mean her any harm, do we?'

'Perhaps she *told* father to get rid of us,' suggested Marko'cain. 'So she could come and live with him.'

Tainto'lilith sighed: a deep, doleful exhalation of regret.

'I wish our eyes had not been opened to these things,' she said. 'The world was so much nicer before.'

Frowning, wedging her head between the taps, she made her very best effort to tell guile apart from innocence. Hot water droplets pattered onto her right shoulder, and cold onto her left.

'She seemed honestly surprised to see us,' she reflected. 'To see that there was such a *thing* as us, I mean.'

'Perhaps she was just play-acting,' said Marko'cain.

'I don't believe so.'

'All right, then, we'll leave her be, and just kill him.' There was a strange new tone in the boy's voice, a cocky impatience, as if the choice between life and death was too straightforward a matter to waste much discussion on. This, too, made Tainto'lilith sad. She racked her brains for a way to save her father, that poor old baby who was, after all, helpless without a woman.

'If we kill father,' she said, 'Miss Kristensen might get killed as well, without us wanting it.'

'How?' The threat of complication was, as Tainto'lilith had hoped, putting a wrinkle on his brow.

'She might throw herself in front of him,' she said. 'Like the brave little squaw in *Sheriff Flintlock and the Rustlers*.'

'One of us could kill father,' suggested Marko'cain, 'while the other engaged Miss Kristensen in conversation.'

'That seems terribly unkind,' sighed Tainto'lilith, glimps-ing a long lifetime ahead of her of keeping her brother's inclinations in check. 'Especially since she is a visitor. I think we should just run away.'

'All right,' he said, standing up in the bath abruptly, a tutu of froth clinging to his midriff. 'But not with the huskies.'

'On foot?' said Tainto'lilith.

'In the helicopter,' declared Marko'cain, clambering out, with such a swagger of purpose that it looked as if he might stride naked to the hangar.

'But we've never flown the helicopter,' protested Tainto'lilith, splashing out of the bath herself.

'We've read the book,' her brother said airily, meaning the pilot's manual they'd often played with when it was too snowy to go outside.

'It's not the same.'

'Of course it isn't. But there is a connection.'

Wrapping towels around themselves, the twins walked to the laundry, where the massive front-loader washing machine was almost finished washing their jumpsuits. The house had gone all quiet, apart from the mechanised sloshing of the water. Boris Fahrenheit and Miss Kristensen had made peace with each other, it seemed.

'Where would we go?' said Tainto'lilith.

'A green place,' enthused her brother. 'Europe. Canada. Russia. Gre-e-e-enland.'

'The names are good,' admitted Tainto'lilith. Then suddenly she started weeping, a stream of hot tears rolling down her face, a lost and frightened look in her eyes.

Marko'cain, catching sight of her distress, was shocked. She had never wept without him before, particularly not in a situation where he himself could imagine nothing to weep about. Awkwardly, he patted her trembling shoulders. Now he too glimpsed a lifetime ahead of him, of trying, and failing, to comfort his sister in her secret sorrows.

'We might get to see a tree,' he said, encouragingly. 'And all the other things that mother used to talk about.'

Tainto'lilith nodded, unable to speak, the tears still flowing down her cheeks. She would be all right in a moment. Behind the big glass porthole in the washing machine, their clothing had begun to spin, an inextricable, mesmerising ring of embroidered pelts. Soon they would be able to put it on again, and cover their nakedness.

And yes, her brother was right, they had so much to look forward to, in the big wide world down below. The Book of Knowledge had a lot of blank pages.